THE
OTHER
WOMAN

HOLLY DOWN

THE OTHER WOMAN

bookouture

Published by Bookouture in 2024

An imprint of Storyfire Ltd.
Carmelite House
50 Victoria Embankment
London EC4Y 0DZ

www.bookouture.com

ISBN: 978-1-83525-504-9
eBook ISBN: 978-1-83525-503-2

For my husband.

PROLOGUE

It feels like I'm inside one of those dreadful horror films and whichever way I turn, there's something awful that I don't want to see, something that is going to change the course of my life dramatically. I stand frozen on the spot, my arms wrapped tightly across my chest where my thin white shirt gives little protection against the wind that is thrashing around us, whipping droplets of rain into my face and destroying my blow-dry, but I'm way beyond caring.

'Kitty?' A voice rasps my name and I'm terrified by how weak my husband sounds; he's so far from his usual deep, booming presence that it makes me want to cry but I fight back tears, aware that I need to hold it together.

I can't bring myself to look at him but I know exactly where he is and exactly what has happened to him. He's splayed on the tarmac roof, his usually luminous complexion drained to an awful grey, his dark T-shirt slashed down the front and sopping wet with his blood, and there *she* is, bending over him, squeezing his hand. As if *she* is in her rightful place by his side.

The urge to grab her shoulders and throw her clear off the roof suddenly runs through me and I find myself considering it for a moment before I clutch my head and let out a howl of pain that comes from deep within. It hurts so much that I have become a person who could even think of murder, let alone someone who could do what I've done. A sob threatens to make me break down but I swallow hard.

'Kitty?' David's voice comes again and I can't help but glance at him and our eyes meet. My husband, the love of my life, my darling David, is dying – it's plain to see. We may have had our ups and downs but that's to be expected when you've been together two decades, especially when we've had someone like *her* forcing her way between us, driving us apart with her schemes and her tricks. I'd like to throttle her with my bare hands, only of course there's no point with David slipping away. I have to think of the future now.

I'm not sure how long I've been rooted to the spot, the shock and horror of what I've done paralysing me, until suddenly I stumble as if I've been released from its grip. Taking a raggedy breath, I know what I need to do and I drop to my knees beside my husband, taking his free hand.

'Ambulance,' he manages to get out but I shush him since it's obvious that there is no time – the time that is left is not for him. I wish I could spend these last moments taking his head in my arms, kissing him softly and telling him that I'll love him forever, but that woman has robbed me of that chance as well. Looking across to where she sits, holding David's other hand with tears streaming down her face, I push my hate deep down inside me and force myself to focus on what needs to be done now. 'It's time for you to listen to me,' I begin.

PART ONE

ONE

KITTY

There is an art to watching someone without being seen. The most common mistake people make is to keep too still – like a lion watching prey – whereas humans are constantly moving when we're relaxed, little things like fiddling with a pen, scratching or slurping a drink.

Like now, I run my finger around the rim of my wine glass and take a sip, grimacing at the cheap acidity even though pure ethanol would probably slide straight down these days. Sitting alone in a pub would usually draw too much attention but this evening it's busy enough that I blend in with the boozy, after-work crowd and besides, David is clearly distracted.

He's perched on a stool two tables away and next to him is a very young, very beautiful woman, hanging on his every word. Of course it bloody is – it's never an old hag, now is it? While I'm dressed in a cheap grey boxy suit, designed for the eye to glide over, she's wearing a sky-blue floral dress with a twist of fabric at the front that exposes a deep 'V' of cleavage, certainly intended to snag the gaze. Her black hair falls in soft waves that must have taken some time to perfect and her eyelashes are so thick they look like the wings of a tiny blackbird fluttering on her face. I snort softly as it hits me that David probably thinks they're real.

Glancing around the pub, I see that I'm not the only one staring, but they do make an attractive pair, and then, there's David. He's a man used to living in the spotlight, accustomed to having all eyes on him. His broad shoulders are relaxed beneath his expensive cotton shirt and as he throws back his head to laugh, I can tell that it's not genuine amusement, just an opportunity for him to perform. His companion is certainly entranced. Their heads are close together, bent over a stack of paper; every so often she makes a note in the margin as if it's a legitimate business meeting and I have to fight the urge to roll my eyes.

'Do you mind if I join you?' A man's voice comes from behind my ear and I flinch at the close proximity before arranging my face into a bland smile and turning to see a stubby, balding man with his shirt sleeves rolled up and a pint in his hand. He nods at the spare stool next to me and says, 'Anyone sitting there?'

I hesitate, weighing up whether he's interested in me or the seat. It *would* be good for my cover to have a man by my side but I really don't want to have to pretend to be flattered while he breathes beer fumes into my hair.

'It's all yours,' I say, against my better judgement as I watch a woman pass David's table and do a double-take, turning on her heel and boldly tapping David on the shoulder.

I see the flicker of annoyance – the jut of the jaw that softens in a blink-and-you'll-miss-it moment – before David smiles broadly and leans his head close for a selfie.

Next to me, the man says excitedly, 'My God, is that David Okine?'

'Shh,' I say as I pick up my wine glass and try to cover my face. I can't let David see me.

'I must get a photo for my sister. She always says he's on her "list". Something about the voice.'

David does have a lovely voice – deep and slow and somehow melodic. I could listen to it all day and, in fact, sometimes I do, thanks to the archive of his old radio shows that was dumped online last year, but before I can agree, the man next to me pushes back his stool and stands with purpose and my panic turns to cold, hard fear. What if he exposes me? Making a snap decision, I grab the back of his hand and squeeze the clammy skin gently.

'Alison,' I lie, forcing a smile.

He falters and I see him glance over at David once more before his eyes return to me and a smile stretches across his shiny, freckled face. I realise he looks like a thumb.

'Pete.' He settles back on the stool and grins, 'Thought I was barking up the wrong tree there for a minute but why else would a woman like you be drinking alone? And no ring.' He glances theatrically at my bare finger. 'You almost let me wriggle off your hook there.' He waggles his finger at me and guffaws and I force myself to laugh along, all the while holding the stem of my wine glass so tight that I fear it might snap. Pete's eyes travel to my glass, 'You want another?'

There's still an inch of straw-coloured wine left in the bottom but I knock it back, enjoying the burn and say, 'That would be lovely. House white, please.'

I watch him shuffle through the throng to the bar before allowing myself another look at David. The selfie has attracted attention and a small crowd has gathered while David preens and purrs. Seeing him in his element takes me back to the first time I saw him. It was hot that night too, the type of heady heat that makes everything feel possible. He was at the centre of his gang, sitting out on the smooth, lush lawn at Trinity. Of course, I noticed his good looks right away – the full lips, dark skin, great bone structure, *who wouldn't?* – but it was the faces of his friends that made me pay attention: the utter captivation.

It was the May Ball at the end of our first year and though it's hard to imagine now, I knew nothing of David. We moved in entirely different circles; I kept to my study group in college while he seemingly knew the brightest and shiniest students from across the whole of Oxford. I watched as his little group ebbed and flowed, bottles of champagne appeared and were drunk, and leggy blondes dropped kisses on his cheek. As I chugged a warm beer alone, it was easy to think our paths would never cross.

It was only a few hours later when he stumbled into the junior common room where I was resting my feet and collapsed in the chair next to mine, his jacket and tie long gone, his shirt open at the neck with a red wine stain the size and shape of a leg of lamb down the front.

There was a long silence and I was sure he was about to lurch away as quickly as he'd come, but after a moment he turned to me and slurred, 'Have we met?' His eyes were unfocused but he gave me what I would later know as his 'television smile'. My chest squeezed out all my breath but I managed to whisper, 'I don't think so.'

'We-ell,' he drawled, 'we should.'

I still remember exactly how I felt, basking in David's glow for the first time as if I were taking a bath in glorious, golden sunshine. It's hard not to feel bitter, since these days I only see him smile like that on the screen.

The gaggle around him is thinning and I realise with a dawning horror that I'm still staring. I stand to leave, planning to slip out of the open door without either man noticing. I feel only the briefest sensation of guilt at abandoning Pete – he is a big, rather unpleasant, boy, after all – but I've only taken a few steps when I hear his confused voice behind me call out, 'Alison?'

I cringe but keep moving, trying not to falter so he thinks I haven't heard but he calls again, louder this time, 'Alison!'

The noise in the pub drops as his voice rings out and I'm forced to stop. It's balmy but I suppress a shiver, feeling as if someone has gripped my shoulders with icy hands. Surely he could read between the lines, put it down to a headache or a family emergency, and enjoy a wine chaser with his pint. I know I would but it turns out that Pete is much more persistent than I've given him credit for.

Turning slowly, I pray David hasn't noticed the commotion and I see Pete standing by our table, holding our drinks. He looks at me, then the wine, and back to me again, frowning as if he's trying to work out a complicated equation. I allow a glance at David and see he's watching Pete with a smirk on his face, my least favourite of his expressions, and then everything seems to happen in slow motion. David turns his head and before I can look away, our eyes meet. Panic courses through me and I'm forced to grab the back of a chair to hold myself upright as my knees threaten to give way.

I feel certain that this is it – David is sure to recognise me and it will be the end of it all – but he barely pauses as he turns back to the young woman and does the universal mime for 'another drink?'.

Everything zooms back to normal speed like a scratched record catching up. The clamour of the pub returns to my ears with a roar and Pete's confused face comes back into focus. I take deep, steadying breaths as I make my way towards him but it's hard to calm down. My whole body is trembling and there are tears in my eyes as I reach his side and lay my hand on his arm. I lie quickly, 'I'm so sorry. I was waiting for you to come back but the queue took a while and I got a call with some bad news.'

He blinks and glances again at the wine, not bothering to look sympathetic.

'Do you mind if I take a rain check?' I ask.

Without waiting for a response, I make for the exit, pushing past warm bodies towards the door. David's companion is now alone, checking her phone with a smug little smile on her face as she waits for her drink. I pass their table and stagger outside into a cloud of cigarette smoke. The close call replays in my head and I feel numb with disbelief that he didn't recognise me. Pausing just beyond the door to gather myself, I breathe deeply, shrinking behind the group of smokers so I can't be seen.

Hurrying around the corner onto a tiny side street, I stop in a patch of shade behind a large, dark-green recycling bin, leaning my back against cold, rough brick. Counting my breaths, I inhale for four, hold for four, then out for four as I think over and over: *I am somebody*. It's my mantra. When Connor, my 'shrink' as the Americans say, first explained the concept to me, I dismissed it as his usual psychobabble, but I must admit, it works. After a couple of minutes, all trace of panic from the encounter is gone and David is banished from my mind. The effect never lasts long but it gives me a chance to think.

Sweat is beading along my hairline and my fingers come away damp. The synthetic wig is like a furnace on my scalp and I long to rip it off but my real hair is pinned up underneath and it would take too long to make it presentable. The bridge of my heavy glasses slips down my nose so I fold them up and put them inside my handbag. Next, I glance back at the main street to check no one is coming, before hooking my finger first inside one cheek and then the other, pulling out the sopping wedges of cotton wool I jammed in the cavity between my teeth and cheek. With a flick of my wrist, they hit the ground together with a squelch.

I can't hang around. I work in telly nearby and people around here know me. Shouldering my bag, I stand up straight and take a final deep breath before setting off for the tube. I'm back in control and I tell myself that at least one good thing has come out of this evening: now I know that not even David – my own husband – will recognise me.

TWO

DAVID

I unlock the front door and stand in the silent, dark hallway, listening for any sign of life. It's only just gone nine; surely Kitty can't be in bed already?

'Kit?' My voice echoes up the stairs but there's no answer. Most evenings at this time she's curled up in front of the TV in her pyjamas watching reruns of *Friends* but I can't hear the recorded laughter that usually rings through the house and sets my teeth on edge. Frowning, I bend to unlace my shoes, easing them off my hot feet and padding to the bottom of the stairs, my socks leaving sweaty imprints on the glossy oak. I try again, louder this time: 'Kitty?'

It's the first time in months she hasn't been home when I've got in. I know I should be pleased that she's getting back out there but I can't shake the niggle of worry in the pit of my stomach. She hasn't been quite herself lately. I check my phone but she hasn't messaged and my finger is hovering, ready to call her, when my eye is drawn to the pile of post on the black marble console table we shipped from Italy. My heart rate ticks up a notch and I tut at myself and shake my head. The whole business from before is sorted, *finito*, and just because a few odd letters have turned up, I can't let my imagination run away with me. Fan mail is par for the course when you're in my position.

Shrugging, I force myself to relax and flick through the stack of envelopes. It's the usual utility bills in their brown envelopes, and there's a thick A4 envelope from my agent that must be the contract I've been expecting. My tension eases until I spot the cheap white envelope at the bottom, smaller than the others with my name written in purple ink, just like the last one – no stamp, no address.

I'm about to open it when I hear her call, 'David?'

I jump at the sudden noise and shove the envelope deep into my pocket, crumpling it into a tight ball.

'Where are you?' I call back.

'In here.'

Her voice comes from nearby on the ground floor where we have the formal dining room. Like every other household on our street, the room is rarely used since we all congregate in the basement kitchens, buzzing around the fridge like flies. Our front room is filled with an oval ebony table that is permanently set for a dinner party for ten, complete with sparkling glasses, silverware and fanned lilac linen napkins stuck into glasses like peacock plumes, but I can't remember the last time we used it. Kitty hasn't exactly been in the mood for entertaining. The shutters are kept closed to keep out prying eyes and as I reach the doorway, it takes my eyes a minute to adjust to the gloom.

When they do, I see Kitty is sitting at the far end, the head of the table, with a large glass of white wine in front of her. Her hair is damp from the shower and her face is somehow both puffy and drawn. Any effort she might have once made for me is a distant memory but I try not to hold it against her. It happens in all marriages, especially ones that have had challenges like ours. And to say this past year has been difficult would be an understatement.

'Why are you here in the dark?' I say lightly as I flick the switch. Her hand goes to her eyes and she grimaces but I paste on a smile and pray she decides to copy me.

'I was just thinking,' she says, and there's a strained silence as I try to discern the mood she's in, wondering if it's going to be one of 'those days', but her face is unreadable.

'Good day?' she asks in a lighter tone that sounds normal, playful even.

'Yes, actually, great.' I smile genuinely, feeling myself relax, and I lean against the doorframe. I'm about to ask her the same question when she takes a large gulp of wine and says, 'Something special happen?'

There's a trap in her tone and I think back quickly, trying to work out what I've forgotten or done wrong this time. Wednesday evening? Nothing comes to mind but then my memory snags on something and my heart sinks. This morning, as I was lacing my shoes and Kitty was sitting on the bottom step wrapped in her tatty dressing gown, hugging her knees, I'd said I would be home after work and maybe we could have a drink in the garden if the weather stayed nice. It wasn't a firm plan, just a possibility, something the old Kitty wouldn't have given a second thought to until the moment arrived, if it ever did, but this new Kitty chalks up scores and settles them as if we're in constant competition.

'Just working on the script for next week's interview.' I keep my voice breezy, hoping to brush right past her anger. 'Should be a big one.'

'Oh?' I can't tell if she's interested or just figuring out how to get her next barb in but I plough straight on.

'You remember that MP, Dick Bell, who was in the news a couple of years ago when an intern accused him of sexual harassment?'

She raises an eyebrow but says nothing. Kitty used to be my biggest supporter and first critic. We'd run through all my questions before an interview, striking out easy ones and redrafting others to make them harder. She helped shape my reputation as a serious journalist but I can't remember the last time she showed one iota of interest, let alone contributed to the script.

'We came up with some particularly juicy questions,' I say, wondering if this will tempt her.

'Very productive.' She says the words with a sardonic curl of her lip and I sense there's more to come as she asks, 'And you did all this from the office?'

I straighten up and fold my arms across my chest – somehow, she knows I've been to the pub. My mind is turning over, trying to work out what has given me away. Perhaps she can smell the beer on me from there or maybe my eyes are a touch pink, although I only had a couple of pints. I consider lying, but in my experience that only makes things worse and she's bound to find me out. For better or worse, my wife has always been the smartest person in any room.

'We were on a roll so we popped into The Stag for one to brainstorm,' I admit.

She takes another sip. It's always been a talent of hers to convey displeasure in a single glance or arch of an eyebrow.

'You know how busy things are with the show right now.' There's a pleading, wheedling note in my voice and I hate myself for being so weak.

'Ah yes, the *show*,' Her eyes flash with fury as she spits out the word.

'Just in general,' I say, quickly realising I've misstepped, 'things are busy in general.'

'No, you're right. Now you're a big TV star it would be silly of me to expect you to be home when you say you will.'

'Kitty.' I rub my face with both hands. 'I'm sorry.'

'Don't be. It's not like I have anything better to do.'

I see the argument unfolding between us. The same old rope where she gave up her career for our potential family while I reaped the rewards with abandon. She never sees that things have been difficult for me too. We both wanted to have a baby, more than anything, but it didn't work out and I have to live with that too. It kills me to see what it's done to our marriage – neither of us foresaw that when we started trying.

'Look, I'm sorry,' trying to circumvent this. 'I didn't realise you had anything planned.'

She picks up an empty bottle of wine that's on the floor and raises it triumphantly. 'I bought wine.'

'Did you eat?'

She dodges my question by posing another of her own, 'Which of your minions did you force to work late?'

I sigh. 'I don't have minions.'

'Oh come on. I see them scurrying after you in the corridors with you striding along like some sort of minor royal.'

'It's not like that.'

'Isn't it? I've seen the way your researcher looks at you. She probably has a commemorative tea towel with your face on it.'

'Nina? That's ridiculous.'

'*Nina*,' she mimics, her face twisted in rage. It's hard to remember that this is the same woman I met at college. The golden girl who smoked joints as we punted on the Cherwell and jumped in nearly naked when the sun went down. I fell in love with her laugh – the low rasp that rang out often – but I can't remember the last time I heard it.

I drop my voice to a whisper, 'I know things have been hard for you; they've been hard for us both. I know you've had to return to a more junior job but you were the one that wanted the career break. You said a break from the stress would give the IVF the best chance, I never put any pressure on you. I know it's hard right now but we'll turn a corner. It's just going to take some time for things to get back to normal.'

'Not for you.' She's straight-backed and stone-faced – brittle is the word that comes to mind; there's nothing soft or warm left. It crosses my mind that it would be so easy to return to the

hallway, to slip my feet into my shoes and set off into the balmy
night, back to the pub or wherever the evening might take me,
and I close my eyes for a moment, practically tasting freedom on
the tip of my tongue. But I'm not a quitter, I never have been. I
cross the room and kneel by her feet.

'No,' I say gently. 'Not so much for me.' I try to take her
hand but she refuses to let go of the wine glass. 'I know it's not
fair that you've had to suffer so much for something we both
wanted and I'm sorry about that but we'll get through this, you
know, together.'

I move to kiss her but she remains stiffly upright and turns
her face away, sighing, and I catch a waft of strong, sour wine on
her breath. Standing up purposefully, I squeeze her shoulder
and say, 'I'm going to make you a bacon sandwich.'

I walk to the door but before I leave, her voice stops me,
'*Together?*'

I turn back, frowning at the odd emphasis, and try a bright
smile, 'Of course, why would you even ask that? We're a team.'

She smiles oddly and I leave for the kitchen but I've only
taken one step into the hallway when a crash explodes by my
ear. Adrenaline floods through me and I throw myself to the
ground, flinging my arms up over my head. What the hell was
that? My mind races from a bomb to a brick through the
window. Perhaps the letter-writer has been watching us from
outside, waiting for the right moment to launch a missile at me. I
take a breath to steady myself then a second wave of panic hits
me. What if I'm not the target and Kitty isn't safe? I get up
quickly, moving to protect her when I hear a strange, guttural
sound: the low rasp of Kitty's laugh that chills me rather than
filling me with warmth.

Turning, I see she's still in the same seat and the wall
behind me is splattered with liquid. Wine fumes hit my nose,
and glancing down I see the floor is covered in shards of
sparkling glass. Only the label of the wine bottle is recognisable

in a crumpled heap by the skirting board. I lift my head to look at Kitty, not bothering to hide my horror and disgust.

'Liar,' she spits.

I open my mouth but suddenly I'm exhausted and my shoulders sag. There's no point trying to reason with her in this state. I shake my head and leave the room, shutting the door behind me and taking the stairs two at a time until I reach the third floor. My study is reassuringly my space.

Letting out a low, shaky breath, I tell myself that it's just a rough patch – understandable really, given all Kitty has been through with the IVF. Without thinking, I turn the lock behind me. I'm not afraid of her – surely not – but my fingers are shaking as I go over to my desk and switch on the shredder. The envelope is still in my pocket, screwed into a tight ball, and I smooth it out.

I read the words with a jolt of fear, 'I'm watching you.'

It may be silly but I can't help but glance around the room, checking there is no one here. But of course, I'm alone and I tell myself that I'm in the safest place I could be: my own home. No one here would hurt me.

THREE

KITTY

The office is quiet when I arrive. The human resources department of Prestige Productions is tucked away on the fourth floor, far from the glass-walled executive floor with its rarefied air and art-lined corridors that David walks. We mere mortals are crammed up here with our squeaky office chairs in a stuffy room that needs a new paint job. I turn on the computer and leave it whirring while I go to the kitchen to make my first instant coffee of the day, needing the buzz to get rid of the nagging hangover behind my eyes. Shame prickles my scalp as I wait for the kettle to boil and I try not to go over last night again, but it's impossible not to and I dig my nails into my palms as I play it back. David deserves better.

When I first got the job here, I was excited to be working in the same building as David. I pictured us ambling to Selfridges' food court for lunch, hand in hand, or going into Soho for cocktails after work on a whim, but it hasn't worked out like that. We're on different trajectories: his star is rising and mine, well, seeing him here just drives home how far apart we've drifted. I try not to dwell on what went wrong. A career break was what I needed, I can't deny that, but I never anticipated returning to work would be so hard. I have a solid CV – an excellent degree and years of experience – but in interviews there was always an awkward silence when they asked the question, 'So, what *exactly* have you been doing this past year?'

The job came through an agency and I made the decision that it would be best for me not to mention my connection to David or be seen with him around the building, since I don't need an accusation of nepotism hanging over my head, or worse, anyone using me to try to get to him – my pride has taken enough blows these past few years. It was my choice but I do sometimes wonder whether he could have put up more resistance. A husband's job is to support his wife, after all, and perhaps he should have put that above his precious reputation?

The kettle rattles and the sound drags me back to the kitchen with its sour milk smell and humane plastic mouse traps pushed up against the skirting board. I pour boiling water into my mug, turning the granules an oily brown, and splash in milk from the carton with 'Kitty' emblazoned across the top in blue Sharpie. I bet David doesn't have to buy his own milk – company policy never does seem to extend to him. The coffee is bitter and hot but I take a much-needed gulp, before carrying it over to my desk just as Karen walks in wearing her bright-red blazer that clashes horribly with her purple pixie crop.

'Morning,' I say.

Her eyes narrow before she pastes a smile on her face and I see her fury that I've arrived before her, as if me being here is a direct threat to her authority. Karen has risen fast through the ranks – a hard-nosed millennial with a point to prove, and her threat level seems to be set at a constant red alert. She hasn't seemed to grasp that the last thing on earth I'd want is her job. She may be my boss but she's still a worker ant, scurrying around the more important people, stealing scraps.

'Good morning, Catherine. Have you uploaded Rupert's receipts yet?'

Kitty, I think but I force myself to smile, 'I'm just about to start.'

'Right-oh. Best crack on. We wouldn't want to keep him waiting.' Karen uses her sing-song voice, which reminds me of a primary school teacher speaking to a class of five-year-olds. I grit my teeth, nod and turn my attention to my computer, hoping to avoid a dissection of last night's telly or some titbit about her dog as she sits on her seat, diagonally opposite me in our bank of four, slurping her takeaway coffee, making a sound like a blocked drain that reverberates in my head and brings my hang-over zooming back into centre stage.

Rubbing my temple in small, circular motions, I pull out Rupert's receipts from their envelope and line them up as if I'm preparing to enter the details into the system, though I have no intention of starting the task just yet. Instead, I open the People Portal and search for David Okine. One of the very few perks of my job is unlimited access to personal details – who doesn't like a good nosy? – and I often scroll through people's profiles when I'm in need of a pick-me-up.

Finding David, I scan his job title, home address, phone number and salary – silly really, since of course I know them all by heart. There's a link to his direct reports so I click through, going slowly to prolong the buzz of anticipation, until I find her. The thumbnail photo looks like a modelling headshot: shoulders turned, face to the camera and head straight on with a slight, self-satisfied smile. *Nina Bello.* I expand the photo and stare into the dark eyes. *What exactly is it that you want?* A sudden wave of nausea hits me and I click the 'close' button. *Like I can't guess.*

Karen clears her throat pointedly and I shuffle the receipts as if I'm working through them. She can't see my screen but the way her eyes keep darting to my face makes me nervous. Before she can say anything, the door opens again and Julie and Matt walk in together, Julie striding ahead and Matt shuffling behind with his satchel slung across his chest like a schoolboy. Julie reaches her spot beside me and drops her handbag on the desk as Karen coughs pointedly and turns her head to look at the clock. It's already 9.37 and I find myself wondering where the time has gone. Julie mutters something about the trains as Matt knocks over his mug full of pens, pencils and elastic bands in his haste to sit down.

'Sorry, sorry,' he says, as he scrabbles to gather them.

'Butterfingers,' Karen sings.

I catch Matt's eye and give a hint of an eyeroll. He shoves everything back into his mug and collapses onto his chair but I swear his lip twitches in the tiniest smile before he drops his gaze and hides beneath his stringy, blond fringe, his face flushed to a deep, brick red. The soft down on his cheeks, the smattering of acne and the fear that emanates from his round blue eyes whenever Karen turns her fury on him, make him appear closer to fifteen than thirty, but he's friendly enough and has always been helpful whenever I've asked him a question. We're not exactly natural allies but I like to think of Matt as my enemy's enemy.

'Here we all are,' Karen says unnecessarily as I turn my attention back to the Portal, taking care to glance at the receipts as if I'm checking something. Here we are indeed: the fabulous four 'people team' as we're known. Karen and Julie, her number two, lead recruitment; Matt the man-boy manages the Portal; and I, the team dogsbody, handle whatever is left. I try to do it with a smile on my face just to piss off Karen but it's hard when I must be the best part of a decade older than the others and I used to manage a team twice this size. I'm not proud but it hurts that I'm only trusted to input receipts and draft responses to HR queries for Karen or Julie to approve. The agency promised that this would be the first step to returning to a position of responsibility but so far the only responsibility Karen has given me is to add a splash of oat milk to her afternoon tea.

I'm still idly clicking on Nina's profile when I realise I've opened her latest payslip. I scan the usual deductions and my eyes land on the figure at the bottom. My stomach twists and turns like a cat in a bag when I see she's paid fifteen grand more than me. I hit the 'back' button, clicking with more vigour now, and find her date of birth, working out that she's thirteen years, two months and three days younger than me, to be precise. My knuckles are white and gripping the mouse almost becomes painful as I try to tell myself that age is just a number rather than a measure of worth, but I can't make myself believe it.

A squeak of Karen's chair brings me back to reality and I force myself to relax my hand and exhale slowly. It's not Nina's fault that she's young and attractive and rewarded for her hard work. She's certainly putting in the hours with the boss – that I can attest to. I let out a snort at my little joke as I return to her profile, scrolling desperately for anything that might make me feel better. I spot her address – Bethnal Green, somewhere trendy, I'll bet – and copy it into Google Street View. Her building is an imposing, historic block where she lives in a ground-floor flat with large windows that open right onto the street. Zooming in on number 17A, I spot a vase filled with an extravagant bouquet, the type men give to attractive women, and I picture David sending them with a cheeky card.

Suddenly I don't want to see any more and I close Google Street View just as Karen's voice comes from behind my right ear: 'That doesn't look like Rupert's receipts.'

My body stiffens as adrenaline hits me and a tremor judders through my arm.

'What is it exactly that's keeping you so occupied?' Karen leans over my shoulder and I am hit with a waft of her sickly perfume that goes straight to my head. With shaking fingers, I hit the 'home' button and manage to get rid of Nina's profile.

There's a tense silence as I suck air in through my nose and try not to sneeze as perfume tickles my nose, waiting to find out how much she's seen.

'Well?' is all she says, as if expecting me to launch into an explanation.

Julie and Matt are looking now too. Heat rises to my cheeks as I scrabble for something to say but last night is catching up with me. Sweat prickles on my back and the room spins as I open my mouth but find no words come out.

'I'm waiting,' Karen says with a little laugh but it's clear she's not amused. My mind is blank and I fear that this is the moment Karen has been waiting for. She's hated me since my very first week when I dared to ask if there was anything more productive I could be doing, back when I cared.

'Did you check that user journey for me, Kitty?' Matt says suddenly, breaking the tension.

I meet his round blue eyes and he gives an almost imperceptible nod.

'Yes,' I say, trying to keep the uncertainty out of my voice.

'And there were no broken links?'

This time his head seems to vibrate in a horizontal motion.

'No,' I say, catching on and feeling a rush of gratitude that I try to convey through my eyes.

'What are you talking about?' Karen cuts in, her voice tight with annoyance.

'I've had a few complaints about broken links on personal profiles so I put in a fix. I asked Kitty to check a couple for me.'

Karen's head swivels from Matt to me and back again. 'Right,' she says reluctantly. 'All sorted, then?'

'Sounds like it,' Matt says.

Karen sighs, not bothering to hide her disappointment that she hasn't managed to pin anything on me this time, and returns to her seat. I take an unsteady breath and fix my eyes on my screen. I don't dare look at Matt again but I can hear he is typing with purpose and I feel a rush of gratitude towards him. I also can't help but go over Nina's details in my head until I know them by rote. She may be growing close to my husband but now I feel like I have something over her too – I know where she lives.

FOUR

DAVID

It's one of those evenings where the heat of the day refuses to die. Friday night and we're in the back of an Uber and my shirt is pasted to my back with sweat. The interior smells like the driver has had a fag out of the window and sprayed air freshener to cover it up, leaving a sickly, almond scent that's deeply unpleasant. On top of that, he's driving like a maniac and keeps glancing at me in the rear-view mirror the way people do when they recognise me. I want to tell him to keep his eyes on the road or else he'll get us killed but I bite my tongue because I don't need a cab driver out there with a story about what a wanker David Okine is.

Next to me, Kitty is staring into space and sighing heavily every so often as if she couldn't care less whether he pulls a handbrake turn into oncoming traffic. We haven't spoken properly since the wine bottle incident and it's taken a couple of days for my anger to dissipate. She hasn't apologised and, given the state she was in, I wonder if she even remembers. I watch her out of the corner of my eye and see her right foot jiggling uncontrollably as her hands flop like two wet fish in her lap. She seems nervous but that's unfathomable since we're just going for dinner with friends.

Taking her fingers in mine, I try to massage some life into her hand but she snatches it back and turns to look out of the window so I can't see her face. I check my watch. We've only been in the car for fifteen minutes and already I can feel blood pounding at my temples.

'What's wrong?' I ask, under my breath so the driver won't hear.

'Nothing,' she says, sighing again, and I wonder whether she's had another bad day at the office. I know she hasn't been enjoying her job recently; it's been harder than she thought to take a step down.

'How was work?'

'Fine,' she says, sounding bored.

'Come on, tonight will be fun. Please.' I feel my energy draining.

We used to see the old gang once or twice a week. The club nights gave way to wine bars then dinner parties, and weekly became monthly, but these are our oldest friends. They were there the day we met, they shared our table at our wedding, we're godparents to one of their kids, for God's sake, but for some inexplicable reason, my wife can no longer stand them.

'Just try,' I say, between clenched teeth. 'For me.'

Kitty sighs again as we pull up at Tom and Annika's and she leaps out before the wheels have stopped moving. I'm slower as I pick up the chilled bottle of champagne from between my feet and get out of the car.

'Cheers,' I say as I slam the door.

'Hey, are you that geezer off the telly?' the driver calls out.

Kitty has disappeared through the gate without a backwards glance and I rub my cheek where a deep-rooted spot lurks painfully beneath my skin as I weigh up what to do. I want to pretend I haven't heard, but there's always the one who calls you a prick online and gets enough reposts that people believe them.

I paste on a smile as I turn. 'That's me.'

'Can I get a selfie?'

'Sure.' I back up to the window and crouch down, turning my face slightly so the spot isn't in shot. He holds up his phone and we both bare our teeth as he takes several photos. My quads begin to burn and my hand holding the icy bottle grows numb but I hold the position until he's got his shot.

'You watch the show?' I say, jarring my back as I stand.

'Nah, mate. Can't stand politics.'

I hold my fake smile as I step back and watch him add a row of emojis beneath the photo – too far away to see which ones – before I give him a wave and hurry up the driveway to the house. We've been instructed to go straight round to the garden so I squeeze past Tom's cherry-red Porsche and through the side gate. The house is one of those deceptive, modern buildings that looks like a two-storey parking garage from the front but when you walk around the back there's three great hulking walls of glass reflecting back at you.

The garden is serene, with tall hedges either side to stop the neighbours snooping, and a rolling lawn that's unusual for London. At the end is a wooden climbing frame and swing set in a tasteful ash wood where the kids are playing. Annika is down there supervising, her feet bare, blonde hair in a long plait and a chunky, cherubic toddler on her hip. The scene looks like a spread for one of those lifestyle magazines that Kitty always rolls her eyes at. Nothing is that perfect, she insists.

'David!' Tom spots me from his station behind the barbecue. His white shirt is open at the collar and his blond hair is combed across his forehead in a side parting, the same style he had the day we met, week one at Oxford, when Tom stuck out his hand and introduced himself by school rather than name,

'Harrow. You?' Eton passed the test but I didn't mention I was a scholarship boy.

I cross the front lawn to the patio where the rest of them are gathered. Caro is sitting at the table in a tent-like floral dress, adjusted so she can feed one of the twins; Ed is jogging the other against his shoulder with bags under his eyes that look like strange pockets of flesh that have been stuck to his face. Kitty stands by the table, conspicuous in her black dress in this weather, a large glass of white already in hand.

'Evening all.' I go over to the barbecue and give Tom the bottle. 'Harrow,' I say with a broad grin, enjoying how he winces slightly even after all this time. 'Good to see you. Those look incredible.'

A tray of steaks is laid out on the metal wing of the barbecue that's the size of a small car and is already whooshing with gas. Tom clasps my hand and shoves the bottle into an ice bucket by his feet with half a dozen others.

'Help yourself,' he says.

I pull out an open bottle and pour some golden liquid into a champagne flute. The first sip goes down far too easily and I allow myself to knock it back, turning away to top it up again, but Tom's eyes drop to the full glass with a knowing smile, 'Long week?'

I raise both eyebrows. 'You could say that,' I reply, and join the others at the table.

Pulling up a seat next to Caro, I kiss her cheek and ask, 'How are the girls?'

'Little devils.'

'Give me a go, then.' I hold out my arms for the little one and Ed bundles her over. She's a red-hot mess of snot and tears but I tuck her against my forearm and bounce until the crying stops. It's my one technique but it usually does the trick.

'The magic touch,' Caro says with a smile and I see a shimmer of tears in her eyes that catches me by surprise. She's mostly been on the stage since drama school, playing loud, brash characters, and it's sometimes hard to remember where they end and the real Caro begins.

'How's the show?' Ed asks.

I launch into a story about last week's interview though it wasn't one of my finest, sensing Ed and Caro will be happy to listen rather than talk in their sleep-deprived state. Over at the barbecue, Tom refills Kitty's drink and I see she's dabbing her eyes. He throws an arm around her shoulder and draws her close. I tell myself I should be grateful that she's opening up but it stings that it's Tom she's talking to and not me.

Annika appears with her three at her heels.

'Kids, time to say good night.' She ushers her children to the table to give each of us a sticky hug in her brisk way and then sends them into the house under the supervision of a broad, Slavic nanny named Olga.

Annika collapses into the seat beside me and gives me an air kiss. 'Tom, I need a drink,' she calls out.

We always wondered what sort of woman Tom would end up with. In our twenties, Kitty and I would rather uncharitably place bets on how long his girlfriends would last, guessing in weeks rather than months, but then he met Annika, already a successful furniture designer and a few years older, with classic Nordic white-blonde hair, ice-chip eyes and an unflappable demeanour and it soon became apparent that she did not find Tom's unreliability charming. She gave him two options: straighten out or get out, and he made the right choice but he's railed against it ever since.

Tom pops another bottle of champagne and fills his wife's glass before topping up the rest of us. Ed eases the sleeping baby out of my arms and both are deposited into a juggernaut of a buggy. The spot on my cheek is throbbing but I avoid touching it, taking regular sips of my drink to keep my hands busy.

A gurgle comes from the pram and Ed leaps to his feet but

the baby falls quiet before he gets there. 'Thank God. If one of them starts up, the other will join in and then we're snookered.'

'Do let's talk about something other than kids,' Caro says, with a sigh.

'Fine by me,' Kitty chimes in a little too quickly and there's a beat of silence before Kitty sighs and says, 'Do excuse me, Caro darling, it's been a long week.'

Caro reaches her hand across the table and we're quiet for a moment until Tom pipes up, 'Get any more creepy letters, Dave?'

Now their heads turn to me in unison and I see the two small frown lines dent Kitty's brow. My fingers worry the sore spot on my cheek as I shoot a look at Tom. He never can keep his mouth shut.

'Come on, *David* please. You know I can't stand Dave,' I say, forcing a smile.

'Evasion, your honour,' Ed says, always the barrister. 'Answer the question, Mr Okine.'

They're all smiling now, except Kitty who is watching me with narrowed eyes.

'What letters?' she says.

'Just fan mail.'

'What fucking letters, David?' her voice is hard and no one is smiling any more. Bloody Tom. I drain the rest of my drink and try to keep my tone light and a hint of a smile on my face.

'Just the usual declarations of love. Who sends a letter these days anyway? It's probably just some troll with too much time on their hands. If you want some real filth, you should see what I get online.'

'Have you given them to the police?' Kitty says, without cracking a smile.

I'm saved from answering by Tom putting the platter of steaks in the middle of the table with a flourish.

'Shit! The salads.' Annika leaps up and disappears inside

while Tom uncorks a couple of bottles of red. My head is starting to swim but the food will help and I'm relieved their attention has been diverted. They're being overly sensitive. Of course there was that whole business with McCrazy, my university stalker who Tom gave a silly nickname to that stuck, but that was years ago and I sorted it. Everyone on TV gets things sent to them. I can't be going to the police every time someone sends me a pair of knickers in the post.

Annika returns with a platter of salads that look too good to be home-made. 'Like you English say, dig in,' she says with a smile.

Tom serves us and the nanny reappears to wheel the twins into the house. We polish off the steak and the red and conversation flows with the alcohol. The light begins to fade and Annika sparks some citronella candles that bathe us in a kind glow. Looking around the table, it's easy to recall the teenagers we once were. The women have barely changed; only Kitty looks paler and thinner but it has been a difficult year. Time hasn't been quite so kind to the men: Ed's lost most of his hair and Tom's jowls and thighs are meatier, but we're doing all right.

People trade stories but soon the plates are cleared and the evening starts to break up as Ed goes to check on the twins.

Tom pushes his chair back. 'I'm just going for a stroll,' he says. 'Anyone fancy stretching their legs?'

'Tom, please,' Annika says, her annoyance evident in her sigh. We all know his code for a smoke.

'Anyone?' he asks one last time before setting off for the end of the garden.

I think about joining him but I see Kitty opening the Uber app on her phone and a moment later she says, 'Two minutes, David.'

'Right.' I turn to Annika and throw out my arms. 'Thank you for a wonderful evening, darling.'

She wraps me in a perfumed hug and says in my ear, 'Take care of yourself.'

I drop a kiss on the top of Caro's head and she blows me an air kiss, and I slap Ed on the back as I pass. 'Let's do it again soon.' They all nod and smile but Kitty has already disappeared around the front before I've even finished my goodbyes.

'Sorry.' I say, raising my eyebrows in her direction, but they wave me away like old friends do and I stagger after her, my steps feeling heavier as I get closer to where the Uber is idling with Kitty inside. It's only ten thirty but I'm drunk and I feel rather stupid. I'm too old for this. Getting in beside her, I slump onto the back seat and hope she doesn't try to talk to me and notice the state I'm in, but thankfully the driver's thumping dance music is too loud for that.

We drive for five minutes in silence and I find myself fighting waves of nausea as the steak and booze percolate in my stomach. I open one eye and see Kitty is looking out of the window, her face turned away from me, so I straighten up, easing my phone from my pocket, hoping that social media will distract me from the battle raging inside my body. I see immediately that I've been tagged in a photo that's getting commented on and I feel the familiar twist of unease as I find the original post, painfully aware that it's usually the bad not the good that grab attention. The photo loads and I see it's me and the driver from earlier and I tell myself it can't be that bad – it was only a short journey – as I read the caption.

'*What a dick...*' Alongside a whole row of aubergine emojis.

A burst of fury makes it through my stupor and I shove the phone under Kitty's nose. 'And to think I gave that wanker five stars.'

It would have been the type of thing we'd laugh about before but Kitty barely glances at the screen before turning back to the window.

'Is something wrong?' I ask gently.

She turns to me and I see defeat etched on her face, 'Is it starting again?'

'What?'

'The letters.'

'No, Kitty, this is different.'

'David, we've spent years putting that behind us. We moved house, for God's sake, and you promised if it started again you'd go straight to the police.'

I feel a simmering reluctance that I can't explain but something tells me that involving the police should be the very last resort.

'How about this?' I squeeze her fingers. 'If another letter turns up I will speak to the police.'

She wipes her cheeks with her fingers and sighs, 'You promise this time?'

Glancing out of the window I see we're getting close to home and I say more resolutely than I feel, 'I promise.'

Kitty sighs but before we pull up outside the house she suddenly adds, 'And listen, I don't want to see Tom and Annika for a while, OK?'

Frowning, I turn to her, feeling confused after such a lovely evening. 'Why not?'

'It's just...' she hesitates and I see she's trying to work out how to phrase something she knows I won't like. 'All that money – the steaks, the wine – it feels so hollow.'

'So our friends being generous is hollow?'

'I knew you wouldn't understand,' she says, her voice harsh.

'You're right, I don't. We've been doing the same things for years and you've never complained before.'

'Maybe that's the problem. Look at us all sitting there playing out the fantasy of living these perfect lives. Take Tom and Annika with their beautiful home and cherubic children.'

Her voice is thick with bitterness and I feel myself pulling away from her. 'Do you wish they weren't happy?'

'Happy?' She lets out a strange laugh. 'You think they're happy?'

I frown; they may have their problems but don't we all? The Uber pulls up outside our house and she leaps out and hurries to the front door. It takes me a few attempts to find the door handle as I grope in the dark, praying the driver isn't watching me in his mirror. When I finally get the door open, I concentrate hard on getting out and walking in a straight line, avoiding looking up at the dark windows that seem to be the empty eye sockets of a skull.

Over the thumping music that continues as I cross the pavement to the steps that lead up to my front door, I hear the driver call out, 'Hey, are you...?'

This time, I don't break stride; instead I jog up the steps and follow Kitty through the front door but by the time I get inside, she's already disappeared. Standing in the dark hallway, alone, a tinging sound rings in my ears and it feels like I'm on sand, slipping and sliding, though my feet are square on the floor. I should never have drunk so much. Tomorrow I know I'll have real remorse, but tonight all I want is for the walls to stop swaying.

Putting an arm on the wall, I take a deep breath, readying myself for the walk up the stairs, when my eyes are drawn to the mat beneath my feet and what appears to be the edge of a small brown envelope peeping out. I squint and try to focus but I can't quite believe what I'm seeing. I crouch down and pull out another cheap-looking envelope with my name in purple ink. Did someone put it through the door while we were out, or has it been there a while, going unnoticed?

I tell myself that if Kitty had spotted it she would have immediately confronted me, demanding I take it to the police this instant. It could have been there weeks or even months, so rather than being anything new, it's old news and I only promised Kitty that I'd speak to the police if another letter turned up. Pleased with this logic, despite my muddled state, I quickly tear it open, wishing I could be strong enough to throw it away without reading it but wanting to know what's written inside.

I saw you with HER.

The final three letters are capitals and have been scrawled over and over so many times that it's surprising the pen hasn't gone right through the paper. I frown as an image of Nina pops into my mind but I tell myself that 'her' could mean half the population and it's hardly a threat. There's no reason to think that Nina could be in any danger.

FIVE

KITTY

It hasn't been a good week – seeing David and Nina together hurt, but if I'm honest with myself, things between me and David haven't been good for a very long time indeed and I can't blame Nina for that. I spent the weekend torturing myself by imagining them together, and first thing Monday morning I make an appointment with Connor rather than waiting for our weekly appointment to roll around, telling myself it's time to start putting myself first. Connor always says I deserve more than being the supporting actor in my own life and I'm beginning to think that he's right.

As I make my way to Connor's office in Camden I feel like a dark cloud is lifting. I've spent too much time alone with my thoughts and it always feels good to share them with someone, even if it's someone I'm paying. Striding along the busy main road, I dodge commuters in their smart skirts, shirts and suits walking to the tube, and go against the grain towards the row of terraced houses where Connor has an office on the first floor, opposite a hangar-sized Sainsbury's, close enough to the heart of Camden that you can live every sight and smell if you crack open the window.

Taking the short flight of steps up to the glossy black front door, I press the buzzer and wait for Connor to let me in. There's no sign or any other indication that it's a psychiatrist's office, but he once told me that's to keep things discreet for his clients. I didn't understand the need at first but I've come to appreciate the anonymity since I've been seeing him much more regularly than I first expected. There's something about Connor that speaks to me in a way others before him haven't, an honesty between us that I've found hard to replicate anywhere else, other than of course, with David.

After a moment, the door buzzes and I push it open and enter the small, stark waiting area, with its white walls and white plastic seats. On the low table in the middle of the room is a dog-eared copy of *Cosmopolitan* that I've read cover to cover several times over. I take a seat on the chair facing the window and watch heads bobbing past over the top of the strip of plastic that's been stuck on to obscure the glass until Connor's soft Irish voice crackles over the intercom, 'Come on up.'

The staircase is steep and narrow and robs me of my breath as I use the railing to pull myself up, thinking back to the first time I came here, when I was in a deep, dark, black hole of despair. I'd only recently stopped working and it seemed that my problems were the only thing going round in my head. It's been almost a year and I feel lighter, more positive, if not wholly recovered but on the right path. The thought makes me smile as I reach the frayed maroon carpet at the top of the stairs until I'm hit by the rush of adrenaline I always get before seeing him. I wonder if everyone feels this way before they see a psychiatrist – do they get a hit of nerves before they open up their darkest secrets like a wound, or do I just have more to hide than most?

I knock gently on the door and Connor calls, 'Come in.'

Connor's office is shabby and impersonal and there's nothing challenging or intimidating about the decor – no heavy books or unusual artwork. The abstract painting behind the sofa, a muddle of pinks and blues, would be at home in any mid-priced hotel chain. Connor's in his usual seat at his small desk that's tucked against the wall where he's writing notes in his large leather book. Paying no heed to the sun streaming through the window, he's in a blue sweater over his shirt and his black hair is combed back, revealing his distinctive widow's peak. He's handsome, but he's one of those men that looks as if he was born in his work clothes. I've tried to imagine him loosened up, perhaps in a T-shirt with a beer in his hand, but it's impossible. There's no wedding ring on his finger and I wonder if he has a girlfriend, though I expect he's one of those types that is married to the job.

'With you in just a moment,' he says with a nod to the seating area in the middle of the room. 'Please, take a seat.'

I sink into my usual spot on the sofa, waiting for him to finish, the scratch of his pen the only noise in the room to accompany the low hum of traffic outside. He always follows the same ritual and I wonder, not for the first time, if Connor once read that a psychiatrist should always make a patient wait in order to appear in control. He strikes me as a man who likes to do things by the book.

'Done. Now you have my full attention.' He shuts his note-book with a snap and strides over on long legs to take the battered armchair opposite me. We are sitting either side of a low coffee table where a glass of iced water sweats. It's a thoughtful touch in the muggy heat and I take a sip, then a gulp, before draining the lot.

'Hot today,' I say, aiming for a conversational tone but Connor just leans over and switches on the fan on the table which whirs into life and circulates the warm air. I kick off my scruffy flats and tuck my feet up next to me on the seat. The silence between us drags but Connor doesn't like to speak first – probably another learning from 'Psychiatry 101'. We have a slightly tetchy relationship but I've found it helps me open up to him. It's when people are too nice that I struggle.

'It's been a good week,' I say. My false cheerfulness is as obvious as if I'd burst into tears and I immediately regret it. Connor raises an eyebrow but he doesn't need to say anything. I try again. 'OK, it's been a fine week. Some things have been more difficult than others but aren't all weeks like that?'

'What has been difficult?' Of course, he latches on to that.

'Work. Karen. You know I can't stand her.'

Connor gives me one of his searching looks and I say, 'OK, so it's not really about Karen. It's David, of course.'

He crosses his legs and leans back: *continue*. I've learned to read his signals and I fear the same is true of him for me.

'He's having an affair,' I blurt out.

I feel Connor's dark-blue eyes burn into mine as my cheeks grow warm. I'll admit it's not the first time I've suspected David of infidelity but somehow this time I'm more sure of myself. Breaking his gaze, I say, 'Well, I don't know for sure but there's this woman at work, his researcher – they seem to be attached at the hip, and she's always smiling this smug little smile...'

To his credit, Connor's face remains expressionless but I stop myself when I realise how petty I sound and brace myself for a rebuke, but Connor just nods and says gently, 'It's hard when we lose trust in our loved ones. It makes us question lots of things we usually wouldn't.'

'Exactly.' We smile at each other and I remember another reason why I like Connor so much: he doesn't belittle me. He makes me feel as if we're on the same team, working towards the same goal, and he listens. We might not always agree but he doesn't shut me down at the first opportunity.

'Do you think you could talk to David about your suspicions?' he asks.

I picture that conversation and the inevitable argument that would ensue and I shake my head.

'Maybe I'm overreacting.' I wind back now I've said the words out loud and heard the absurdity. 'They went for a drink together one night after work last week. It was probably entirely innocent.'

'Don't dismiss your feelings. It's important to acknowledge them and find a way to confront them or move past them. Is there something specific that has made you feel this way?'

My cheeks grow warm and I fiddle with the fan, pressing the button to move it onto the highest setting. 'I've just seen the way she looks at him.'

Connor doesn't respond immediately and in the long silence I begin to feel foolish. Really all that's happened is David went for a drink with a colleague, something we've all done, even me in a former life. Obviously Karen, Julie, Matt and I do not go out for drinks but it's hardly a crime. I open my mouth to back down but Connor cuts in.

'And is there anything that David has done to suggest he's reciprocating?'

I think of the way he pulled his chair close and turned on the charm so she must have felt like the star of the show but I can't mention that or Connor would know I was watching them and he certainly wouldn't approve of that.

'She's very attractive,' I mutter.

'I think it's fair to say it's inconclusive but let's put that aside for now since we're here to focus on you and the things you can control. How would you feel if David were having an affair?'

I try to imagine it and find my shirt sticking to my lower back. I tug it loose, going for another sip of water but finding the glass is empty. David is all I've known my whole adult life and I dread the day I fear is coming, the day I'm forced to make a choice between him or me. Connor spots my unease and holds up his hand, 'OK, I see that's difficult for you. Let's go back a little further. Do you mind if we talk about your father? I think you mentioned in one of our previous sessions that he left you and your mum when you were small?'

My jaw tightens with annoyance as I feel him unearthing memories I'd rather were left buried. 'I'm not sure I see how that's relevant.'

'Perhaps it's linked to how you're feeling now. Can we explore it a little further?' I'm sure I spot superiority in the slight upturn of his mouth as if he senses he's on to something. Connor always seems to enjoy going back to my childhood and picking at it like a scab as if he hasn't achieved anything in a session unless he's related it back to one of my parents.

'Fine, but that happened when I was a baby,' I add, 'and he died when I was three. I don't remember him.'

'Things that happen when we're young have a ripple effect across a lifetime. Is there something you remember about that time?'

I try to delve into the deepest recesses of my memory but my father has always been a blank outline, a cartoon figure that my mum liked to complain about. *Wastrel. Good-for-nothing. Coward*, were some of the choice names she'd call him, when as far as I could tell, his only failing was to dare to return to his wife. She never talked about him and there weren't framed photos around but if I asked she would turn the pages of a tatty album and point him out in newspaper clippings she'd stuck in a book. He was head of the local council and she seemed to like the aura of power it gave him, but in my mind's eye, all I can see is a regular man, standing at the edge of a group, neither smiling nor frowning, wearing an ornamental gold chain around his neck.

'He had a moustache,' I say, grasping at the one feature that stands out.

Connor waits for more, tapping his long fingers together.

'He was much older than my mum.' I remember the maroon suit and dodgy glasses. He probably couldn't believe it when a young woman like her showed interest in him. 'And Mum said he was smart.'

'And how do you feel when you think about him?'

I rake my memories but I can't dredge up a single emotion.

'I was too young,' I say. 'All I remember are photos and things my mum said.'

'What did your mother say?'

'She said I must have got my brains from him.' That was all he gave either of us, she used to say with a slight curl of her lip, as if she'd expected so much more and felt like she'd got a raw deal, but I don't tell Connor that. It felt like the cause of a distance between us, something in me she simply couldn't understand, and it seemed to cause a deep-seated resentment in her that I could never resolve.

Connor pulls a tissue from the box on the table and I realise a single tear has slipped from my left eye and fallen down my cheek. It's been a short round but I feel like he's won, although I know that's stupid. I dab at my eyes and blow my nose. Our sessions always follow a familiar pattern: I talk about David and Connor delves into the deepest recesses of my childhood, extracting a memory I thought I'd forgotten. Initially I hated his interjections, but I must admit, it seems to help. Somewhere, deep inside, the swirling mass of feelings that's always felt padlocked shut is slowly loosening, as if one day we'll pull on the end of something and the whole lot will cascade out of me. It's what keeps me coming back. I want to get better, for David.

I think we both assumed the night of the May Ball would be a one-off but that summer we both happened to stay in Oxford. *What luck!* David manned the phones for his college's annual fundraiser – getting the highest pledges of any student across the whole university – and there was nothing for me at home, so I stayed up, making some extra money as a college cleaner. I'd wear the apron and hairnet while we made love and David would laugh himself silly.

It was an Indian summer and the last week of September was particularly hot. David knocked on my door at three in the morning, drunk and stoned, rambling something nonsensical about Harrow. He half collapsed on my bed, twisting his body at an odd angle, and I was close to calling for help when I realised he was trying to fish something out of his pocket. The ring itself was only costume jewellery, not even sterling silver, but when he squeezed it over my knuckle, it felt like I was levitating above my body. I can't remember ever being so happy. I still wear it; I couldn't take it off even if I wanted to. Some people have diamonds, others have strings of pearls but I don't care – I have David.

Connor coughs pointedly, 'Where were you?'

I blink a few times and turn my face into the fan. I know Connor will be disappointed if I say I was thinking of David in the midst of his breakthrough.

'Just thinking about my dad,' I say, but his eyes narrow and I can tell he doesn't believe me.

He shifts in his seat and glances at his watch. 'Our time is almost up but, you know, I think we've made some good progress.'

His praise gives me a small lift and I sit up straighter in my chair, placing my feet back on the floor and into my shoes.

'I think we've established that having suspicions in a relationship is normal. You can sit with them without letting them ruin your relationship, especially when you don't have any evidence to back them up. You just have to acknowledge them.'

I turn this over in my mind and a slow smile spreads across my face.

'You're absolutely right,' I say and I leave the room, feeling pleased that Connor hasn't dismissed my feelings; in fact, it seems like he's telling me to go and gather evidence to establish whether my suspicions are the reality. I feel like he's given me permission to investigate Nina further.

SIX

DAVID

Kitty left early this morning and I must admit, it was a relief to be alone. After an interminable weekend spent trying to hide the intensity of my hangover while Kitty haunted our house like a ghost, it finally felt like I could take a full breath, so I rolled over in bed and gave myself a lie-in.

I can't remember a time when it's been this bad between us but nothing I do seems to help, and this morning I have other things on my mind. The Dick Bell interview is this week and it's probably the biggest moment of my career to date. I've been trying to land him for months – persuading, wheedling and eventually begging his press secretary until she finally agreed that now *is* the right time to rehabilitate his career. It's going to be a huge moment for both of us; he needs the show as much as I need him.

I decide to walk to the office to feel the sun on my skin. A couple of people have a second look as I stride by and I admit to feeling a small glow of pleasure in being recognised. Fame can be fun when people only have the chance to admire from afar. When I reach the main doors of the Prestige building, I stride through the security barriers feeling like a man on a mission and whistle softly as I take the stairs to my first-floor office, stopping by Angela's desk to check for messages on the way.

'Good morning, Angela.' I give her a broad smile as I approach her desk. She's wearing one of her usual bold power suits, today in a post-box red. Angela has been my assistant for ten years, coming to Prestige with me from the radio show where I made my name, and I sometimes worry that she knows me better than anyone, Kitty included. She turns to me but the frown on her face doesn't lift.

'What's wrong?' I ask.

'You're not going to like it.'

'What?' My mind is spinning through options of what it could be. Angela isn't one for melodrama.

'Dick Bell has pulled out of the interview.' My stomach plummets and I put a hand on her desk to steady myself. It's the worst thing she could have said.

'What?' My voice comes out as a squeak. 'When? Why didn't I know about this?'

Angela holds up her hand and waits until I fall silent. 'His press secretary just got off the phone with Stanley ten minutes ago and he came straight here looking for you. I tried your mobile but there was no answer.'

I pull my phone from my pocket and see there's a missed call from the office line and Angela has left a message. 'Yes, of course, sorry, Angela,' I mutter.

'Stanley said to go straight up when you turned up.'

My good mood is shattered and I take a deep breath, nodding as I hang my head and set off for the senior executive floor, taking the stairs to give me some headspace before I step out onto the thick carpet. As I pass the bank of assistants, a young man in a narrow tie with a trendy haircut pops his head up and calls out, 'He's expecting you.'

I nod grimly, not needing to be told that Stanley is going to hit the roof, and continue to the walnut door with his nameplate on the front. Taking another deep breath, I knock once and wait for him to call, 'Come,' before stepping inside, dread churning in the depths of my stomach. Stanley is hunched over his computer, the top of his bald head winking at me, shiny and pink. He continues typing for a moment, keeping me waiting, before looking up, his eyes huge behind a pair of wacky glasses in a bold red, and says, 'David, what a fucking disaster.'

The first time I met Stanley was at an awards do. I spotted this balding, skinny man in a black and white checked suit – he always does like to make an impression – and the first thing he said to me was, 'That face ought to be on telly.' We hit it off right away and years later, when I came to him with the idea for *Confessions*, he said yes without question. A spot of flirting usually goes a long way but today it's plain that he's not in the mood so I keep my questions to the point, 'What did they say?'

'He's out. That's it.'

'But there's a signed contract in place.' My voice sounds desperate and I vow to calm myself as Stanley's eyes narrow and I feel my insides turn cold.

'There is, David, but apparently you promised Dick a full script and they've just found out they're not getting one.'

'I never promised...'

He pulls in his chin so even on his skinny frame he has a thick double chin, looking more than ever like an earthworm rising up from the mud.

'I may have said they'd get a rough outline of the questions but I never said "script".'

'David, what the fuck were you thinking? "Unscripted". "Honest". Those are in the tagline of the show, for fuck's sake.'

I bow my head, biting back the retort that of course I know the tagline for the show, I was the one who wrote it.

'The teasers have been running for weeks and are getting good traction. We can't pull it now. This could be the end of the whole show – absolute catastrophe, David. The ratings have been waning and it's been too long since we had a hit. You must know how much we need this. How much *you* need this.'

It's always the truth that hurts the most and every word is a sucker punch. I've known for months that the show has been struggling, with audience numbers declining and the calibre of guests falling short, but I've kidded myself that no one else has noticed, that it's just me worrying too much. Hearing Stanley confirm that I'm close to the edge is excruciating.

'I'll fix it.' I say the only words I can and he nods.

'You do that, and do it yesterday. Get on to Dick and I'll speak to the lawyers and see if there's anything we can pin them to but don't get your hopes up on that front.'

He lowers his glasses and my insides turn to jelly but I hold his gaze. 'This is your chance to stay relevant.' I swallow hard and nod before he dismisses me with the words, 'Now get to it.'

I scurry back to my office, feeling embarrassed to even think of the way I strode in here – whistling, for God's sake, as if I was untouchable. Nobody is irreplaceable in telly, I should never have forgotten that – it's what Stanley said to me the day *Confessions* was commissioned. Returning to my office, I'm struck by how small it is compared to Stanley's and the glass walls mean there is zero privacy, but I still felt like I'd made it when I first walked in. I remember how bloody pleased with myself I was, but now I just wish there were proper walls so I could hide behind them. But there's no time to feel depressed; failing is not an option so I pick up my phone, pressing the button for Angela's line and she answers on the first ring.

'Yes, David?'

'Can you get me Dick Bell's publicist on the phone, please?'

'Hold a moment.' A repetitive beeping comes down the line while I wait for Angela to find the number and ring through. I sit forward in my seat, preparing myself for a difficult conversation, getting ready to swallow my anger and turn on the charm.

The line connects and I take a breath but it's Angela's voice that comes through again, 'They're not taking your calls, I'm afraid.'

My anger rushes back, 'What do you mean? We've been working on this for months. They can't just not take my calls.'

'She said it's not a good time.'

'Of course it's not a good time. They're fucking me.'

'Is there anything else I can do for you, David?' Angela asks in a clipped voice and I remember too late that she doesn't like bad language, 'Sorry, Angela,' I say contritely, 'Nothing else for now.'

The line goes dead and I rock back in my chair, wondering how the hell I'm going to salvage this. There's a tap on the door and I look up, expecting Angela with a coffee and some soothing words but it's Nina, with her hair pulled up into a tight bun on the top of her head and a berry-red lipstick on her full lips. Shaking my head, I tell myself I shouldn't be noticing her lipstick when my whole life is on the line but she does look excruciatingly pretty and I silently berate myself for behaving like Tom. I must be spending too much time with him.

'Everything OK?' she asks gently in a way that suggests she's already heard what's happened. News leaks in this place like water through a sieve, especially bad news, and I feel heat rising to my cheeks as I picture people passing it on with glee.

'It's a fucking disaster,' I say, my voice sounding thicker than usual.

She comes in and closes the door, hurrying over to the desk and pulling up a chair beside me, taking my arm and looking at me in a way that makes me sit up a bit straighter, as if she believes I could do anything. 'What can I do?'

I shake my head as I desperately try to think of ways to get through to Dick, but I've already used my only Westminster contact to get him in the first place and I'm all out of ideas. Nina rubs my upper arm and I close my eyes, determined not to cry although I can feel the pressure of tears behind my eyes. 'I don't suppose you know Dick Bell?' I say, half joking but with a pathetic shred of hope.

She lets out a strangled laugh, acknowledging that it's a ridiculous suggestion – Dick Bell and Nina are from completely different worlds.

'Sadly not,' she says. 'I don't get how he can just pull out like this. I thought he'd signed a contract?'

'He knows we're not going to sue him. There'll be some loophole his lawyers have found.'

'Have you spoken to his team?'

'They're not taking my calls.'

'We could go to his office?'

'And sneak past Whitehall security?'

'Or wait for him outside?'

'Like the gutter press?'

She has no response to this and we descend into silence. A black gloom overtakes me and I slump forward, resting my head on my hands. If it wasn't eleven in the morning I'd suggest the pub so we could drown our sorrows and I'm considering suggesting it anyway when Nina suddenly asks, 'Didn't you two go to the same school?'

I shake my head, thinking back to the pages of research we have on him. 'No, he went to Harrow.' As the name of the school leaves my lips, a surge of excitement runs through me and I sit up straighter.

'What?' asks Nina.

I don't answer and instead rifle through the ream of notes on my desk, searching for Dick's early life until I land on the right page. A wide smile spreads across my face when I see he was only a year ahead of Tom; I can't believe I haven't thought of this before. I take my phone out of my pocket.

'What are you doing?' she asks.

Holding up my hand, I find Tom's number and press call,

listening to it ring as Nina watches on. I think it's going to ring out but he answers with, 'Dave, what's happening?'

'Tom, how are you?' I say, ignoring the 'Dave'.

'Shit,' he says. 'The weekend was a total washout.'

'That good?'

'Annika had me cleaning out the garage all day Saturday and then we had an awful dinner with her business partner last night. The Norwegians are all so bloody sensible.'

I laugh but get to the point: 'Tom, I need a favour.'

He groans, 'Tell me it's not going to land me in prison, or worse, in trouble with Annika.'

'It's not. I just wondered if you know Dick Bell from school? He was the year above you.'

'The Right Honourable Bell-end? Of course I know him. Played squash with him a couple of weeks ago, in fact, at the club. He's not as bad as you might think actually, for a man of his heft. I beat him of course, but it was closer than I'd like.'

'He was meant to be on the show but he's got cold feet and won't return my calls. Do you think you could have a word?'

There's a pause and I hold my breath. Tom may be my best friend but he's always been a man to weigh up what's in it for him in any given situation, and he's very protective of his powerful friends. He's always known which side his bread is buttered.

Tom lets out a strained laugh, '*Confessions*, for a disgraced MP? You've got to be kidding me.'

'Why? The show gets good ratings and surely it's time for him to get his side of the story across?'

'The show's great, but come on, we both know that Dick will get crucified.'

'Not necessarily. I'll give him a fair trial but it's down to him what he says. Yes, it might restart the fire all over again, but it could be his only option to rehabilitate his career.

Tom sighs and I can tell he's weighing it up.

'Just get him to call me, that's all I ask. Please.'

He lets out another long sigh and says, 'OK, but only because it's you.'

'You won't regret it. Thank you, Tom. I owe you one.' A wide smile breaks out on Nina's face and I notice her teeth are a blinding white.

'You owe me more than one,' he says and ends the call.

I hang up and Nina lets out a shriek that makes me smile, but I don't want to get carried away so I try to dampen her excitement, 'He hasn't even called yet.'

'You'll persuade him,' she says. 'Who can say no to you?'

Our eyes meet and I feel a flicker of something pass between us as Nina stands; I wonder for a moment if she's going to hug me but she just says, 'I better go and finalise the script. We're going to need it.'

I watch as she walks to the door but before she leaves she hesitates and turns back towards me, picking something up off my desk and peering at it before holding it out to me.

'David, what's this?' It's a small brown envelope from the top of my in-tray with my name written on the front in purple letters. It's been such a topsy-turvy morning that I somehow haven't spotted it.

'No idea,' I say as my heart pounds, now for a very different reason. 'Why do you ask?' I try to deflect her question as I wonder how the letter got there. You need a security pass to get into the building and Angela guards my door like a bulldog.

'It looks weird. Who writes in purple ink? Is it a fan?' She smiles in a teasing way but I don't feel like laughing any more. Since she's looking at me expectantly, I gingerly tear it open, trying to keep my expression neutral as my stomach churns and I feel my good mood draining away.

Inside, written in purple again, it says, 'She better watch her back.'

I feel a cold chill run through me as I stare at the words to avoid having to make eye contact with Nina. Is she the woman it is referring to? Should I warn her that someone might be watching her? I open my mouth to say something but the words die on my lips. What do I really know? I have no idea whether this even involves her and the last thing I want is to frighten her unnecessarily. That wouldn't be fair.

'Well?'

'It's just a good luck message for the show,' I say, and her smile widens though I can't shake the feeling that the letters may be a warning I shouldn't ignore.

SEVEN

KITTY

Thursday is my favourite night of the week, though I would never admit that to David since he finds it so stressful. I have my *Confessions* routine: a bottle of white and a Chinese takeaway in front of the TV. I find that there's something truly decadent about washing down unctuous kung pao noodles with an ice-cold Pinot Grigio while David picks apart his subject, tearing meat from bone to get to the raw truth beneath. And tonight is a doozy – David has managed to get Dick Bell to appear and it's been advertised all week like a prime-time fight. Why is it that these disgraced MPs always think they deserve more lives than a cat?

I may be biased, but David is an excellent interviewer. He's always had an eye for detail, even in his younger days when his mind was more often somewhat clouded by some substance or other. That first night we met, in the common room at the end of the May Ball when there were more alcohol fumes coming off David than a Christmas pudding, he squinted at me and asked, 'Are you here with anyone?'

'No one special,' I answered vaguely, hoping that would satisfy him, but he didn't let it go. 'Who were you with earlier?'

Feeling a stir of annoyance that I swallowed, I shrugged and replied, 'I've just been wandering.'

'Alone?'

Lifting my chin and ignoring the rush of heat to my cheeks, I said, 'Yes, alone.' The truth was, I enjoyed my own company – I always had – and I didn't need a self-serving group around me, parroting to each other how wonderful we all were, like most students did, David included. But instead of frowning or treating me like a social pariah, a slow smile spread across his face and he said, 'So I have you all to myself? Lucky me.'

There's no hint of that smile now as David appears on the screen and walks to the swivel chair in the centre of the dark studio as the theme music plays. I tap my fingers in time on my knee as he sits, crosses his legs and studies his notes while he waits for his cue. It's a clever set – just the spotlit chairs in a cavernous space with nothing to distract the viewer from the words being exchanged. The camera pans the room showing the outline of the live audience and then returns to David as the music reaches its crescendo. His jaw is set and I can see he's nervous – only a wife would notice but I can see the tension in his shoulders.

The music stops and David lifts his head with perfect timing, giving the viewers an easy smile to let them know they're in safe hands before beginning in his smooth tones, 'Good evening and thank you for joining us. Today I have Richard Bell in the chair, Member of Parliament for Haverford West and the former Secretary of State for Environment, Food and Rural Affairs. Richard, good evening.'

The camera pans to Dick Bell who is pink-faced and trussed up in a suit that's straining across his thighs and paunch, and he says, 'Good evening, David.'

I pour my first glass of wine and take a large swig, trying to dampen my fluttering nerves.

'Let's start with explaining to our viewers why you're here,'

David says and Dick nods. 'You resigned from your cabinet position in September 2019 following an accusation of inappropriate behaviour from a junior member of your staff.'

'That's correct,' Dick says, grinning as if it's a quiz show and he's about to play for the jackpot.

David leans forward, resting his elbows on his knees and closing the gap between them, intensity blazing in his eyes. 'Richard, as you know, this show is about honesty. It's a chance for you to get your side across without judgement. There's no script. You tell your side and let our viewers be the judge. How does that sound?'

'Fantastic.' Dick lets out a little laugh, wiping his hands on the front of his meaty thighs, and I can't help thinking that the narrow pinstripes were a mistake. He looks nervous.

'When did you first hear that Ms Taylor was making a complaint against you?' David begins with.

'About a week after she left, Internal Affairs got in touch. I assumed she'd decided to go off travelling with her mates or something, like most students, and I was absolutely flabbergasted to hear that she felt I'd behaved inappropriately during the brief time she was with us.'

'Flabbergasted?' David cocks his head and I make the same motion with my wine glass, sloshing some over my hand and licking it off.

'Yes, appalled. Horrified. Utterly shocked. However you want to say it.'

'You had no idea that Ms Taylor was unhappy with your conduct?'

'None whatsoever.' Dick sits up in his chair and stares down the barrel of the camera, looking as if he thinks he's on to a winning point. 'You've heard her story – everyone's heard her story – she said that I squeezed her shoulder and it made her uncomfortable. Do you know how many people I meet every day? Ten, twenty, fifty some days, and how many of those do you think I might make inadvertent contact with? A brush of the shoulder or a tap of the arm. Does that make me guilty of something?'

Dick's face turns red with indignation and David leaves a long pause as I steadily drain my glass.

'That's what we're here to discuss,' David says sharply before continuing, 'OK. Let's run through the sequence of events we know about and you can give your version.'

Dick nods but shifts back in his seat and his eyes narrow warily.

'June first, Ms Taylor joined your team.'

Dick waves his hand again.

'June second, you "liked" Ms Taylor's Facebook photo from the album "uni shits and giggles".'

David looks up and catches Dick's eye with pure disdain, and there's a moment where colour rises in Dick's cheeks and his mouth flaps like a fish before he splutters, 'You need to understand the nature of my work. I have a team of twelve working across four social media accounts on all the major platforms. I'm posting up to ten times a day on each account and engaging with hundreds of messages. It's not an aspect I enjoy but it's part of the modern job and there's no way one individual can be across it all.'

'So you're saying that you, personally, did not "like" the photo?'

'I have no recollection of "liking" any photo but it's not impossible it was me. I try to engage with my constituents as often as I can across all social media but there's not enough hours in the day—'

'It was a photo of Ms Taylor in a Lycra bodysuit.'

'As I said, I have no recollection—'

'It was "liked" at 2.34 a.m., so what you're saying is that one of your team was trawling through Ms Taylor's online photos in the early hours of a Friday morning, just a few hours after she joined your office on an internship.'

Dick runs his hand through his hair. 'I really can't speculate on who was involved, given I have no memory of the situation.'

David seems to suck in a deep breath and lets the exchange hang in the air before continuing. 'OK, let's move on. June fifth, you asked Ms Taylor to join you at the Commons bar after work.'

'I often go to the bar with my team to celebrate successes.'

'Were the whole team there this time?'

'Not the whole team, as I recall, but I'm sure I invited them. It's usually an open invitation.'

'Who was present on this occasion?'

'It's a busy bar. I'm sure I spoke to lots of people that evening.'

'Who was sitting at your table?'

Colour is rising in Dick's face. David remains motionless. 'Just me and Rosie, but there was nothing untoward...'

'But you did have another intern at the time, Rory Douglas – do you remember him?'

Dick frowns as he nods. 'Of course, red hair.'

'How long did Mr Douglas intern for you?'

'He completed the programme and stayed for the whole summer. Must have been seven or eight weeks.'

'And how many times while he was an intern in your office did you invite him to the Commons bar?'

'Really I don't see what that's got to do with anything. We must have been in the bar together dozens of time over that summer.'

'But how many times did you invite him?'

'As I said, it was an open invitation.' Dick waves his hand and I slurp my wine.

'Well we've spoken to Mr Douglas and he said that you never once asked him to join you in the bar. He did however recall you inviting Ms Taylor to go with you on several occasions and, as he put it, "not giving up until she said yes". Is that your understanding of what happened?'

Dick is shaking his head so hard his jowls judder. 'No that isn't my understanding.'

David sits up and looks directly at Dick who wriggles in his seat. 'But you did go for a drink, alone, with Ms Taylor?'

'We weren't alone. There must have been twenty or thirty people I knew in the bar that night.'

'Did you sit together alone at a table?'

'Briefly.'

David ploughs on. 'Let's go to June seventh, a few days later, when you stood behind Ms Taylor on the pretence of looking at some work on her screen, and placed your hand on her shoulder.'

'The pretence? I *was* looking at her work.' Dick shifts in his seat but his shoulders drop and he seems to relax a little as if he's back on solid ground. 'As I said at the time, I may have touched Ms Taylor's shoulder but that's the way I am. I'm always hugging and putting my arm around people. My wife says I'm like a Labrador, full of exuberance.' He glances up from under his stringy hair as if he expects a laugh but the audience is silent.

'So you admit you did touch Ms Taylor?'

'It's possible. I'm sure I've even clasped your shoulder this evening but I don't hear you complaining.'

'Surely you can see how that's different?' David's voice is quiet but persistent. My wine is warm now but I don't want to get up for ice. This is the moment. The shoulder squeeze was the incident the press focused on. The left-wing papers wrote about personal space and the microaggressions women suffer, while the Tory tabloids ripped Rosie apart and called her an oversensitive 'snowflake'.

'How is it different?' Dick asks.

'Ms Taylor was a 21-year-old intern in her first job. You're an MP with over a decade of experience, a figurehead, and you're responsible for a large team. You must see the imbalance of power in that situation.'

'Of course, I'm aware of my position.' He draws himself up, looking like a puffed-up bird fluffing its feathers. 'But I don't see how a brush of a shoulder or a handshake is relevant to that. Are you suggesting that I should stop being friendly because I'm an MP?'

'Our definitions of "friendly" may differ.'

'It was a pat on the shoulder!' Dick is angry.

'Did you ever stop and think that workplace harassment is not always grabbing genitals and name-calling? It can be something more subtle than that, something insidious.'

David doesn't look down at his notes or back to the camera. He keeps his eyes fixed on Dick and I can almost see the sweat forming at Dick's rising hairline.

'Is it not your responsibility, as a boss, as someone who invites interns into your place of work, to behave in a way that makes everyone feel respected?'

'People do feel respected. I must be doing something right since I have had thirty or forty interns over the years.'

David cocks his head and says lightly, 'Yes, I know. As I mentioned, we spoke to Rory, the other intern in your office that summer, and he told us that all the junior staff have a nickname for you – do you know what it is?'

A single bead of sweat forms on Dick's forehead and glistens in the harsh lights as he flaps his mouth, his face reaching a shade of purple. 'I don't see how that's relevant at all. I can't control what junior members of staff say behind my back, and anyway, there are always bad apples.'

'They call you "the octopus",' David says, his lip curling in disgust as Dick seems to slump down in his seat. I raise my glass, a smile playing on my lips as I think, *Got him.* Dick Bell will

forever be associated with a creature with eight legs and tenta-
cles, however much he tries to distance himself from the allega-
tions; looking at his sweaty face and the wild flash of panic in
his eyes, it's clear he realises that the damage has been done.

David turns back to him, like a shark scenting blood. 'Do
you see that each of the alleged incidents may on the face of it
seem small – a comment here, a passing touch there – but the
impact can be devastating? Rosie Taylor has been unable to
pursue a career in politics, she's been publicly hounded and told
us that she's suffered huge amounts of stress and been unable to
work full time since. Do you still think your behaviour was...'
David pauses and then says with utter disdain, 'friendly?'

Dick opens and shuts his mouth, his face almost purple and
his stringy hair stuck down with sweat. Finally he says in a
heavy, resigned tone, 'As in the statement I made at the time, it
is not my recollection that I did anything untoward. The accusation came out of the blue and caused great personal upheaval
and I can't possibly comment on hearsay.'

David waits until he's finished before asking, 'Are you
sorry?'

Dick flounders like a giant whale stuck on a beach. 'I'm
sorry that my actions have been misunderstood, if that is indeed
the case.'

'So it's the misunderstanding that's the problem, not your
actions?'

'There are many people who share my view that I behaved
perfectly reasonably. The furore meant I had to leave the cabinet, which was regrettable, but the party took no further action
and chose to publicly support me.'

David sits up straight and turns away from Dick as the
camera pans to his face. 'I think that's the perfect moment on
which to finish. We have a credible complainant who stood to
gain nothing by speaking out about her experience. And yet, the
man in the chair sees nothing wrong with his actions and

continues to enjoy the support of his party. As always, I leave you to be the judge. I've been David Okine and tonight, you've been here for Richard Bell's *Confessions*.'

The show ends with a final shot of Dick tugging out his earpiece and striding off the set as music booms and the credits roll. I feel a surge of pride at how well David's done, and as the alcohol swirls inside me I have a sudden urge for shots. Why not celebrate David's triumph, I think, as I lurch over to the dusty shelf of spirits above the microwave.

Running my finger along the shelf, I sing to myself, *Eeny-meeny-miny-mo*, my finger stopping on a dusty bottle of kirsch, bought one Christmas to soak cherries in for a cake, only I never got round to making the cake. I unscrew the cap and knock back a few swigs. The sweet liquid slips down like syrup and I close my eyes, running my finger along the shelf, landing this time on a hexagonal bottle of Bols Blue that I picked from an off-licence shelf one evening as a joke. I knock back first one shot, then a second for luck. Finally, I gulp a couple of mouthfuls of single malt, enjoying the scorch as it goes down. I buy that for David.

It only takes a few minutes for the full impact of the alcohol to hit and I'm forced to use the walls to stay upright. My fingers and toes are tingling and there's a lovely warmth in my heart that spreads through me. I feel high on David's success. I want to go out, to be part of the crowd around him that basks in his glow, and as soon as the idea has formed, I can't dispel it, however much I tell myself it's a bad one. I need to go and join the party. I feel a jolt of righteous anger: why shouldn't I be there to enjoy his success?

I'm sure *she* will be there, so why shouldn't I?

EIGHT

DAVID

There's a ripple of applause as I enter the green room, a windowless room that's bare of furniture apart from a couple of chairs and a coffee table, and much less glamorous than it sounds. Nina is the first person to approach me, still holding her clipboard which gets stuck between us as I wrap her in a hug and crush her to me. We're both grinning as we pull back and she says, 'You smashed it.'

I already knew it had gone well but I feel my shoulders drop as the relief hits me that she agrees. In the first season of *Confessions*, I'd pop into the green room for a few minutes and then hurry home where Kitty and I would open a bottle of red and curl up on the sofa to dissect the show, going over it line by line. She'd always have insightful observations that helped me improve my technique, and that moment of peace would help me wind down. These days, I'm not even sure if she watches.

'Bloody brilliant, David,' one of the sound technicians says, and there's a pop of a cork from somewhere in the room; a moment later, someone presses a glass into my hand. The bubbles go up my nose as the room fills with crew and other Prestige staff members and I circulate, accepting praise and pats on the shoulder as we all congratulate each other on a strong show, but my eyes keep searching for Nina as if they're moving of their own accord, and every couple of minutes her dark eyes meet mine and I feel a tug of desire deep in my core that shocks me.

I don't want to admit how much I want her but I tell myself it's the halo effect of having a good show. Like a footballer scoring the winning goal, there's a high that needs to be slowly managed or else I could go off the deep end. I've seen it happen many times over where an actor or musician performs and then is filled with such a buzz that they lose their mind for a brief window that's enough to damage the rest of their life. So far I've avoided all the usual temptations – drugs, booze, sex – but only because I've had the one thing I truly wanted waiting for me at home.

There's a raised voice from somewhere that makes everyone look around and my stomach lurches as a frisson of panic rushes around the small room that's now packed with my colleagues. Everyone cranes their neck, trying to see the source of the noise, as people raise their eyebrows and look at one another, trying to laugh off any fear that something's not right. I search out Nina for reassurance, but I see a frown on her face as she stares at the doorway, shaking her head at someone as if warning them away.

Turning slowly, I hear another yell and this time the words are clear, 'Where's David?' and I feel terrified but I tell myself not to be silly, what can happen to me in a room full of friends and colleagues? Everyone here is on my side.

'Out of my way,' the voice yells again, and I see people moving aside as a gap forms in the crowd.

Nina turns to me and grimaces and I brace myself as I see Dick Bell striding towards me, his face puce and his head down like a bull. I wonder if he's going to hit me but he stops just in front of me and jabs one of his sausage fingers into my shoulder, speaking with such venom that spittle flies from his mouth and lands on the front of my shirt, but I decide to ignore it and give him his chance to vent. People always feel a lot better when they've said what they feel they need to, and deep down I know it's not me he's angry with, it's himself.

'You have a fucking nerve,' he says. The background noise in the room drops to a hush as everyone stops what they're saying, desperate to catch every word of Dick's rant, conscious that the fireworks are about to start. I duck my head, waiting for his words to rain down on me like blows.

'You've always been a scheming maggot, a pathetic little shit-muncher.'

There are a few titters around us; I shoot one of the cameramen a sideways look and he quickly wipes the grin from his face. The team know the drill when a guest is unhappy. We have protocols in place, because it's a hard-hitting show – I'm meant to ask the difficult questions, and not everyone likes getting grilled. I long to sigh and say, *What exactly did you think I was going to ask?* But I know from experience that will only wind him up more.

'I remember hearing about how you tried to worm your way into the right circles. Cosying up to all the chaps from school whose parents had money and status, the things you desperately craved coming from the balls of Mr Nobody from Nowhere.'

I meet his gaze and see his pupils are so dilated that his eyes look pure black and the whites are cracked with tiny red veins. His words have found their mark and I feel heat and fury rising inside me, but I can't allow him to see that he's got to me.

'Dick, please,' I say, trying my best to sound reasonable, but he cuts me off.

'I know your type, boy.' I raise my eyebrow at this since he's only a year older than I am, but he wants to put me in my place. 'You would do anything to shake off your past but, you know, some shit leaves a stink. So now your tactic is to invite people onto your show and try to ruin them with your lies and deceit. You are a disgrace.'

'It was a good show.' I can hear I sound defensive but I want to shut him up. 'You'll gain respect for facing the accusations head on. It's all good press, as they say.'

'You played me like a fool,' Dick says, his eyes narrowing, and he leans close enough to me that I can smell whisky on his breath. He's clearly had a little snifter already to pick himself up and I hope it won't carry him away. 'I didn't come to join your little party, I just wanted to tell you in person exactly what I think of you.'

Nina chooses that moment to glide between us with two full champagne flutes in her hands.

'David, Mr Bell,' she says politely. 'Can I offer you a drink?'

I take mine with a thin smile and Dick stares at the second glass she's holding as if she's trying to force a glass of cold vomit into his hand.

'Do you think this is something to celebrate?' he demands, and I feel a flicker of horror as his eyes rest on Nina.

'Is my humiliation funny to you?' he asks, stepping closer to her, and she immediately drops the polite smile that had been on her lips.

'Dick, shall we go somewhere a bit quieter and talk about this,' I say.

He blinks at me and rocks on his heels before flinging his arms out, 'Let them all hear, what have I got to hide? I've just been buggered on national television, after all.'

'It's not all bad,' Nina pipes up from behind me, and I shoot her a look. It's better to stay out of the firing line when someone's in this sort of mood.

'What did you say?' Dick asks, his face turning redder still.

'You're getting a fair bit of support online,' she says.

He pauses and I see a flicker of interest in his eyes. 'What are they saying?'

'"FreeDick" is trending,' she says, keeping her eyes down. 'I think it's a reference to an old film—'

'I get it,' he interrupts, 'but what exactly are people saying?'

Nina scrolls on her phone and reads, '*Is it a crime now to touch someone's shoulder? Clearly the woke police are on the case.*'

Dick's frown lifts and Nina goes on, 'This one says, "*That man deserves a medal for keeping a straight face. What a loud of bollocks.*" And there's one here that just says, "*Dick Bell for PM.*"'

A grim smile is spreading across Dick Bell's face and it's like he can already picture the provocative podcast he will release, and the presenter slot he'll be offered on the right-wing news channel and a column in one of the tabloids. I have a horrible thought that one day we might appear on the same reality TV show, and I vow that if I'm ever forced to stoop that low I'll quit television. The noise levels have risen again and Dick is glancing around. 'Now where did Sarah get to? I need her to get me a summary of the comments.'

He accepts the glass from Nina and begins drinking it as she takes his elbow and steers him from the room in the direction of his press secretary who has been hovering nervously in the doorway while the whole scene played out. Sipping my champagne, I long to knock it back as my fingers shake from the adrenaline, but I resist the urge since I'm in a room surrounded by my colleagues. I'm about to join a conversation about next week's interviewee when Nina reappears.

'Do you want to take a minute?' she asks, and I nod gratefully, heaving a sigh of relief as she leads me out of the back exit from the cramped room and along one of the corridors, where we step into an empty office and Nina starts laughing, 'Well, that was awkward.'

'You were brilliant,' I say. 'I was a puddle and you rescued me.'

'Men like that just need their egos stroking,' she says, slipping her hand inside her black leather handbag and pulling out a silver flask. 'Care to join me?'

She unscrews the cap and takes a sip before offering it to me and I knock back a couple of gulps, wincing at the burn as the tequila hits the back of my throat. I wonder if this is the moment to mention the letters to her. If there is any risk to her I know I should say something but tonight is meant to be a celebration. We've both worked so hard that I feel like we deserve one night to celebrate. Tomorrow, I vow, I will sit her down and tell her everything I know. Tonight, we have fun.

We're standing close together, passing the flask between us and our hands touch; instead of flinching and moving away, we both keep the contact for a brief moment, but long enough that everything is communicated in that moment. I know then that I could kiss her if I wanted to, and that realisation fills me with a thrill of excitement that reminds me of being a teenager. I'm disappointed that I've become such a cliché but I can't deny that being so close to someone where our mutual attraction is palpable is exhilarating.

A loud banging on the glass partition makes me jump and for a moment I have no idea what it could be but then I turn to see someone slapping the glass. Who is it? Subtly stepping back to create more space between me and Nina, I peer through to see the production team are outside the glass walls of the office.

'Pub?' one of them yells, and I glance at Nina, not wanting to leave without her, and she gives a small nod.

'Coming,' I call out, feeling better that we're together since what harm can come to Nina when I'm by her side?

NINE

KITTY

Sitting in the back of the Uber with alcohol swirling through my system, I try to remember why I thought this was a good idea.

I glance at myself in the driver's mirror and my stomach lurches as I wonder who the hell is looking back at me before I recall that I hurriedly put on my disguise as I swigged peach schnapps from the bottle. It's not meant to be an attractive look but this evening I appear almost clownish with the thick layer of apricot foundation that I smeared on and the brown eyeshadow that's not quite even. The wig is a librarian's mousy bun and it's hot and itchy, but I tell myself it's better that David doesn't recognise me – I don't want a scene.

As we join the traffic heading to central London I tip my head back and try to still my thoughts. When we pull up outside the pub, I'm no clearer on what my plan is.

'Have a good night, yeah?' the driver calls out, sounding unsure as I open the door and almost fall onto the pavement. Pulling myself up quickly with the handle, I say, 'You too,' and try to walk with some dignity through the crowd that's spilled out of the pub. I get a few odd looks as I edge through the door and into the throng inside but I push my glasses up my nose and walk with my head held high, making my way towards the bar, feeling nervous as I discreetly try to scan the room and locate David.

Doubt assails me as I don't see a single face I recognise and it crosses my mind that they might have chosen another bar to celebrate in, or David might have left already, but then my gaze lands on Nina. She's sitting alone at a table in the corner, wearing a skin-tight black dress and her hair is in long braids that are pulled into a top knot. Her make-up is as heavy as usual but it's impossible to deny that she's the most beautiful woman in the room. She'd be the most beautiful woman in any room.

Lurching forward, I decide I need another drink, but I keep watching Nina and it doesn't take long before I see her eyes land on someone behind me and her whole face lights up like a Christmas tree.

'Who's next?' The barman yells and people surge forward but I remain rooted to the spot, sensing that the person she is watching is right behind me. A cold sweat breaks out and I feel my boxy grey suit sticking to my arms and legs, the lining a cheap polyester that seems to fuel the furnace. Someone pushes past me to take the space that's opened up at the bar; I find myself staring at the back of David's head and feel a rush of fury. My own husband has queue-jumped while I've watched him making eyes across the room at his colleague. I'm tempted to tap him on the shoulder but I don't; instead I stand so close I could lick the back of his neck. The thought makes me giggle but thankfully it's too loud in here for him to hear. He orders a pint and a glass of fizz and I stand with my arms folded across my chest as he waits for his drinks, glancing over at Nina every few seconds and grinning inanely. He's so preoccupied he hasn't noticed that his own wife is standing right behind him.

Once he has his drinks, he edges out of the queue and in the fifteen paces back to the table, I watch a constant flow of people move in and out of his orbit, clapping his shoulder or shaking his

hand. It's clear who is the star of the show, and when he reaches
Nina, she beams up at him with the same adulation. Standing
by the bar, hammered and alone, dressed in what can only be
described as a Halloween costume, I have the sudden clarity to
see how ridiculous I have become and the mismatch between
us, and the shame I feel is crushing. If I were a braver person, I'd
admit that David and I are no longer meant to be, but the
thought only spurs me into action to get myself a large glass of
wine.

Once I have it in my hand, I take a few big gulps and feel a
little calmer before I turn to see that their table is empty. My
stomach twists as I scan the room, hoping to find David chatting
to someone else, but as I check the exit, I notice Nina slipping
out of the door. Surely they're not leaving together? Panic hits
me as I down the rest of my drink in three gulps and hurry after
them, knocking into several people as I cross the room, and yank
open the door, stepping out into the cool air.

Stepping through the crowd of smokers, I spot them
rounding the corner and I'm forced to sprint the short distance
along the pavement, arriving just in time to see them getting
into a black cab together. Where are they going? Suddenly I no
longer care if David realises it's me and I set off sprinting, but
they slam the door and the cab drives away. Its rear lights disap-
pear around the corner but for some reason I keep running,
turning onto the main road where I race along the pavement,
until I stumble and land hard on my knees. A sob judders
through me and I try to hold the tears back. Are they really
leaving together, right in front of my nose? Something within
me snaps and I decide I'm not going to let them walk all over
me. I'm not going to give up just yet.

I'll admit that I'm not really thinking straight, but one thing
is clear in my mind: I recall Nina's exact address in Bethnal
Green from when I checked her payslip. Taking out my phone,
I open the Uber app again and I'm about to enter the address

when it crosses my mind that it might not be a good idea to have digital proof that I followed them, so I switch to Google Street View, spotting a McDonald's on the corner right by Nina's flat and putting that into the app instead. It's only three minutes later when I'm on my way and I'm not more than ten minutes behind them.

We pull up outside the bright windows of McDonald's and I hop out, blinking as my eyes adjust to the garish light, before I see a 24-hour shop where I duck inside and buy a quarter-litre of vodka that I swig from the bottle as I walk towards 17A. The building Nina lives in has the look of an old asylum – 'Calling all lunatics!' I'm giggling as I stagger along the quiet street, my voice ringing out, but the main road is not far away and the sound of traffic and voices carries down the street so I don't feel alone. When I reach the flat, the lights are on but the blinds are closed so I can just see a sliver of light.

At first, I hover on the other side of the street, peering over, but soon I realise that I can't see anything from there and David is either inside or he's already left so I approach the front window, stepping behind the short, spiky hedge and pressing my face to the glass. I try to peer through the gap between the blinds but I can only glimpse the edge of a cream sofa and an inch of floorboard. Perhaps David dropped Nina at home and left immediately. They always drink heavily after a show to release the tension after a live recording so I wouldn't be surprised if she's passed out on her bed fully clothed – that must be it. Feeling a little reassured, I put my ear to the glass but I can't hear anything.

There's no one else walking along the street and I suddenly feel unsteady on my feet so I sit heavily on the stone step outside the front door and drink my vodka in small sips. I know I should leave but I can't summon the energy. What am I doing? David isn't even here, I tell myself. As soon as I build up the strength, I'll get up and leave this place since I know I shouldn't

be here, but the vodka is sliding down far too easily and I'm
suddenly exhausted. I feel myself slipping into sleep when I
hear a voice that drags me back – David's deep laugh rings out
and I push myself upright, grabbing the edge of the windowsill
to peer into the slit of light between the curtains.

I close one eye, and then the other, but I'm struggling to see
straight and my vision is blurry. I'm certain there's movement
inside the room and I try desperately to make out what's going
on. Something doesn't feel right. I'm struck by the wild thought
that maybe I should knock on the door to see if I can help, but
then there's a loud crash from close by the window and I leap
back in panic. Without thinking, I jump to my feet and run
away as fast as I can, something telling me to get the hell out of
there.

TEN

DAVID

It's 1 a.m. when I stumble out of Nina's front door, the exhilaration and joy I felt a few short hours ago having evaporated completely, and now a deep sense of shame crawls over my skin like maggots on rotting flesh. My stomach roils and my heads pounds as the amount of alcohol I've drunk catches up with me and a scary voice screams inside my head, *What have you done?*

The street is quiet now and there feels to be more of a malevolent air to the lone figures I spot in the distance, as if the only people left awake are those up to no good. I keep my head down and hurry along Nina's street until I join the main road where a brightly lit McDonald's dazzles my eyes and I instinctively turn away, hurrying to get as far away from Nina's flat and what I've done as quickly as possible.

How could I have been so stupid? I feel like falling to my knees and curling into a ball right there on the grubby pavement but I know I need to keep going and get back to the safety of my own home. The night has gone from being a glittering success to a total failure in a couple of hours, and I feel like I've risked everything I've been working for, put it all on the line, due to

one loss of control. Checking my phone, I find the battery is
dead but there's no one I can call anyway – I need to deal with
this on my own.

A sob judders through me as I spot a car coming towards me
and I tell myself to get it together, now's not the time to fall
apart. Holding out my arm, I think the car is going to cruise past
but just as it reaches me, the driver slams on the brakes and
pulls up in the bus lane. I'm not sure if it's a genuine minicab
but the young guy in the front calls out, 'Where you going?'

Holding up the two twenties, I say 'Islington,' and he nods
to the back, 'Get in.'

We drive in silence while music blares and he nods along to
it while I stare out of the window, not really seeing the dark
houses and brightly lit takeaways that we pass as I think about
Nina. Poor, young, vulnerable Nina – she didn't deserve to
meet someone like me. And Kitty, what will she do when she
finds out about what I've done? Panic courses through my body
and I catch the driver's eye in the mirror before he returns to
looking straight ahead.

Silently kicking myself I tell myself I need to keep a low
profile. The driver doesn't appear to have recognised me and I
know it's better to keep it that way. Earlier this evening it was a
nightmare at the pub; the unwanted attention made me feel like
a circus freak by the end, although that feels like an eternity ago
now, but perhaps that contributed to what I did. The hours of
feeling invincible, being put on a pedestal, may have made me
think that the normal rules don't apply to me. Even as these
thoughts run through my brain, I'm shaking my head, since the
only person I have to blame is myself.

'Next left,' I say as we get close to my house, the journey
feeling like it's passed in an instant.

The car screeches around the corner, going far too fast, but I
find I don't care, almost wishing we'd hit the kerb and flipped
over, anything to stop me having to deal with my actions this

evening, but we make it onto my street. When I say, 'Just here,' the driver slams the brakes on and I toss him the notes and leap out, hurrying towards my front door.

I step inside to a silent hallway. All of the lights are off so I assume Kitty must be in bed and I pray she is fast asleep so I don't have to face her now. I unlace my shoes and tiptoe up the stairs as quietly as I can. Pausing outside our bedroom, I strain my ears, bracing myself for the inevitable questions: where have you been? Who were you with? What were you doing? I know that I'm in no fit state to answer any of them with the amount of alcohol still in my system, the pressure behind my eyes that's the start of my hangover, and the squirming guilt that's threatening to overpower me.

I need to think, and I need to drink a pint of water and take two paracetamols immediately, but I also want to climb into bed and sleep. I know it's cowardly, but instead of opening the door to our room and facing Kitty, I return to the stairs and creep up another floor to my study, breathing a small sigh of relief as I step into the cool and tidy room. Unbuckling my belt, I leave my trousers in a heap on the floor and curl up on the small sofa where I usually read. There are no blankets in here but I've left a cashmere sweater hung over the arm and I wrap it around my legs, ignoring the ever worsening pressure in my head as my eyelids grow heavy and I slip into sleep. My last thought before I enter oblivion is Nina.

* * *

I wake the next morning to grey streams of light filtering into the room and needles of pain shooting up my legs. I'm in a foetal position on the sofa and need badly to stretch out. There's a glorious moment where all I remember is the success of the show and I feel uplifted, but then the rest of the evening comes back to me like a series of punches to the gut and I suddenly think that I might be sick. Pushing myself up, I stagger out of the room and back down the stairs. All I want to do is go to the bathroom and then get into my own bed. I don't think about facing Kitty until I fling open the door and see that the bed is empty and I stop in my tracks.

Where is Kitty? Several thoughts hit me at once: perhaps she didn't come home; maybe she's already left; and I am absolutely desperate for a piss. I deal with the easiest one first and hurry through into the ensuite where the toilet seat is up, suggesting Kitty hasn't used it since I last did, and I frown as I relieve myself. Something doesn't feel quite right but then my whole body feels wrong and memories of last night threaten to send me into a spiral, so I concentrate on gulping water from the cold tap and digging around in the cupboard beneath the sink until I find a packet of paracetamol. I wash down three for luck.

Deciding I will deal with untangling everything later, I return to the bedroom and collapse onto the smooth, cold sheets that are tucked in the way I make the bed – Kitty doesn't bother tucking the duvet under the mattress but I like it to be pulled tight. It crosses my mind that I made the bed after I rolled out of it yesterday morning so Kitty can't have slept in it, but as a swirl of confusion and worry begins, I close my eyes, fighting it off, promising myself that I'll work it out when I feel better.

* * *

When I next wake, the sun is blazing through the window and I sit up too fast, thinking I'm late for work, before the hangover hits me. My mouth feels like I've been licking a litter tray but the paracetamol has done its job and all that's left is a feeling of pressure behind my eyes. Checking my phone, I see it's still dead and I've been too drunk to charge it, but Kitty has an old-fashioned alarm clock on her side of the bed so I lean over and see it's after 11 a.m. I still have no idea where she is and I can't bear to think about last night but it's not the time for that now – I need to get to work. There's always a debrief after a show and Stanley will want to talk about the early numbers, so I'll just have to work out what I'm going to say to my wife later.

I shower and dress in a crisp white shirt and walk to work to clear my head, forcing all negative thoughts out of my head and repeating to myself that no one knows what I did. The sense that everyone is watching me is just paranoia and all I need to do is get through today and then I can come up with a plan of how to deal with the fallout. It's already lunchtime when I arrive at Prestige and I go straight to my office, praying I can get inside before anyone spots me when I hear a voice say, 'David Okine, my hero.'

Turning slowly, I plaster on a grin and spot Stanley coming towards me with his arm outstretched. I grab his hand and he pumps my arms saying 'David, what a show. What a bloody show. You had the audience eating out of your hand, and the figures...'

He trails off and my heart gives a skip despite everything and I ask, 'How are they?'

'You haven't heard?' He smiles so his bald head looks like a watermelon split in two and I can't help but copy him. 'They are fucking fantastic. Best of the series so far.'

My heart soars and I glance around, looking for someone to tell, but the corridors are empty as everyone must be out at lunch, and I realise Stanley is still gripping my hand. 'Great news,' I say, pulling my hand away. 'It's been a real team effort. Some fantastic individual contributions. Nina Bello in particular, my researcher, did sterling work with the script.'

'Funny you should mention her,' Stanley says.

My body sends a warning spike of pain into my temple and I wince. 'Why's that?' I say, making sure to sound neutral while my mind is racing. What does he know?

'Why don't we step into your office?' Stanley doesn't wait for a response and takes my arm, steering me into my office and closing the door behind us. I feel an ominous lurch of worry as he says. 'Listen, it's none of my business, but there've been a few rumours doing the rounds this morning.'

'Rumours?' The pain is now throbbing at both sides of my skull.

'People saw you and Nina leaving the pub together and then you're both late this morning. They're putting two and two together and getting—'

'Five,' I say, louder and angrier than I intend but deciding that attack is the best form of defence. 'That's absurd. She's a colleague, a junior colleague, and we may get on well but it's purely a professional relationship.'

'And last night...?'

My face feels warm and I choose my words carefully, aware I need to avoid the truth at all costs. 'Last night we were all a little worse for wear and I felt it was my duty to make sure she got home OK. You must understand that.'

'Of course. Look, say no more. I'm sure when Nina eventually turns up she'll set the record straight.'

I feel another painful lurch and my head spins. 'She's not here?'

'Hasn't come in yet. Probably just one too many, you know how it is.' Stanley winks and then glances at his watch, 'Look I best be going.' He offers his hand again and we shake once more. 'Good man for last night – keep up the excellent work.'

He leaves the room and I slump into my chair, letting my head hang. Only last night I felt on top of the world and now I feel like a piece of chewing gum stuck to the bottom of someone's shoe. Both Nina and Kitty appear to have disappeared. I close my eyes, pushing my thumbs into my eye sockets and trying to force the nausea back down inside, wondering how the hell I could be so careless with them both.

There's a gentle knock on the door and I sit up quickly. Angela is in the doorway, her eyebrow slightly arched as she looks at me. She doesn't need to say anything since I know every frown line on her face and what each of them means.

'You don't know anything about Nina, do you?' she asks, and I catch a hint of disapproval in the tension in her shoulders.

I meet her gaze and say emphatically, 'Not a thing. We shared a cab and I dropped her at home.'

Angela gives me a long look.

'And then I went home. To my wife.' I hold her gaze until she nods and I feel a rush of relief that she believes me. Angela's like a pit bull – short, powerful and relentless when she wants to be, and I feel better knowing she's on my side.

'What's happened to Nina?' I ask.

'No sign of her this morning, which is not like her. Not like her at all.'

I shake my head in agreement; she hasn't taken a day off sick since I've known her, even taking holiday is a rarity for her.

'Has anyone called her?' I ask.

Angela looks over the top of her glasses at me as if I'm a simpleton. 'First thing we tried. Not answering. Again, not like her. That phone is usually glued to her palm.'

I give a weak smile, wanting this conversation to be over now. Thankfully Angela seems to sense this and says, 'Not to worry. Joe is popping over to her flat on his lunch break to give her a knock. They're close. He's a good lad.'

'Joe?'

She gives me another withering look and says, 'Stanley's assistant. They've been dating for months. Do you go around this place with your eyes closed?'

Hearing that Nina's in a relationship fills me with bitter envy that I try to suppress. Nina is within her rights to date whoever she pleases, although I must admit it hurts. I wish I could shrug it off but my hangover is overpowering and I let out an anguished groan that makes Angela relent and say, 'Shall I bring you a coffee?'

'You are a lifesaver. Cappuccino, please.'

Angela disappears and I plug my phone into the cable on my desk and wait for the screen to come to life. Congratulatory messages ping in about the show, and my social media mentions are through the roof, but there are no calls or messages from Kitty. I try her phone but it goes straight to voicemail so I leave a message for her to call me immediately. I then send a text and WhatsApp but nothing comes back – I can't even see when she was last online. She must be at work; I pick up the desk phone, my fingers hovering over the numbers as I wonder whether to call. Our rule of not speaking in the office surely doesn't extend to emergencies? We only came up with it to protect our privacy, and it seems ridiculous now when I need to reach my wife.

Jabbing the button for the switchboard, a smooth voice answers and I ask to be put through to her line. The ringing seems to take place on the inside of my skull, like the hammer inside a bell hitting the sides, but when it stops it's a man's voice that says, 'Kitty's not here right now. Can I take a message?'

I slam down the phone and my hangover seems to worsen; I find myself clinging onto the edge of my desk, head down, praying no one comes in. The wave passes and I scroll through my messages – it's all praise and jokes until I land on a message from Tom: *We need to talk.* That's all – no context, no explanation, but I know he isn't going to be happy with me. My head is killing me but I decide the distraction might be good so I hit 'call' and he answers on the third ring.

'David.' From the tightness of his voice, I hear from one word that he's pissed off. 'What the fuck were you thinking?'

'What do you mean?' I say.

'Bell-end.'

'Oh.' I exhale and try to sound contrite. 'I'm sorry, mate. He walked right into it.'

'I vouched for you and you set him up.' Tom's voice is clipped with anger and I can tell he's spoiling for a fight, but surely his righteous anger is misplaced since Dick seemed placated by the end of the evening.

'Come now, I'm a journalist. He must have known I would ask hard questions. I had to do my job, he can't have thought—' I'm backpedalling, and Tom cuts in with a stream of angry accusations about how I've damaged his relationship, but I pull the phone away from my ear because through the glass partition I see Angela approaching, striding with her arms swinging and no coffee in sight.

'Listen, Tom. I'm sorry, I really am but I've got to go. When I have a minute, I'll call Dick and explain that you had nothing to do with it.'

'You think he cares about that? You just don't think about anyone else, do you? That's the last time I do you a favour.' Tom hangs up as Angela opens the door. Any guilt I feel about Tom immediately evaporates as I see the look on her face. My heart plummets as she closes the door behind her and comes around the back of the desk, resting her hand on my shoulder in a sympathetic manner. Fear constricts my throat and I can barely squeeze out a word but I manage to rasp, 'Kitty?'

Angela's eyebrows draw together in confusion and she says, 'It's Nina.'

My first feeling is relief and I manage to sit up straighter. I don't know why I've had such a dark sense of foreboding since I saw the empty bed but I silently thank God that nothing bad has happened to Kitty as I wonder where the hell she is. I should have asked Tom if he'd heard from her – maybe I should call him back if he's still speaking to me? Or I could ring Caro?

'David.' I glance across at Angela, having forgotten for a moment that she was there. Our eyes lock and I feel a surge of fear and confusion. It's clear she's about to drop a bomb on my head and I brace myself as best I can. Does she know about last night? Does she know what I did?

'I'm sorry to be the one to tell you, David, but Joe just rang from outside Nina's. He's with the police...'

'The police?' The fear returns.

'I don't know the details. I just heard that there was a lot of blood. It looks like Nina was attacked last night.'

The floor falls away. I press both my hands into the desk. A hundred questions rush into my head but when I try to speak, a sob jags my words. Angela squeezes my shoulder and I try to pull myself together, but another sob takes over.

'Is Nina OK?' I ask the question but I already know the answer from Angela's face, which is a death mask of shock and horror. 'I'm so sorry, David, I know you and Nina were close, but it's not good news. Joe said he called an ambulance but it was too late.'

Angela tiptoes around the word, but the fact that Nina is dead hits me like a punch in the gut, immediately followed by the almost as painful realisation that I must have been one of the last people to see her alive. Panic turns my breaths to gasps as I try to get control of myself but I find my thoughts are running away from me. What will people think? What will they say? I'm going to be the prime suspect or else everyone is going to blame me for doing nothing about the letters. Each of these thoughts hits me like a sledgehammer to the head but I try to control myself while Angela is here.

Taking a deep breath, I force myself to think about Nina instead of my own problems. How could this happen to someone so young, so vibrant? I try to think of the last thing I said to her, how we left it, but I find my mind is a blur.

'David?' I realise Angela's been talking but I haven't heard a word. Giving myself a mental shake I turn to her and focus on her face.

'Sorry, what was that?'

'The team. Do you think you should say something?'

I open my mouth but find myself unsure of what to say. I don't feel like the right person to lead the team, not today. 'I think it's best if I wait until I've spoken to Stanley. If there's a police investigation—'

'Of course there'll be a police investigation – she's been murdered, David.' Angela gives me another of her looks and I quickly wipe my eyes to stop any tears from falling. 'I know, you're right. I should probably ring HR...'

Stanley reappears outside my office and flings open the door, 'David, I've just heard. What awful news.'

'Awful,' I echo, not trusting myself to say anything else.

'We were just talking about what to say to the team,' Angela interjects, and I'm grateful when Stanley says, 'Don't you worry about that. I've spoken to HR and we're sending the whole team home, of course. It goes without saying but we will do whatever it takes to aid the police with their investigation. David, you head home and I'll give them your number. I'm sure they'll be wanting to speak to you first since you dropped her home last night.'

A shiver runs through me and I want to yell that I have no more information than anyone else, that I had absolutely nothing to do with it, but I find myself nodding and muttering thanks as Angela says something about getting me home and strong-arms me out of my office, along the corridor and outside where the sky has clouded over and the air feels heavy. Blinking, I simply stand and try to take in what has happened as she hails me a cab.

'Just go straight home and don't speak to anyone,' she says as a car pulls up.

What would I do without Angela?

'Your phone,' she says, handing it to me, and I realise I must have left it on the desk. 'I'll ring if I hear anything more.'

'Thanks,' I manage, and she gives the cab driver my address

and slams the door. We join the afternoon traffic and I slump in the back, trying to calm the panic pulsing through me that's making me want to leap out into the busy road. It is impossible to think that between the time I left Nina and this morning, someone else killed her – I'm sure the police are going to find it hard to believe.

Panic is making it difficult for me to think straight, but my mind goes to the letters. Maybe they were more serious than I gave them credit for – perhaps someone's been following me. I let out an anguished groan when it crosses my mind that I might have led them straight to Nina. What the hell have I done?

ELEVEN

KITTY

I'd rather not relive the horrors of this morning. At forty years old, you'd think you'd be beyond waking to a concerned voice saying, 'Madam. Excuse me, madam, but are you OK?'

And as I extricated myself from a tangle of leaves and twigs, brushing mud and dew from my clothes, and tried to reassure the man in the suit that I was fine, tears of shame prickled my eyes and I vowed that I would never, ever wake up in a public park again, although I'm aware that some things should go without saying. The man was eager to help but I managed to brush him off and hurried away, seeking refuge in a local Starbucks and washing off the grime and residue of orange foundation in the sink in the loo. The horrible wig was long gone, but that could only be a good thing.

It was already after nine and I decided the grey suit could pass as work wear so I went straight to work, smoothing my crumpled trousers and trying to finger-comb out the worst of the knots in my hair, trying to ignore the black hole in my memory where the end of last night ought to be. An awful feeling of dread and shame sat heavily upon me and I knew something had happened, something terrible, but I was in no fit state to try to piece it together. Instead, I ordered a large coffee and tried to cut through the lingering alcohol, although I was certain it was radiating from every pore.

By the time I reached my desk, Karen and Matt were already working and I felt Karen's gaze linger on me as I took my seat and booted up my computer. Although I'd done my best to make myself look presentable, in the harsh office lights I was aware that every flaw must be obvious so I was trying to hide behind the screen, opening my browser and reading the online reviews of *Confessions* to distract myself, when Julie came running in, and squeaked, 'Have you heard?'

'Heard what?' Karen pounced right away, a gleam of excitement shining in her eyes at the prospect of gossip.

'It's truly horrendous,' Julie said, pulling a face to warn us to arrange our expressions into concern rather than glee. 'A junior researcher, Nina Bello, has died. *Murdered,* is what they're saying.'

Karen jumped up, her hands flying to her mouth, while I remained absolutely motionless at my desk, feeling as if cement had been poured into my veins and was being pumped around my body. In that moment, we reacted with a mix of shock, horror and a glimmer of exhilaration, but very quickly HR mode kicked in and Karen started talking about internal and external comms and how best to deal with the press. A flurry of activity began around me while I sat staring at my computer, unable to move or think anything other than: *Nina is dead, Nina is dead, Nina is dead.*

Last night was the drunkest I've been in a long time, maybe ever, and only flashes of the evening have come back to me. I remember *Confessions*, the noodles, the wine – *oh God, the wine* – and deciding to go to the pub, but after that there are only snippets of memory and I'm not sure what order they go in. I definitely got an Uber and was at the pub at some point but I'm struggling to piece it all together. I put my head in my hands as

something comes back to me that I know is important: I was at
Nina's flat.

An instant message pops up from Matt: *You OK?*

Dragging my eyes from the screen, I see he's watching me
over his monitor with a worried frown on his face, but all I can
do is give a frantic shake of my head and push back my chair,
leaping up, overcome by a need to get out of there. David must
be desperate to get hold of me, and though I know he won't
come barging up here, I feel a sudden urge to be outside in the
fresh air, away from the stuffy office, the soundtrack of
muttering and clicking keyboards and Karen's omniscient
glare.

'I'm not feeling well,' I blurt out, and the others pause what
they're doing, glancing up at me with expressions ranging from
concern to exasperation. 'I think I need to go home.'

Karen nods once, instantly dismissing me, turning her attention back to her screen while saying with a sigh, 'Fine just log
your absence on the Portal.'

I should probably be worried about my job but all I feel is a
swell of relief as I hurry out to the lifts and jab the button, but
before it arrives I hear the soft squeak of trainers on the tiles
behind me. Praying it's not Karen, I turn slowly and see Matt.

'Are you OK?' Matt says.

'I think it's a bug,' I say. 'I just need some rest.'

'It's obvious you're upset. Do you know that woman, Nina?'
he asks and panic rushes through me. I'm not sure how honest
to be and I search Matt's eyes for any hint of how he'll react.

Letting out a shaky breath, I say, 'Only a little, but it's really
hit me. I just can't believe she's...' I can't finish the sentence;
Matt steps closer and wraps his arms around me and I'm
grateful for the touch. I lean into his stocky body, enjoying the
warmth and weight of his arms until he finally lets go.

'I'm so sorry,' he says.

'I hardly knew her. It's silly...'

'It's not silly, it's totally understandable. It must be such a shock. Is there anything I can do?'

I shake my head but he persists, 'Can I help you get home? I could come with you if you need a friend.'

I smile at him gratefully. 'I'll be fine, thank you. I'll get a cab.'

'Let me walk down with you, at least.'

'I'm fine, honestly.' Instinctively, I reach out and squeeze his hand. 'I just need to get home.'

'Look, take my number, and if you need anything you can give me a call.'

His persistence makes me take out my phone and I wait while he types his number into it. I try to shrug it off, but it does feel better to know I have someone to call who isn't David.

'Promise you'll ring if you need anything?' he asks.

'Promise.' I smile briefly and he walks back to the office as I jab the button for the lift again and the whoosh of nausea returns. Why is it taking so long? In a minute the doors ping open and inside are two men in suits talking about tennis. I press myself against the wall, willing myself not to be sick, as the lift descends. Their inane banter feels like a screwdriver digging into my brain and I squeeze my eyes, trying to block them out, until the lift stops on floor three and they leave. I feel a rush of gratitude at the silence until my own thoughts start screaming: *what did you do?* The gap in my memory fills me with terror and when the doors open on the ground floor, I rush outside, almost running and gasping for breath.

The sky is a flat grey overhead and the temperature has dropped, but I'm grateful for the fresh air, sucking in hard through my nose as spots of rain hit my face. Taking out my phone, I ignore the texts and missed calls since I can't face reading them now and instead, I find Connor's number and hit 'call', needing to sort out my head, but it rings out and his recorded message kicks in, a new one that I haven't heard before: *I'm afraid I'm unavailable this week but I will continue with all my usual appointments next week. Apologies for the inconvenience and do keep working on the things we've discussed.*

The line goes dead and I stand there, motionless, in disbelief. How can it be that he is unavailable when I need him most? Calling again, I wait and listen to the message but it plays out exactly the same way and I'm still nonplussed. I wonder what I can do – surely there must be some way to get hold of him. But just as I'm considering what that could be, I spot David's tall figure being bundled out of the building by his assistant. I'd know him anywhere despite the dark rings under his eyes and the chalky undertone of his skin.

Fear ripples through me as I realise there is nowhere to hide, but before I can move, they've bustled past me towards the road and Angela is hailing a cab. Looking at David, his eyes appear unfocused and his movements are jerky, as if he's not in full control of them as she deposits him into the back of the taxi. I wonder if he's only just heard about Nina. He looks worse than I feel and not in a fit state to provide the support that I need. Where the hell is Connor? I try breathing deeply but I notice a security guard in his luminous vest glancing over at me so I stride out to the roadside, suddenly desperate to get home. It only takes a minute to flag a black cab, and I slump on the back seat and try not to hyperventilate.

I try to remember what happened at Nina's but all I know is I sat on the cold concrete step outside her flat while the light was on inside. She must have been at home. Did I go in? The thought fills me with terror but the stretch of nothingness in my memory scares me even more. Why can't I remember? What did I do? I feel a strange impulse to hit my arms and legs and slap myself until the voice in my head goes quiet, but I force myself to sit up and put my hands in my lap, telling myself to act normally. Then in the mirror I see the cabbie's eyes dart to me and he frowns.

'You're not going to upchuck, are you, love?'

I shake my head but I'm not really sure if that's true.

'You've gone a bit green around the gills. Don't go messing up my leathers. I've just had them done.' He taps on the white sign on the glass that reads, '*Soiling charge: £150.*'

The word 'soiling' turns my stomach and has me looking for a place to stop. 'Here's fine,' I say, and he's clearly pleased to be able to get me out of the cab as he jerks to a stop. I shove a tenner through the glass and hop out onto the pavement. I'm still a twenty-minute walk from home but I set off on foot, readying myself for the conversation that I know has to happen between me and my husband.

TWELVE

DAVID

I made it back home just as the heavens opened and I've been listening to the rain tapping on the window as I wait for Kitty to return. I'm sitting on the bottom step of the stairs, checking my phone every few seconds and trying not to hyperventilate as panic courses through my veins and I try to think calmly and logically to work out what might have happened last night. Of course it was a messy evening – we were celebrating, under-standably – but whatever else happened, Nina was fine when I left her, absolutely fine.

Squeezing my eyes shut as an unbidden image of Nina pops into my head – I'm not ready to confront the absolute horror that she is actually gone – I tell myself to try to think like the police. Of course they are going to want to know my every move, since I was the one who took her home, but surely they won't think I had anything to do with her death? I'm a fucking celebrity, for God's sake. I don't want them wasting their time on me when there's a killer out there, but something tells me I'm in for a very rough ride.

Pressing my palms into my eyes, I mutter to myself, 'Think, man,' as I try to work out exactly what I can and should say to the police. What information can I give them that will put them onto the right track? Snatching up my phone again, there is still no message from Kitty and I slam it back down in disgust. I need to talk to my wife. We may have had our ups and downs but she's been my sounding board for the last twenty years and she's the smartest person I know – she'll know what to do. I pace along the hallway and lean against my front door, letting my legs slide from under me. Sitting on the wooden floor, I pray for her key to slide into the lock and the door to open and for her to be there and to tell me that everything will be OK.

But how can she say that when Nina is dead? A moan comes from deep inside me as I think of her – so beautiful and vibrant and now gone. Tears spring to my eyes as I remember the time she brought in doughnuts for the whole team when we didn't win the first BAFTA we were up for just to cheer us up. Why would anyone want to hurt her? Someone must have been waiting outside. They must have watched me leave and forced their way inside. I really want there to be an explanation that has nothing to do with me, but I feel a heavy responsibility that I can't shift.

I stop pacing. Perhaps whoever it was wasn't there watching Nina – maybe they were there watching me. Someone has been getting uncomfortably close and although they've never actually threatened me, there's always an undertone of menace when someone's putting anonymous letters through your front door.

Could McCrazy have killed Nina? I'm shaking my head as I think it but a little voice inside is whispering, 'She is batty.' Batty, but not dangerous, but then again, who knows? Perhaps seeing me with a woman like Nina could have tipped her over the edge. Kitty certainly thinks McCrazy is someone to be feared – look at how she reacted to the letters. I realise I need to do something; I can't just stay at home, waiting for the world to burn, so I pick up my phone again, scrolling to Tom's number, the man with the limitless contacts. He's the one that convinced me that McCrazy has moved on with her life, but I can't take his word for it any more. I need to look into the whites of her eyes and ask her if she had anything to do with Nina's death.

Pressing the 'call' button, I listen to the phone ring until Tom answers with a terse, 'Yes?'

'Harrow, it's me. Where are you?'

There's a long silence before Tom says, 'I'm laying low because Dick Bell is baying for my blood. I can't think why.'

Thinking of Dick is like trying to look through a piece of cloudy glass – I find I can't bring him into focus.

'I can't even think about Dick Bell right now, Tom.'

'Ah yes, other people's feelings are not something you dwell on,' he says snidely, but I can't rise to his barbs, I have bigger things on my mind.

'Listen, one of my colleagues was murdered last night.'

I hear him draw in a sharp breath and there's another long silence before I add, 'And I dropped her off at home after the celebrations in the pub.'

Tom still doesn't speak.

'So I need to figure out what actually happened or else the police are going to think it was me.'

A strange noise comes down the line; it takes me a moment to realise that Tom is laughing, and an icy feeling spreads through me.

'I hardly think it's funny.'

The noise stops and Tom says, 'Sorry, I've always had a twisted sense of humour, you know me. It is quite the pickle.'

I find myself grinding my back teeth and I cut in, 'Tom, is there anything you know about McCrazy, anything that could link her to Nina Bello, my colleague?'

He whistles down the phone. 'You think McCrazy is involved? In murder?'

'Would it be so ridiculous after everything she's done?'

'I told you before, she's sorted herself out.'

'How can you be so sure?'

'I'm a good judge of character.'

I realise I'm not going to get anything helpful out of Tom in this mood. 'Look, is there any way you can get hold of her address?'

'Why?' he asks.

'Why do you think?' My hand is holding the phone painfully tightly and I force myself to let out a breath. 'Thanks for nothing,' I say, about to hang up when I hear his voice again.

'I'll see what I can do.'

'Thank you.' I open my mouth to apologise for the Dick Bell situation but I see Tom has already hung up and I let my hand fall, aware he's furious with me but certain he'll come round. He always does.

Suddenly I freeze, hearing a soft thud of footsteps from outside, and I strain my ears, my heart pounding as for some reason I imagine the police in full combat gear approaching with a battering ram, and then I hear the key in the lock and I rush forward and open the door. My wife is on the doorstep, her blonde hair tugged back in a bun, but the rain has plastered the strands that have come loose onto her forehead and there are smears of mascara under her eyes. Her face has the telltale puffiness of a hangover.

'Where have you been?' I say, my voice tight with anguish.

'Hello to you too.' She won't meet my gaze and pushes past me, kicking off her sodden ballet pumps at the bottom of the stairs and heading down to the basement kitchen. 'I need a glass of water.'

The state of her hair and the whiff of sweat that came off her as she passed me makes me certain she never came home last night, and she must have called in sick at work or else she'd be in the office. I want to demand that she tell me what's going on but after what I did last night, I know my anger is hypo-critical.

'Where were you last night?' I ask.

'I could ask you the same question,' she fires back as she fills herself a glass of water from the tap and downs it in several gulps before dabbing at her face and hair with a tea towel. She's clearly hung-over and I can see from the way she's carrying herself how guarded she is, so I force myself to perch on one of the stools by the kitchen island, clutching the edge of the marble worktop in an effort to hold on to the world and not get carried away by my anger.

'I went to the pub with colleagues, like I always do after the show,' I say, trying to keep my tone level.

'And after? Did you come straight home?' she asks lightly, but I hear in her voice that I'm on shaky ground.

'I was home just after one. Where were you?'

Kitty laughs and digs around in the fridge until she finds a packet of ham that she opens and starts peeling off pink strips and shoving them into her mouth. As I watch her, I try to remember the last time I found my wife sexy. It's hard to imagine that I thought she would help me when all she's doing is antagonising me further. I wonder if she takes pleasure in this as she looks at me and smiles.

'Nicely avoided,' she says. 'Well, I will tell you the truth, since you asked. I waited for you and when I got sick of waiting here like a lemon, I decided to go out.'

'Where?'

'What business is that of yours?'

My fingers ache as they lose the battle against the hard marble. 'You're my wife.'

'When it suits you.'

I jump up and go to her, grabbing her wrist as she goes to shove another handful of ham into her mouth. 'Stop. Just look at yourself. This is serious – my colleague, Nina, has been murdered and I'm asking you where the hell you were.' Her eyes betray her and the realisation nearly floors me – there wasn't even a flicker of surprise, she already knew. My grip on her arm loosens and she shakes me off, eating the ham and flashing me a slightly deranged smile. I feel a jolt of fear run through me as a thought crosses my mind that I can't believe I'm thinking.

'You didn't—' A loud rap on the front door cuts me off and both of us look around then back at each other. Before we can say anything, there's more banging and we hear a shout, 'Mr Okine, are you there? It's the police.'

Adrenaline shoots around my body and my face grows warm as I picture our neighbours hearing them and posting online that I'm in trouble with the police. It would only take one message for the whole world to know that something was going on and before long I'd be on the front page and my name would be trending online. We all know how bad news spirals. Kitty catches the expression on my face and smirks, 'Nervous?'

Ignoring her, I hurry back up the stairs before they yell again, and open the front door to a man and a woman in plain clothes with serious expressions. The man is tall and thin and pasty, while the woman is dark skinned and approximately as tall as she is wide, carrying a metal briefcase. 'How can I help?' I say, trying to sound casual when panic is racing through me like wildfire.

'Can we come in, Mr Okine?' The woman says.

I open the door wide and grin, stupidly, as if I'm about to give them a tour of the house. 'Of course, come on in.'

Leading them into the ground-floor dining room, I pull back two chairs, gesturing for them to sit. The woman eyes the crockery and glassware – all set out perfectly – and raises an eyebrow. 'We're not interrupting anything, I hope.'

'Not at all,' I say, taking a seat myself and wiping my sweaty hands on my trousers. 'My wife likes to keep it set up, just in case...' I tail off as I realise that they're not here to talk about our social life. Remembering Nina, I wipe the smile from my face and say in a more sober tone, 'Of course, I will do whatever I can to help you catch whoever did this.'

'Thank you, Mr Okine,' the woman says, sitting next to me. Her partner sits beside her as she carefully moves the glasses and plates, clearing a space in front of her and placing her brief-case on the table, snapping open the locks, which sounds like two gunshots and makes me flinch, before opening the lid and removing a notebook and pen.

'Call me David,' I say, because that's what they say on TV.

'OK, David.' She doesn't sound any friendlier. 'I'm Detective Hopping and this is Detective Green. We're here to ask some questions about your movements last night and your rela-tionship with Nina Bello—'

There's a loud crash from the basement and we all flinch. Detective Green, the male detective, gets to his feet and drops his voice, 'Is someone else at home, David?'

My heart is hammering from the shock but I try to act unfazed. 'My wife. I left her emptying the dishwasher so maybe something slipped from her hand.' I raise my voice and call out, 'Are you OK, darling?'

'Why don't you continue here and I'll go and check on Mrs Okine?' Detective Green says. Hopping nods as I close my eyes for a moment and silently scream on the inside. God knows what Kitty will say in the state she's in.

Hopping flips open a notepad. 'Were you with Nina Bello yesterday evening?'

I look at Hopping's bland face and try to work out what she knows, or suspects, and I nod.

'Where were you?'

'We went to the pub. After the show.' I realise she might not know which show, so I start waffling. 'I present a live political interview show that went out last night—'

'I'm aware. Let's stick to when you last saw Nina, shall we?'

Heat flares in my cheeks and I drop my head.

'Which pub were you at?' she asks.

'The Stag, just behind the main office. The whole team was there.'

Hopping nods as if she's heard this before and I realise that lots of people saw us there together.

'Can you remember when Nina left the pub?'

I wish I could tell her that I have no idea, that I finished my pint and came home to my wife, but to my shame, that's not the truth. And to lie would be absurd: there were too many witnesses and the taxi driver would be sure to come forward when he saw the story in the paper – driving a celebrity and a woman like Nina, would be hard to forget.

I try to chase away those thoughts – I need to focus.

'We left at the same time and I realised she'd had a bit too much to drink so we shared a cab.'

Hopping doesn't look up from her notes this time but we both know her internal alarm bell must be ringing. I've watched enough TV to know that I've just become the prime suspect if I wasn't already.

'What time was this?' she says.

'Around twelve.'

'Can you be more precise?'

'It was a couple of minutes before twelve. I remember looking at the time.'

'And did you order a cab or hail one from the street?'

'I flagged one down.'

'Can you recall any details? Licence plate? The driver's name?'

Shaking my head, I say, 'It was a black cab.'

'That area has plenty of CCTV so we'll track down the driver.'

This sounds slightly threatening, and I nod as a trickle of sweat runs down my back; I sit up straighter, hoping it won't soak through my shirt and make a mark.

'And what happened when you got to Nina's flat?'

She fixes me with her brown eyes and I know this is the part where I need to tread very carefully. How can I say 'we had sex' with my wife only a few feet away? She'd leave me in a heartbeat and I cannot and will not allow that. We may be going through a bad patch but Kitty means the world to me, she always has. My chest constricts and it feels as if I'm holding my breath although I'm forcing myself to breathe steadily in and out through my nose.

'She was a bit worse for wear, so we both got out so I could help her inside.'

'Did you ask the driver to wait?'

I shake my head. 'She wasn't very steady on her feet so I didn't know how long it would take.'

'How long it would take to help a woman from the cab to her front door?' I hear her scepticism and I can't shake the feeling that she already thinks I'm guilty.

'I'd been drinking too,' I say, defensively. 'I wasn't thinking straight but I just knew she needed help and I could hardly have imagined all this would happen.'

There's a long silence as my words sit heavily in the air between us. I glance at the doorway wondering what the hell Green is talking to Kitty about but there's no sign of him and they're evidently too engrossed in their conversation to hear. Hopping shifts in her seat and says, 'Would you say you were drunk?'

Knowing I need to head this off, I say quickly, 'I'd had a few drinks but I wasn't drunk. Tipsy, perhaps.'

She repeats, 'Tipsy.'

The word sounds absurd and I let out a strange giggle.

'Is something funny?' she says.

'God, no. Sorry.' I sigh and rub my face with both hands. 'It's been a long day.'

She nods as though this is a more acceptable response

before continuing, 'Can you tell me what happened next, David? After you left the cab with Nina.'

'I saw her inside and then I got a cab home.'

'Did you go into her flat?'

There's a pressure on my chest as if a piano has been rolled on top of me, but I need to keep breathing evenly. This is the killer question, I know. The moment when you're watching a TV drama when you sit up in your seat and pay attention. I think quickly, not wanting to pause for too long but considering all the angles. There'll be forensics of course, her entire flat will be being picked apart, probably as we speak, for every little hair and fibre – I'm in an impossible position.

'Briefly,' I say, and Hopping's pen seems to waver before she jots this down.

'Nina lay down on the sofa and I headed home,' I add, and a memory comes back to me that makes me blurt out, 'I got her a glass of water from the kitchen. She took a few sips and I left it on the floor beside her next to a wastepaper bin in case she was sick.'

'Did you have sex with her, David?'

My eyes go to the door but there's still no sign of Green or my wife.

'No!' I say emphatically. What else can I say?

'Did you engage in any form of physical relations?'

'I didn't touch her. I left her on the sofa and went home.'

'Did you lock the door behind you?'

'Yes, no, I...' Guilt runs through me as I try to remember, but find I can't. Did I leave the door open for someone to attack her? Could it be my fault? I squeeze my eyes closed and search for a memory of turning the key and returning it in some way. 'I think it was a Yale that locked when I left.'

She writes something down and I'm relieved that she moves on. 'And you say you got a cab? Did you order one or flag one down again?'

THE OTHER WOMAN

'I walked to the main road and waved down one that was passing.'

'A black cab?'

'No, a local minicab.'

'Make? Model?'

I try to think back but all I can remember is a car and I shake my head.

Hopping sighs.

'It was dark and I'd been drinking,' I try to explain.

'So you said.' She sounds disappointed.

She flips back over her notes and I wonder if she's finished asking her questions, but then she looks up at me.

'Is there anything else you'd like to tell me, David? Anything at all that might be relevant?' The way she says it fills me with a horrible guilt and I long to blurt out that I did sleep with Nina, but I'm too afraid that Kitty will hear. Shame floods through me as I realise how cowardly I'm being, but I don't see how admitting it would help Nina now and saving my marriage has to be my priority.

Hopping closes her notebook and I feel a rush of relief that we're almost done when she lifts the briefcase back onto the table with a thud.

'I'd like to take a DNA sample to rule you out of our inquiries,' she says. 'Is that OK?'

I feel as if all the blood has drained from my head and I'm glad I'm sitting down or else I might fall over. Of course I should have known this was coming and of course, I should never have lied to the police, but now I have no idea what to do. Will my DNA be found on Nina's body? What will Hopping do if she discovers that I've lied? I think about confessing but my eyes stray to the doorway and I think of Kitty downstairs. Perhaps she can hear every word we're saying. I feel a sudden resolve to tell her what happened myself – she deserves to hear it from me and be the first to know.

'Is it mandatory?' I ask.

The look Hopping gives me tells me that I've asked the wrong question. 'You can refuse and I can arrest you on suspicion of Nina's murder and take a sample at the station, if you prefer?'

She says it lightly but there's a steeliness in her voice that chills me. It's as if the ground opens up and I feel like I'm falling as I quickly say, 'No, no, of course, whatever I can do to help.'

Hopping smiles coldly and I realise that she doesn't like me but I know I've got bigger things to worry about. She opens her briefcase again and lines up her equipment on the table before pinging on a pair of blue rubber gloves. I wiggle my eyebrows in an attempt at humour but she just says, 'Open your mouth, please.'

I open up and shut my eyes, desperate for the humiliation to be over. There's barely a tickle on the inside of my cheeks before Hopping deposits her sample in a plastic tube and says, 'All done.'

We hear footsteps on the stairs and Green appears in the doorway with Kitty close behind him. My face feels hot as Hopping fiddles with her briefcase and I pray that Kitty can't see what she's doing. I don't want her to think so little of me.

'Mrs Okine has answered all my questions,' Green says with an easy smile that Kitty returns.

'You have my number if you need anything,' she says. 'And sorry again that I have to dash off.'

'You're going?' I say, trying to keep the surprise and anger from my face. I need to speak to her but I can't let the police know we're not on good terms.

'Yes, remember, I have that appointment?' Our eyes lock as I try to remember what she's talking about – it could be hair or nails or her therapist, she has so many appointments. I try to plead with my eyes for her to stay since there's so much more we need to say to each other, but she just gives me a bland smile and a jaunty wave. All I can do is nod and murmur, 'Oh, yes, of course. I'll see you later?'

'See you later,' she says dully, and we hear her walk to the door, followed by a slam.

'Your wife was very helpful,' Detective Green says, returning to the table and pulling up a chair. 'She mentioned you've been the victim of a stalking campaign?'

Hopping sits up a little straighter and jots something down in her notebook. I suddenly feel very silly that I haven't mentioned the letters before now. It can only help my case that there's someone else out there that could be involved, even if it does make me look rather negligent since I did nothing about them.

'Yes, someone has been putting anonymous letters through the door.'

'And this is recently?' she asks.

Nodding, I say, 'Yes, a handful over the last couple of months.'

'And you didn't think to mention this before?'

'Sorry,' I murmur but secretly I'm pleased that she's showing interested in another line of inquiry. I don't know if it's just wishful thinking but I detect a slight shift in the mood in the room, almost as if they are now regarding me more a witness than a suspect. I breathe a little more easily and wonder why I didn't mention it before when it could at least provide another avenue of investigation.

'And did you report this to the police?'

I shake my head and Hopping sighs, but I cut in, 'I get a lot of attention from fans so I try not to catastrophise, although this did feel a bit different.'

Hopping looks up. 'In what way?'

I search for the word and land on, 'Personal. It felt personal.'

'What did the letters say?'

Feeling myself flush I say, 'They started off saying "I'm watching you" but then they started mentioning a woman. One said, "I saw you with her" and another said, "she should watch her back".'

Hopping and Green exchange a glance.

'And you think this "her" might be Nina?'

When I nod, I notice she is writing furiously in her notebook so I nod more vigorously.

'Could someone have been following you last night?' Green says and I detect a little more warmth in his tone.

'It's definitely possible. In fact, I think there was someone at the pub who seemed to get in my way whenever I tried to get to the bar. A woman.'

'Did you recognise her?' I think back to the crowded room and the woman with the dull mousy hair but I can't recall any features. I'd like to say it was McCrazy, to throw her to the wolves, but something stops me. I'm sure McCrazy is shorter than that woman for one thing, and I want to talk to her myself before the police do. I want to catch her off guard, before she's had chance to script her lies. 'No, I didn't recognise her but she was hanging around. There was something off about her.'

Hopping glances at Green and something passes between them that I don't understand. There's certainly been a shift in energy in the room since the stalking was mentioned and I kick myself for not bringing it up sooner to divert their attention from me.

Both officers stand. 'We will be verifying everything you've told us, David, and do expect more questions in the coming days. As I'm sure you're aware, this is an extremely serious situation, and currently you are the last person to see Nina alive so I'm going to ask you not to leave the city without speaking to us first. Do you understand?'

I nod my head, just glad they're leaving.

'Can you give us your contact details? Email, phone, everything.'

Taking my wallet out of my pocket, I pull out a card with shaking fingers and slap it on the table in the hope that neither of them will notice the tremor.

'Thank you, David. We'll be in touch.' Hopping leaves the room but Green lingers. He turns to me and acts as if he's just had a thought.

'I hope you don't mind me asking,' he says. 'But can you tell me how you're getting on with your wife at the moment?'

In that moment, I want to punch him on his long, bulbous nose or ask him how he's getting on with his wife. Instead, I shrug and say, 'We've been married fifteen years, so you know how it is.'

He laughs but says, 'Maybe, maybe not. Tell me.'

'Ups and downs, but mostly we're very happy together.'

'Your wife mentioned some fertility issues?'

I wonder what other secrets she's been spilling but I just nod. 'Those have been the downs, but we're getting through them. My wife is a strong woman.'

'Must have been tough, though?' I wonder how this could possibly be relevant to their investigation but I grit my teeth and force myself to answer levelly.

'We made the decision to move on a few months ago and things have been better since then.'

'Glad to hear it.' He gives me a lopsided smile and lumbers after Hopping on his too-long legs with his too-short trousers. I follow them out into the hallway and wait by the door as Hopping turns back and hands me a card. 'If you think of anything, call me.'

I nod and watch as they walk to an unmarked car, only shutting the front door when they start getting inside. Sinking down onto my knees, I rest my forehead against the wood and breathe deeply until the panic starts to ease. They've got hold of the end of a thread and I fear that very soon, everything is going to unravel.

Just then, my phone beeps and I glance at the screen. It's a message from Tom and a small smile tugs at my lips when I see it's an address, but it quickly fades when I see that McCrazy lives less than a mile from my own front door.

THIRTEEN

KITTY

My hangover is making me desperate so I set off to Connor's office beneath my umbrella, flinching at every car horn and leaping out of the way of strangers as they cross my path, as if one of them might be about to grab me and drag me away. I've tried not to think about Nina's murder but it's impossible not to picture her pretty face covered in blood, and full body tremors keep juddering through me. Surely, *surely*, I'd remember if I'd been involved in any way; the thought of it chills me, despite the hazy sun trying to fight its way through the grey clouds.

Connor may not be answering his phone but I've decided to take matters into my own hands. A nasty acidic burp escapes my mouth as I hurry along the road towards his office. I'm sure he'll understand as soon as I tell him the circumstances – it's clearly an emergency. My sessions with Connor are never easy but we have made progress over the year and he's the one person I can think of who may be able to help me work out what happened last night. Reaching the nondescript door, I push the buzzer and wait anxiously. What if he's not there? There's no answer, and I lean on the buzzer letting it sound for ten, twenty seconds as my heart pounds.

Finally a voice crackles over the intercom, 'Who is it?'

'Connor, it's me,' I yelp, before realising how crazy I sound and starting again in a lower register. 'It's Kitty. I'm sorry to drop in on you like this but I really need to see you.'

There's a long pause before Connor's voice comes back, sounding tight with worry, 'I'm afraid I'm not taking appointments this week. I've had a personal matter come up.'

'Connor, please.' I hate to beg but I'm desperate. 'I wouldn't be here if it wasn't an emergency.'

There's another interminable pause before I hear him sigh, 'Can you wait downstairs for ten minutes?'

'Thank you,' I breathe. 'Of course.'

He buzzes me in and I take a seat in the small waiting area, not bothering to pick up the magazine, just tapping my foot on the floor as I count down the minutes. After ten, I leap up and hurry up the stairs.

'Hello Connor,' I say as he opens the door and I notice his black hair looks wet as if he's just come out of the shower. Maybe I caught him after exercise or perhaps he'd been in bed? It feels almost intrusive even just thinking about Connor's personal life.

'I think you'd better sit down,' he says, and nods to the sofa. 'Are you OK? You look dreadful.'

A surge of anger runs through me and I want to scream that of course I'm not OK, given the circumstances, and no thanks to him. Aren't therapists meant to be there for you in your hour of need? Where the hell has he been? I open my mouth to say something but Connor stands up and comes towards me and different words come out.

'David's colleague has been murdered.'

Connor's eyes grow round before resting on me uneasily, 'That's terrible.'

'It's the one I mentioned to you.'

He lifts his chin, challenging me to go on.

'The one I thought he was sleeping with.'

He closes his eyes for a moment and when he opens them he says evenly, 'I think you ought to be careful about making an accusation like that unless you're absolutely certain, given the circumstances. In our last session you said you didn't have any proof.'

'I wasn't to know this was going to happen,' I say sulkily.

Connor rubs his eyes before looking at me again. 'Over the course of our sessions, how many women do you think you've accused David of sleeping with?'

My cheeks grow warm and I open my mouth to object but only a small squeak comes out.

'Ballpark?' he asks.

'A few,' I say, tugging at a loose thread on my trousers.

'Five? Ten? More than ten?'

I don't look up at him and say in a quiet voice, 'More than ten.'

'I haven't kept an exact tally but I wouldn't be surprised if the number doesn't run to twenty.'

'Lots of women throw themselves at him.' I say, folding my arms defensively. It's the truth though I'm starting to feel very uncomfortable. It's as if Connor is telling me off though he doesn't even know the half of it. We stare at each other as I feel a burst of anger that Connor isn't simply accepting what I say – he's meant to be on my side, and neither of us speaks. The silence seems to simmer in the room until Connor looks away first and says, 'I'm sorry but I need to ask you an important question.'

I swallow hard, anticipating what is to come.

'Did you have anything to do with it?'

Hearing his suspicions hurts, despite sharing them myself, and I squeeze my eyes shut, poking at the black hole in my memory, trying to mentally retrace my steps to Nina's front door, but I find everything is jumbled. My heart thuds in my chest as I try to work out what to say to Connor. I'd like to say no, but something inside stops me. What was I doing there?

'Kitty?' he asks sharply.

A small sob escapes my lips and I fight to hold it in. 'I don't think so.'

He sighs heavily. 'Think?'

'I was drinking and things are a bit hazy.'

'What do you mean, hazy?'

'I can't remember exactly what I did but I have no reason to think I was involved.'

He looks horrified. 'Don't you think you would remember?'

I meet his gaze and nod hard, wanting to feel his certainty, but how can I be sure when I have a hole in my memory for the time when Nina was murdered, and I know I was at the scene. There's a long silence while Connor and I observe each other. I can't help but feel I've gone down in his estimations, and when he speaks again he catches me off guard.

'Did you know that you've been coming to these appointments for almost a year?'

'Yes,' I say, narrowing my eyes, wondering where he's going with this.

'And we've made some fantastic progress. It's been eye-opening to go back to your childhood and try to work out together where some of these deeply buried feelings are coming from. I'm really proud of the work we've done.'

I sense the 'but' that's coming and feel a twist of worry so I try to cut in, but Connor raises his hand to silence me and continues, 'But I think we might have reached the limits of what I can do here.'

Panic rises inside me and I almost cry out 'no'. How can Connor think now is a good time for us to part ways? Surely he can see that I'm not in a good place, and it crosses my mind that he wants to wash his hands of me in case I'm implicated in what happened to Nina. I rack my brains for what I can do or say to change his mind – I can't lose Connor, not now.

'I'm sorry,' I say. 'Please don't end our sessions. I still need you.'

'I think you're ready to take the next step.' He smiles but it doesn't reach his eyes and I panic at how calmly he's detaching himself from me, feeling like I'm entering freefall.

'I've found our sessions invaluable. For the first time in years I feel like I'm making progress. We're really getting somewhere.' I take a deep breath before continuing in a lower, steadier voice. 'Look, please, can we continue? I'd really like to talk about my mother.'

There's a flash of interest in Connor's eyes and I know I've hit on something. It's what I've been holding back all these months, the one piece of the puzzle I've kept to myself. Connor has pushed me to go there, of course, and I've always said I preferred to focus on the here and now, but I can see that I'm left with no choice but to give him what he wants.

'Go on,' Connor says.

'And will we continue next week?' I ask, not willing to give in until I have his commitment.

Connor tilts his head to one side and presses his fingers together. The silence stretches until he finally nods and I allow myself a brief smile before taking a deep breath. Reeling back through my hazy memories, I immediately land on the one I know I should start with and I begin softly, 'It was the night before I went to Oxford; one of my teachers was driving me down the next morning. I was in my room packing what little I had into a suitcase I'd got from a charity shop when my mum came in. It was late...'

I can still see her now, all dressed up with a face full of make-up, sitting on the edge of my bed, holding one of the books I'd bought for my course in her hands and roughly flicking the pages. 'Util-... utilitar-... What is this crap?'

'Utilitarianism. It's a theory of morality. The greatest good for the greatest number.'

'That's a wee mouthful. So how does that work when it's at home?' Her eyes snapped to me, and for a moment I felt like she was vaguely interested in something I had to say and I felt a rush of pleasure suffuse me.

'You make decisions based on what will produce the most happiness for the most people.'

'As opposed to?'

I pulled myself up, pleased to show off what I'd learned in my philosophy class. 'As opposed to any theory of morality that has an intrinsic good – something fixed that is right or wrong. With utilitarianism, anything can be the right thing to do as long as it makes more people happy than sad.'

She seemed to consider this, tipping her head to one side and staring off into the distance, before smiling widely and ruffling my hair. 'You know, I rather like that. I think Don will like it too.'

I wrinkled my nose. Don was her latest man on the scene, a businessman who wore dodgy suits and seemed far older than my mother, and he'd made it clear he preferred it when I wasn't around. The feeling was mutual, but I let it pass without comment because I didn't want to break the spell since it felt like we were having a normal conversation – a mother asking about the subject her daughter was going to study the night before she went to university. I wanted it to continue, to share with her my worries about leaving and whether I would make any friends, but she stood up.

'Don't wait up,' she said, leaving my room as quickly as she'd swept inside and slamming the front door a moment later. I must have drifted off, and when I woke early, ready to go, she still wasn't home and she didn't return before Mrs Hodgson arrived and beeped the horn. I left for Oxford without saying goodbye.

'And then?' Connor asks, tilting his head, and I can tell he's intrigued.

'And then nothing,' I say. 'It was the last time I ever saw her.'

There's a long silence and I stare out of the window, refusing to allow myself to cry. When I returned from Oxford after the first term, an Indian family were living in the flat and they had no idea where she'd gone or who she'd gone with. Eventually, I tracked down Don's ex-wife and she said they'd moved to Edinburgh and we were both better off without them.

'What happened to her?'

I shrug as if I have no idea, but I did once bump into her old hairdresser who asked me how I liked my new stepsister. I didn't let on that it was the first time I'd heard of her but hearing that I'd been so readily tossed aside for a new family tore me apart. I've always pictured them living in one of those upmarket townhouses, somewhere I wouldn't have fitted in, playing happy families. My mum probably helping her new daughter with her homework the way she never helped me.

'We just drifted apart when I went to Oxford,' I say.

'Do you wish you never went?'

'I can't change what happened, but I got carried away believing that Oxford University would be a golden ticket to the fucking chocolate factory.' I realise how angry I sound and let out a short laugh as if I'm joking.

'And it wasn't?'

I twist my mouth into a contrite smile. 'Well, I did meet David.'

Connor doesn't smile. 'You did.'

'But no, Oxford wasn't a trip to the chocolate factory, not for me.'

'What exactly did your time at university break that wasn't already broken? Your relationship with your mother?' He lifts his voice and poses the question innocently enough but we both know that relationship was long since spoiled and I shake my head.

'Not that,' I say.

'What then?'

My mouth feels dry and when I speak again the words come out in a croak. 'Me.'

Connor looks sad now. 'And then you met David.' Usually I'm happy to return to the topic of my husband – back to safe ground – but there's something in the way Connor says his name that sounds ominous. He goes on, 'David came into your life at the worst possible time.'

I frown at this. 'David was a bright spot in the dark. A rainbow in a storm.'

Connor shakes his head. 'You must know, deep down, that your relationship with David is not normal.'

I open my mouth to protest but only a strange whine comes out.

'Your mother's rejection left a great void in your life and, consciously or not, you filled it with David.'

My face is hot but I can't feel my hands and feet.

I think of warm cider in the sun, roll-up cigarettes, walking hand in hand through Christ Church meadow, and I shake my head.

'What David and I have is special.'

'Come now,' Connor says, and the look he gives me makes me want to slam my fist into his face. I wish I'd accepted his request earlier to end his sessions since he clearly doesn't know me at all.

'I would do anything for David,' I say, fury boiling in my veins, and I get up and leave without another word. My anger making me worry what exactly I might be capable of.

FOURTEEN

DAVID

I arrive at the address Tom gave me by late afternoon when people are starting to make their way home from work.

McCrazy lives in a ground-floor maisonette in a pretty row of terraced houses behind Angel station, and as I walk down the street, it chills me to think that it's only a fifteen-minute walk from my house. We're practically neighbours. I'd been expecting a more down-at-heel neighbourhood and it's unsettling to see the well-cared-for brown-brick houses with their fresh white window frames and distinctive front doors painted different colours giving the street a cheerful vibe.

She has a peppy orange front door and I stand outside, peering through the front window, trying to make out anything inside, but all I can see is a pair of floral curtains. It's hard to imagine that the same person who put up such a bright, happy print has spent years intermittently trying to ruin my life, but that's always been one of my problems – not seeing Catherine McCollum for who she really is. Even the first day I met her – the day I made the biggest mistake of my life – I took her for someone who would be thrilled to have a supporting role in my life, never for one moment dreaming that she would fancy herself the leading lady.

It was one of those wonderful Oxford days where the sun beats down on the leaden spires and the streets are crowded with tourists, but inside the quads it is peaceful and serene. The kind of day where the students laze out on the perfectly manicured grass, staring up at the cloudless sky as they leaf through library books and think of themselves as the next Oscar Wilde. I recall sitting out on the lawn in the afternoon sun watching a group of boys play croquet and getting pleasantly drunk on cheap fizz as I looked around at my friends and realised how lucky we were. The chosen few that had banded together, a heady combination of good looks, wealth, public school pedigree and even one or two famous last names. It was the type of crowd I'd aspired to belong to my whole life and finally I'd made it.

Tom was the ringleader of the croquet game, schooling a couple of the younger boys by sending their balls flying into the hedgerow whenever they gave him the chance. Ed and Caro were sitting nearby, Caro in the centre of the group and Ed hanging at her shoulder, interjecting in her conversation every now and then and trying to sound clever. I seem to remember there was a row – one of Tom's latest dates got the hump and stormed off – leaving the rest of us to ponder exactly how Tom managed to keep sleeping with women when it was no secret how he treated them.

Whooping and cheering broke out as Tom brought his ball home and the croquet game descended into a cross between a wrestling match and a rugby ruck. As the rest of the boys drifted off, Tom plopped himself down in the middle of the group, red-faced and sweaty, and draped his arm around Caro's shoulder, giving her an easy grin as Ed scowled. It's strange now to think of us as teenagers together – so young, so full of dreams, with so much ahead of us. I may not have had the same pedigree as the others, but I knew then I was destined for big things and I was exactly where I was meant to be.

It was the night of the May Ball and we must have gone back to our rooms, pulled on our formal clothes and returned to Trinity for dinner, drinks, dancing – even a spin on the Ferris wheel that had been erected on the quad, though the rest of the evening is a strange blur. I was under the influence of booze and whatever Tom had in his pocket wrapped in cling film, and I find I can't extract a single clear memory until I woke up, in McCrazy's single bed in her college room and peered over at her, trying to work out who the hell she was.

Shame and a horrendous hangover sent me pinballing around her room, gathering my things as quickly as I could and apologising as I walked backwards out of the door, still shirtless, desperate to put the whole evening behind me. She never even told me her name. As I slowly made my way down the stone stairs and worked out which college I was in and how to get home, I put the incident behind me and assumed I'd never see her again, never dreaming for a second just how wrong I would be.

Term ended without incident, and while my crowd returned to their family homes or disappeared on Caribbean holidays with their parents, I stayed in Oxford for my college telethon – the college call centre that involved flogging sponsorship opportunities to alumni. The money was good and it was preferable to returning to a cramped flat in Peckham, a place I'd successfully avoided since I was sixteen, but it was deathly dull. No one I knew stayed up, and I didn't let on that my summer plans were much more pedestrian than theirs, so I spent my evenings drinking cans of beer on the bank of the river and counting down the days until the summer was over, feeling for the first time the lustre of Oxford dimming.

It was on one of these evenings, on my way back to college, weaving a little from the booze buzzing in my system, that I spotted a girl I recognised sitting under a tree with a book in the botanic gardens. I'd already called out and waved when it dawned on me that she was *that* girl – the girl from the night of the ball. It was too late to pretend I hadn't seen her after all because she'd closed her book and was looking up with a wide smile on her face, revealing a very English set of teeth – slightly yellowing with twisted eye teeth. She wasn't like the glossy girls I usually hung out with, but I had no one else and she was happy to see me and in my desperate state, that was enough. Sitting down beside her, I remember saying, 'I think I ought to introduce myself properly, I'm David,' as her murky blue eyes flashed with excitement.

I'm ashamed to admit that boredom and booze drove me back to her room several times over the course of that summer, and each time I'd creep out drenched in regret while she'd sit up, rubbing sleep from her eyes and give me one of her vacant grins, thanking me far too earnestly for staying over. It wasn't exactly my finest hour, but I was young and foolish and it was the long holidays when the normal rules of Oxford didn't seem to apply. Then the new term began, my friends returned, and a fresher named Kitty joined the college and everything changed. For me, that summer was consigned to the depths of history the moment it ended. I never thought I'd be the one hanging around outside McCrazy's front door all these years later.

As I approach slowly, with a feeling of trepidation making my legs feel like jelly, I reach Catherine's door but I don't knock right away. Instead I breathe in deeply to steady myself, trying not to dwell on the fact that behind this door is the woman who's plagued me for twenty years. It hasn't been constant, but just when she's slipped to the back of my mind, I'll turn around and find her ordering a blueberry muffin in the queue at the coffee shop behind me with her lopsided grin on her face. She always pretends it's innocent enough but I'm not a man who believes in coincidences. Could she have begun following me again? Is it possible that she was at Nina's flat last night? I can't bring myself to think what that might mean but I raise my hand to knock – I need answers.

After rapping three times I wait, my heart hammering in my chest. There's no response and I get a sinking feeling but I try again, knocking harder and longer than before. There's another long silence as I press my ear to the door but then I hear a soft, swishing noise like shuffled footsteps on carpet. I breathe as quietly as I can, trying to inhale as much air as possible through my nose without making a sound. She must be right behind the door, listening, the same way I am. It makes me shudder to think of her being so close. Suddenly I'm exhausted by it all and I feel a flare of anger; I'm sick of playing her games after all this time and decide to try it my way.

'Delivery!' I call out in a loud, obnoxious voice.

There's a pause before I hear a barely audible, scratchy voice say, 'I haven't ordered anything.'

'It's flowers. Maybe a secret admirer.' I try to keep my tone playful, putting on a strong London twang.

She doesn't act right away and I begin to wonder if she's walked away, but then I hear the gentle click of the lock and the door opens a crack. Taking my chance, I jam my foot inside, glimpsing a sliver of her pale face, her mouth open in shock, before I give the door a hard shove and she stumbles backwards without making a sound. I close the door quietly behind me and we face each other in her narrow hallway, both breathing hard.

'Hello Catherine,' I say, and a snide question slips out before I can help myself, 'Still kidding yourself that we're married?'

A strange look crosses her face and something twists inside me as the familiar vacant smile crosses her face and she says, 'Hello David, it's lovely to see you again, but just so you know, I go by Kitty these days.'

My mouth falls open and I feel the odd urge to laugh that

sometimes comes when you hear something that shocks you to the core. I had hoped to find her much better than the last time we met – Tom had told me I would but he's badly mistaken – here she is, still convinced that we are married and going by the name of my actual wife.

I long to grab her by the shoulders and try to shake some sense into her but I know it won't work. Our brief fling twenty years ago has planted some sort of seed in her brain that has grown over the years as if it has a life of its own. I never really understood how or why, only that somehow when I tried to end our dalliance, she decided to re-write the ending into her own happily ever after, but it has become a nightmare for us both.

As I meet her intense gaze, I almost feel sorry for her since I can tell that this woman isn't faking it – she truly, madly and deeply believes that we're married. I've been told that she suffers from a form of paranoid delusion called erotomania but the words never were important to me, it's the impact that matters. And I can't feel sorry for someone who has caused so much pain to me and everyone I love, and I have to fight to keep the horror from my face so I don't antagonise her as I wonder: did you kill Nina?

PART TWO

FIFTEEN

CATHERINE

I wasn't expecting David – and I certainly wasn't expecting him to barge into my hallway – but as I drink in his beautifully tailored suit and box-fresh white shirt, I think how nice it is to see him. It always is.

Glancing down at my own attire, I feel a rush of shame, since I changed into my pyjamas the moment I got back from Connor's, planning to spend the evening on the sofa with the telly for company and nurse the remnants of my hangover.

'I haven't been feeling well today,' I say, thinking I need to explain why I'm not dressed, but David barely glances at me and doesn't bother to ask how I am. I must admit that rankles, but I put it down to a bad day – he must have heard about Nina, after all.

'Is there somewhere we can talk?' David demands, his eyes darting behind me, and I wonder where I should show him to. The living room is the cosiest but it's messy in there, and the kitchen is tidy but the wooden dining chairs are uncomfortable after a while. Then there's the bedroom, but I'm almost certain David would not be amused by that. Before I can answer, David grabs a fistful of my dressing gown sleeve and tugs me into the living room and I gasp in shock at how forceful he's being.

'Here?' he says, and I squeak, 'David, please, let go of me.'

He drops my arm as if I've burnt him and refuses to meet my eyes. 'Sorry,' he mutters, as I survey the state of the living room and decide it's not too bad. Quickly folding the blanket I left on the sofa, I gesture to him, 'You can sit there,' but he ignores me and takes the small armchair, leaving me to sink into the sofa cushions.

'Would you like some water or tea? Or I could make you a coffee?' I ask but he shakes his head sharply.

'No water, no tea, no coffee. This isn't a social visit.'

I pick up a cushion and hug it to my chest. David and I may not always see eye to eye but there's no need for him to be so short, we do go way back after all. Spotting a loose thread on my sleeve, I begin winding it around my fingertip, watching as the skin turns white like a small pearl as I brace myself for what David is here to discuss. Biting my lip, I wonder how much he knows – has he spotted me following him? Does he realise I was at Nina's house last night?

'I thought we had an agreement?' David demands.

I frown, thinking, *I thought we were married*, but I don't say that aloud; it will only make David angrier, and he doesn't wait for a response.

'Have you been sending me letters again?'

My mouth drops open slightly since that is not what I expected him to say, and I can meet his eyes and say honestly, 'No, I haven't. You have to believe me, please, David. I've done exactly as you asked after the last time I had an episode.'

A look of scorn crosses his face and he bursts out, 'You may call it an "episode" but I think of it as a reign of terror that you have inflicted on me and my wife. Turning up at our house, following us in the street, putting your bloody poison-pen letters through our front door. Don't you realise how serious this is?'

Shaking my head, I say, 'David, I haven't written you any letters. I've been seeing Connor every week like I agreed and I tell him everything. He's been helping me, actually, and I'm getting my life back on track. I'm sorry I'm not as mentally strong as you are.'

'This isn't about mental strength!' He's practically yelling and I want to tell him to keep his voice down. My neighbours will be home and the walls of these terraced houses are very thin.

'It's about human decency. All I ask is that you treat me and Kitty with respect.'

I flinch at the sound of her name on his lips but I don't utter the retort that's on the tip of my tongue – I give David nothing but respect, he's my world. David leans forward in his chair, resting his elbows on his knees and clasping his hands. He looks tired – there are deep lines beneath his eyes and his lips are chapped – he needs to look after himself better, but that's another thing I don't say.

'Listen, Catherine,' he says, dropping his voice, and I swallow hard, feeling certain that I know what topic we're coming on to.

'Do you know my TV show?' he asks.

'It's prime-time television, hardly a secret,' I say lightly, but he doesn't smile.

'Have you heard of one of my colleagues, Nina Bello?' I shake my head without even flinching, but all I can think is, *Our colleague, don't you mean?*

'Should I have?' I ask innocently. It was a stroke of luck when the temping agency called and said there was a position in the HR team at Prestige Productions. Of course I knew that David was their star presenter and Kitty, his wife, the finance director – such a power couple. It tickled me to imagine working alongside them, declining their holiday requests and querying their sick leave, but I had no intention of actually joining the company until I read that Kitty was taking a sabbatical. I'd been in and out of work myself due to my own issues, and it felt like fate that I was now well enough to return and reclaim my rightful place by David's side.

I haven't said anything but suddenly David's hands dart forward and grab the lapels of my dressing gown. The air rushes from my lungs as he shakes me roughly and I feel my teeth chattering together.

'Do you think this is funny?' he says.

'No,' I stammer, as tears prick my eyes, I certainly don't think it's funny but I must have smiled at the thought of me and David together. How stupid I am, of course it didn't work out like that – it never has worked out how it should have.

David lets me go as suddenly as he grabbed me and I sink back into the cushions. 'Nina is dead, did you know that? Did you follow her? Did you do something to her?'

He sounds desperate and I'm shaking my head as hard as I can, wishing I knew for certain that what I'm saying is true.

'I never... I wouldn't... How can you even think...?'

Tears slip onto my cheeks and I rub them away with my fingertips. David and I are soulmates and it hurts so much that he could think so little of me. I need to convince him that there's no way I could be involved in something as grubby as what he's suggesting. I know that now isn't a good time to mention my role at Prestige – he'd hit the roof – but I land on Matt and our last conversation. Clearly there's potential there, so it's only a slight exaggeration and I'm certain it will improve David's opinion of me.

'Things are going well for me,' I begin. 'I've got a job and a boyfriend. His name's Matt and we work together. You can call him if you like.' Pulling my phone from my dressing gown pocket, I scroll to Matt's name and offer it up to him, praying he doesn't call my bluff as I stare into his eyes, almost daring him to challenge me.

He sighs and looks away first. 'Just tell me the truth. Have you been following me?'

I realise he's close to believing me and I say, 'I wouldn't do that to you, David.'

'You did before.'

His words take me back to when we met – that long, lonely summer when Oxford was deserted and I was stuck, feeling numb and confused since I no longer had a home to go back to. I was hired as part of the cleaning team but the rest of the college staff treated me like an outsider; I was a student, after all, only working for the summer, while most of them had been born on the outskirts of Oxford and had long lived in the shadow of the university. I didn't know it until I saw him again but I needed David – he was like a tall glass of ice-cold water and I drank him in.

What we had may not have been a normal relationship – even I knew that – but we shared things that I don't think he told anyone else. Neither of us felt like we fitted in, not at Oxford and not at home – we were outsiders, each playing a part. We'd both grown up in difficult situations, born to single mothers who didn't pay us the attention we deserved, and we'd both escaped to hallowed institutions of learning where our differences stayed with us as if they were carved into our skin. We understood each other and that was why the last time I saw him at college was so hard to take. I never got over it.

It was the end of our third year and I'd spent the day at the library revising for finals – an ordinary day. I'd woken early, eaten a cooked breakfast in hall and walked along the sunny street to the library where I found a desk tucked away in the bowels of the building, nestled among the stacks of books, and worked all day. It was dusk when I finally packed up and set off back to college, taking my time to enjoy the fresh air, when someone touched my shoulder and I swung around in surprise. I was utterly delighted to see David but he didn't return my grin and said in a serious voice, 'Have you got time for a drink?'

I felt like my feet didn't touch the ground from that moment until we pushed open the door of the King's Arms and stepped into a wall of boisterous noise. Groups of students – boys in rugby shirts and girls with puffy blonde fringes – sat too many to a table, chatting and laughing without a care in the world. Several heads turned as we came in, and I felt eyes following us across the room and my smile widened. Finally, David was by my side and we were together for the whole world to see. It felt good not to be his dirty little secret – I deserved more.

'What can I get you?' he asked.

'White wine, please.' I'd developed a taste for it at the formal halls I went to, often sitting alone or with foreign students who needed someone to show them around.

All of the tables in the pub were taken but while David went to the bar, I found a couple of stools in the back room and pulled them together so our knees would be touching. Through the window I watched students cycling by and finalists walking back from exams in their gowns. I'd been so focused on the papers I'd sit in the next two weeks that I'd been neglecting David. I'd only been by his room once or twice and I hadn't actually seen him in days. When he came over with the drinks, I studied his face. He looked tired – the strain seemed to show on his forehead and I longed to smooth it out with my finger, but I knew he wouldn't appreciate that so I accepted the wine and sipped it slowly.

'How's your revision going?' he asked.

'Good, and you?'

'Terrible.' He rolled his eyes and we laughed. I liked that. Us, sharing a moment, like we had so many times back in that summer in first year. 'I'm desperate to avoid a Desmond.'

I smiled but I was disappointed by his lack of originality. It was a well-worn joke around the town – *Desmond Tutu*, 2:2 –

and I was sure David would do much better than that. I'd spoken to students in his study group and he had a good reputation by all accounts. David took a big gulp of his pint and then a deep breath – I could see he was building up to saying something and I stayed quiet, letting my eyes convey that he could tell me anything.

'Look, Catherine.' He sounded earnest and I leaned forward, nodding eagerly. 'I need to ask you something. No, I need to tell you something. You need to forget about me.'

I felt my face growing hot and I opened my mouth, but I didn't know what to say. Suddenly the laughter in the room sounded louder and the stares felt more direct. A pretty blonde girl nearby leaned over to her friend and whispered something, and they both collapsed into giggles. I was sure they were talking about us but David went on, unperturbed.

'I've spoken to a few people and they said I should speak to you one-on-one, and explain the impact your, um, persistence is having on my life.'

'Persistence?' My voice was small and my head felt like it was on fire. I knew my cheeks would be bright red and I saw that the two girls next to us were quiet now but still staring.

David rubbed a hand across the top of his head and I suddenly wished we were back in my room, lying in bed, and I was touching those tight curls, drawing them out between my fingertips.

He cleared his throat and I knew he was about to say something I wouldn't like. 'I'm sorry, there's no other way to say it. I know things are hard for you but it's been hard for me too. We're about to finish uni and all I want is for us to go our separate ways with no hard feelings. Please, can we do that?'

I blinked back hot tears and nodded, not trusting myself to speak. David had been such a big part of my student experience. It was almost our two-year anniversary and now he was pushing me away for absolutely no reason at all when I was the only one who understood him. As I nodded I tried to work out why he would say something like that, and then it hit me – it must be the exam stress, it was getting to everyone. He didn't actually mean it, he couldn't. I reached out and touched his hand, stroking the cool skin gently.

'No!' He snatched his hand away.

It was the turn of the perky brunette on the next table to burst into giggles while her blonde friend looked on with a smirk. I wanted to smash my glass into her face.

'This isn't a date,' David said. 'We're not friends. You need to get it into your head that we are nothing, and if you don't stay away from me I'm going to call the police.'

It was as if he'd punched me. I struggled to catch my breath, gripping the edge of the table as I wheezed. David jumped up but he watched me, horror etched on his face, and then sat back down, speaking again in a low, pleading voice, 'Please, calm down. It doesn't need to be like this. We can part ways as friends if you just agree that this is the end of it.'

A tear fell and, inside my head, a voice screamed that it was impossible, we meant more than that – he'd given me an engagement ring, for God's sake – but I felt myself nodding. The heat of the pub and the attention of the audience around us were getting too much. I just wanted to get out of there.

'Thank you,' David said. 'And good luck with finals.' It was the perfect moment for a hug or even a handshake, and I saw his indecision over whether to touch me, but in the end he stuck his hands in his pockets and gave me a curt nod. 'Goodbye.'

My insides screamed at the indignity of it, that he hadn't deemed me worthy of a simple pat on the shoulder after everything we'd been through. I waited until he'd left the pub before draining the last inch of my wine and following him, checking he'd gone around the corner before hurrying after him. It was quieter now and I saw him up ahead at the crossroads, his sky-blue jumper moving between people on the other side of the

road and approaching a figure waiting in the halo of light under
a street lamp. Her hair shone – that ridiculous, unnatural silvery
blonde – and his arm slipped around her waist. *Kitty.* I felt a
scream rising inside me. That was the last day I did any revision,
and it was me that got the Desmond. David, of course, got a
first.

'Earth to Catherine,' David says and takes my hand now,
squeezing it painfully, but all I can do is stare and think, *oh, so
you can touch me now.* His fingers grip tighter until suddenly I
cry out, 'David, let go, you're hurting me.'

He looks me very deliberately in the eye, and when he
speaks, his voice is low and menacing and it crosses my mind
that I've never seen this side of him before.

'You need to stay away from me, away from my family, away
from everyone who knows me. I never, *ever* want to see you
again. Do you understand?'

I stare down at my hand, where my fingers are turning pink,
and say, 'I understand,' but then David and I spot the ring at the
exact same moment and before I can snatch my hand away, he
tugs it towards him and holds the thin metal band up to the
light.

'What the fuck is this?' he asks, his voice tight with anger.

Feeling my face flush, I try not to think of the night when he
gave it to me. He may have been debilitatingly drunk but no one
could ever deny that he brought a ring to my room and gave it to
me. That is a fact I hold on to every single day but I know that
David won't want to hear it so I quickly think of a lie.

'This? It's just a bit of tat my mum picked up at a market
stall, but it has sentimental value.'

He hasn't taken his eyes from the ring and his face is
contorted in disgust, as if he's staring at something grotesque,
until he drops my hand and says wearily, 'Just stay away
from me.'

Suddenly I feel a surge of anger that makes me grit my teeth and raise my chin. Why should I let him sit here, in my home, and accuse me of horrible things when he's the one who fed me lies and promised me things he never meant to give? Even after all these years his betrayal still hurts.

'You're here accusing me,' I say, 'but I don't see the police anywhere. They don't appear to share your concerns, but I bet they've been to your house.'

I see from the look on his face that I've hit the nail on the head and I force out a laugh. 'It sounds like you might need to look a little closer to home.'

'What do you mean?' he asks.

'I hear your wife has had some time off work. Perhaps she's not exactly in the most stable frame of mind right now.'

'Don't you—'

I interrupt since I don't want to hear any more from him. 'And just look at yourself! Do you think these are the actions of a right-minded person? Turning up here with your wild accusations. Perhaps you ought to look in the mirror.'

He jumps up from his seat and I feel no pleasure at having hit my mark.

'Never contact me again,' he says as he storms out of the house, slamming the front door behind him.

I remain on the sofa, breathing slowly and deeply until my heart rate returns to normal, but I can't shake the squirming worry I feel. Perhaps David is right that I am a horrible person. Maybe I did do something to Nina. Those thoughts make me want to go to the fridge and take out a bottle of wine and never stop drinking, but that's what got me here in the first place.

Taking out my phone, I see the contact I offered up to David is on the screen – Matt's number. He did say to call him if I needed anything, and my finger hovers over the 'call' button as I wonder if I dare. People say that sort of thing all the time and no one ever really means it, but he did give me his number and I can't deny that I could do with a friend right now. Taking a deep breath, I tap the button, deciding that there's only one way to find out.

'Hello?' Matt answers on the second ring.

'Hi, it's Kitty. I hope you don't mind me calling, it's just you said—'

'Kitty! How are you doing?'

He sounds genuinely thrilled to hear from me and I sink back into the chair, relief washing over me as I say in a shaky voice, 'I'm OK,' and then I correct myself, 'Actually, I'm really not. Sorry, it's just been a bad day. Losing an old friend is incredibly painful, especially one that meant so much.'

He sighs heavily. 'I'm sure, I'm so sorry for your loss.'

'Thank you,' I say, but he has no idea I'm talking about David, not Nina.

'Do you want to talk about it or something else? I'm happy to listen if you just need to talk, but if you need distracting, I guarantee I can talk about rubbish for hours.'

I feel a smile tug at my lips, 'Something else, please.'

'Then let me ask you one question – does the name Gary mean anything to you?'

I can't help but burst out laughing at the mention of Karen's bulldog that we've been subjected to hours of her droning on and on about while we're meant to be working.

'You know,' Matt says. 'I've always thought we might be on the same wavelength.'

'What wavelength is that?' I ask.

He drops his voice and I can hear a smile in his words, 'The wavelength that thinks that Gary ought to be euthanised.'

Another laugh surprises me and I say, 'Cancelled, not euthanised. I don't wish the dog ill.'

'Oh I do,' he says gleefully. 'That dog is the bane of my life. If I have to hear about his diet or his latest Instagram post one more time I might start trolling him. *Gary, your backside looks big in that romper.* That kind of thing.'

I can't help laughing. 'You've been on his Instagram, then?' I say, teasingly.

'I *live* on his Instagram and I'm not ashamed to say it. It's so damn compelling.'

'Did you see "Gary rides a skateboard"?' I ask.

Matt laughs and says happily. 'Gotcha! And of course I did. You know, the thing that annoys me most about that video is that it's not even a bloody skateboard. It's a snowboard that Karen's tied to a rope.'

We're both laughing and I manage to get out, 'The bit where Gary rolls onto his back on the grass and she's Photoshopped in snow...'

As my laughter fades, I realise that Matt has managed the impossible – I haven't thought about David or Nina for at least five minutes.

SIXTEEN

DAVID

Seeing Catherine only made me more confused and I rushed home, desperate to talk to Kitty, but she wasn't here. Now it's 5 a.m. and I should be asleep but the bed is empty beside me and my phone is gripped tightly in my hand as I will her to ring.

I have no idea where the hell my wife is or what she's doing and I'm on edge, certain the police are going to realise that I lied about what happened with Nina and return to arrest me at any moment. I feel absolutely awful about sleeping with Nina but I know for certain that I had nothing to do with her death. A sob suddenly chokes me as I remember how happy she was as we said goodbye. She may have been tipsy but she thought that was the start of something, not the end, and I hadn't the heart to tell her that it was one giant mistake and I would never leave my wife, not for her or anyone.

Rubbing my face with my hands, I tell myself that it doesn't matter any more. Nothing matters to Nina because someone snuffed out her life and I need to find out who that was. A cold dread crawls over me as I think about trying to tell the police the truth, and I have a very bad feeling that whatever I say and do, they are going to try to pin this on me. Even if I call them right now and say *I'll hold my hands up – I lied – I did have sex with Nina*, they're not going to say *Thank you, Mr Okine, how helpful*. No, Hopping would delight in snapping the handcuffs on my wrists and twisting every detail of the case until a jury would be in no doubt of my guilt, and it certainly won't help Nina.

Sweat pours from me and my T-shirt clings, wet and cold, to my back as I toss and turn in the covers, trying to get comfortable. I realise I'm getting worked up but I have no idea what to do or think. Last night I waited up for Kitty until almost two before deciding it was time to try to sleep, but my spiralling thoughts kept me awake. I have no idea where she is or what she's done – I can't believe she could be involved but a little voice keeps whispering *Why isn't she here?* Her phone is switched off and none of our friends have seen her. I alternate between imagining that Kitty had something to do with Nina's death and worrying she might have suffered the same fate.

Just as I'm drifting off, a text buzzes through on my phone that jolts me awake. I push myself up onto one elbow and squint at the phone, my eyes taking a few moments to adjust to the light from the screen, before I see it's a message from an old colleague, one I never got on with, and my heart sinks that it's not Kitty. I tell myself that he's probably just messaging me to congratulate me on the Dick Bell interview – my phone has barely stopped since it aired – but as I sink back into my pillow and tap on the message, I see he's sent a link to an article in the *Daily Mail* and I frown in confusion. I've already read the *Mail*'s review of the show – 'Okine Eats Bell for Breakfast' – but I click on the link anyway, and see immediately that it's not my review.

The page loads and the headline '*Confessions* Executive Found Dead' makes me forget to breathe as an image of Nina fills the screen. It's a formal headshot that must be on her LinkedIn profile, and a gagging sound comes from my throat as I stare. It's a fantastic photo of her and it's horrible to imagine people all over the country drooling over her as they pore over the lurid details of her death. A sudden wave of nausea hits me and I sit bolt upright, groping for the light switch as my heart hammers in my chest. There's a glass of water on my bedside table and I sip, telling myself to calm down: Nina was murdered, so of course there was going to be press coverage. Scrolling, I see the article is mostly made up of images; they must have got access to her Instagram since there are photos of her in a bikini on a beach and one of her dressed up as Wonder Woman holding a large glass of wine. I feel like firing off an email of complaint at the crassness, but I tell myself it probably won't help my cause to draw attention to myself.

There are no new details but it does say that the police have said that the circumstances are suspicious and the investigation is ongoing. I'm grateful that other than the headline, there is no other mention of *Confessions* and certainly nothing that might link me to the situation. I'm almost at the end of the article when the final photo loads. It's grainier than the others and the lighting is terrible. Nina's face comes into focus and I realise the photo was taken in the pub after the show, and next to her is a blurry figure that must be me. The heat drains from my body and I wrap the duvet around me, shivering. I can't help but feel like it's only a matter of time before someone publicly points the finger at me and detonates my career, and although I know that's nothing compared to what happened to Nina, it still fills me with terror.

Outside, the lilac dawn is stretching across the sky but I remain in bed, refreshing the article again and again. I know that if the police check my phone it's not going to look good, but I need to know every detail that's out there – perhaps I'll come across something solid I can use to exonerate me when the police come knocking, which of course they will. My sweaty finger leaves a greasy smudge on the screen as I scroll to the comments. I know I shouldn't read them – hate and bile is all I'll find – but their speculation and theories is the only new information I have to go on.

TV tart. Mouthy bitches wanna b careful

Seriel killer on the lose. Lock up yo women!

Mine already is mate… in the kitchen. Ha ha

Most of the comments focus on Nina's appearance or job, and reading nasty words from people who don't know her fills me with rage, but I can't stop until another text message arrives and I'm surprised to see Annika's name. We rarely message each other directly, preferring to use Tom as a conduit for making arrangements. She and I don't meet up independently so the only thing that comes to mind is that she must have news about Kitty and I read the message impatiently.

Can we meet this morning? It's important.

My lack of sleep makes it hard for me to process why Annika might want to see me. Perhaps she's seen the story about Nina, but I can't see why that would make her want to meet. We are friends, but only because she's Tom's wife. I can count on one hand the number of times we've met just the two of us. It crosses my mind that she might want me to be the face of one of her furniture lines, though she's never asked me anything like that before and I decide that, whatever it is, I have to focus on finding Kitty.

I text back, *Could we do it in a few days? I've got a lot on.*

She replies immediately, *No.*

I feel a flicker of annoyance but Annika always has been direct. A follow-up message pops up a moment later with the name of a café near her house and a time: 9 a.m.

OK, is all I can bring myself to reply.

Giving up on sleep, I stagger to the shower, using a zingy lemon scrub to try to wake myself up, but it doesn't work. When I catch my face in the mirror, I see it looks gaunt and drawn, but I decide I have more important things to be worrying about right now so I don't bother with my usual regime of creams and scrubs.

Throwing on black jeans, a fitted black T-shirt and a pair of sunglasses, I set off to meet Annika early, grateful to get out into the morning air after the long night. It's strange to see people going about their day, knowing that they either haven't seen the story about Nina or have written it off as one of those everyday tragedies and already forgotten about it. Nina doesn't deserve to be a side note. I go on foot, wanting to avoid public transport and cabs where someone might recognise me, and I walk at speed so no one has a chance to really study my face. The thrill of fame wears off quickly, that I can attest to, and at times like this when you need to be incognito, it can be downright scary.

Trying to clear my mind, I avoid looking at my phone or making eye contact, but halfway to the café I catch sight of a headline on a paper tucked under someone's arm: 'TV Researcher Stabbed to Death' and I stop so abruptly that someone slams into my back.

'Watch it, mate,' the man says as I mutter an apology and duck out of his way, feeling as if all the air has been sucked from my chest.

Finding a quiet spot, I lean against the wall, breathing hard as I try not to imagine Nina's body punctured by stab wounds and covered in blood. Of course I knew something awful had happened to her but I hadn't let myself imagine anything so brutal, and the concept of murder felt abstract before I saw the word 'stabbed' in black and white. Sensing a woman hovering nearby on her phone, her eyes sliding to me in a way that makes me certain she recognises me, I push away from the wall and break out into a brisk jog. Once I begin, I find myself wanting to run and keep going until my legs give out, though my work shoes slow me down.

Moving my body is the only thing that's given me any respite from my thoughts but sooner than I'd like, I join Hampstead's busy high street and the foot traffic forces me to slow to a walk. We're meeting at Annika's local coffee shop, a chichi bakery with natural wood floors and a garish pink and orange plastic flower wall behind the counter. I make sure I've got my breath back by the time I step inside. The clientele are mostly mothers and dog owners, and I feel conspicuous as I join the back of the queue; I can't shake the feeling that I'm about to be arrested at any moment. Even here, I feel like the police may barge in and handcuff my arms behind my back, and someone would be sure to get a picture – smartphones have made everyone paparazzi.

As I wait to be served, a woman in the far corner of the room catches my eye, lifting her phone over her shoulder and pointing it at my face, before holding it out for her friend. The two of them study the photo and laugh. I grind my teeth, grimacing, but for once I don't care if she posts a photo of me looking stressed online with the caption #constipation – I just want to get out of there.

There's no sign of Annika, and as the queue inches forward, I open my *Times* app and spot the story immediately. The language is less sensationalist but it's there in black and white: 'Journalist Murdered at Home'. My finger hovers but I hesitate before I click on the story. I know my mind is all over the place but I can't help worrying whether it makes me look guilty to read multiple articles about her death? Or is it worse to avoid the coverage entirely? Surely as a concerned colleague and friend – and I would describe myself as both – I would follow the progress of the case? *Make a decision, Okine.* My whole arm jerks from the shoulder as I tap my thumb on the story, but before I can read it a voice in my ear says, 'David?'

I recognise Annika's clipped accent and turn to see her at my elbow, dressed in a pair of black running leggings and a blinding white shell jacket. Her hair is in two plaits, making her look younger than early forties, but her face is make-up free and the dark rings and fine lines are more prominent than usual. I kiss both her cheeks and say, 'Darling, so nice to see you,' while being vaguely aware of the woman in the far corner raising her phone once more for another picture. There should be a law against photographing strangers or at least a strong moral deterrent like there is about snapping other people's kids.

'Oat flat white,' Annika says across me, and I realise we've reached the front and the young man with long hair and a droopy moustache is looking at us expectantly.

'Black Americano,' I say, noticing the man's eyes dart to me briefly but immediately swing back appreciatively to Annika. She always has been striking.

'Any pastries or cakes for you guys?'

'Not for me,' Annika says. 'David?' I shake my head. I haven't been able to stomach anything since I heard about Nina.

The coffee machine hisses and spits as we wait for our drinks.

'How are you? How are the kids?' I ask, but Annika brushes off my attempts to chat with a curt, 'Fine.'

'I'm sorry about your colleague,' she says suddenly, and I realise she must have seen the coverage, but it still throws me off guard.

'It's awful, truly. She was a wonderful woman.' My face grows hot under Annika's stare but she gives my arm a squeeze and says, 'The police will do their job.'

I nod, wishing I shared her confidence but I can't admit that I'm terrified that they will stick it on the wrong man. I wish I could open up and tell Annika everything that's happened but I can tell there's something else on her mind and I couldn't bear her judging me.

'Have you heard from Kitty recently?' I say, although it's a long shot. Annika and my wife have never been close and their personalities are polar opposites. Where Annika is calm and controlled, Kitty is tempestuous and wild.

'Not since you came over for dinner,' she says, and we lapse into silence. Small talk has never been our strong suit. The man hands over two cardboard cups and Annika steers me by the elbow towards the door. 'Let's walk.'

She doesn't give me much choice and we emerge outside where the sun is already beating down – it's going to be a hot one. My shoes aren't suitable for tramping about on the Heath but we cross the road and head towards the entrance and I don't object. Annika marches straight up a sloping path that cuts across a wide expanse of grass where there are fewer people and I hobble alongside her, sure my feet are already swelling in my tight leather shoes, casting envious glances at her fluorescent-orange trainers. I shouldn't have run all the way here.

It doesn't take long before I feel my breath catching and sweat starting to bead along my brow. I open my mouth to ask her what this is all about when she veers onto a bench and sits down. Relieved, I slump down beside her and surreptitiously try to suck in lungfuls of air, not wanting her to see how unfit I am.

Annika sips her coffee and watches me with her head tilted and her blue eyes fixed on my face. I try to work out if she's angry or sad or happy but it's impossible – she has never been one to wear her emotions on her sleeve. Cold is how some people describe her, but I've always thought of her as sensible since she doesn't throw herself into situations as if she's tied herself to the mast of a ship in a storm, allowing herself to be tossed about by the waves. Instead, she keeps her distance and calmly assesses the situation, only acting at exactly the right time. It's stood her in good stead over the years. Her marriage has remained rock solid despite Tom's flakiness, and her business has skyrocketed. I shift under her gaze, uncomfortable as sweat drips down my back.

'Is this about the interview with Dick?' I say. 'I know Tom isn't happy with me—'

Before I can finish Annika makes a 'pfft' sound through her teeth.

'That is between you and Tom,' she says, making it clear that she couldn't care less about the interview. I wonder if she even watched it. 'It amuses me all of those rules and hierarchies that exist between you. Grown men but still looking up to someone because they were house captain twenty-five years ago.'

Fives captain, in Tom's case, I think, but she sniffs and I decide it's not the moment to correct her.

'David, in all the time I've known you, have I ever asked anything of you?'

Frowning, I sense a request that I won't like is coming so I try to stall. 'Well, I don't take my godfather duties lightly, I'll have you know.'

She smiles a watery smile and my chest tightens with panic – she looks like she might cry. Kitty's tears I can cope with; I've even had Caro sobbing on my shoulder a fair few times, but I've never seen Annika anything other than dry-eyed and I'm not sure what to do as I awkwardly try to put my arm around her, but she shifts forward in the seat out from under my embrace and says sharply, 'Just answer my question.'

I say in a hoarse voice, 'No, you've never asked me for anything.'

She takes another sip of coffee and I copy her, though I barely taste it as I gulp it down, waiting tensely for what she has to say.

'All I want is for you to be honest.'

'Of course,' I say, but she grips my arm, digging her fingers in painfully.

'No, David, not "of course". I know you and Tom have your schoolboys' code. I have never understood the traditions in this country and the way these school rituals—'

'Whatever it is, I'll answer truthfully,' I say, cutting her off, having heard many times how the Norwegian school system is far superior to ours.

'Promise me.'

'I promise.' Finally, she releases her grip and I take a deep breath, bracing myself for her question.

'Is Tom having an affair?'

Relief hits me and I feel weak, as if I could slip onto the ground into a puddle. Exhaling loudly, I let out a shaky laugh and Annika says, her voice tight with anger, 'Is something funny?'

'No, of course not,' I say quickly, but I'm thrilled I don't have to lie to her. 'No, he's not.'

She turns to face me and there's fire in her icy eyes. 'Are you certain?'

I think back to the times when Tom has been sleeping with someone – women from work, mostly, or ones he met on the apps – and the amount of detail I'd have. Not only would I know their name, occupation and bra size, but he'd tell anyone who'd listen about their sexual proclivities and anything vaguely funny or embarrassing they'd got up to, however crude. I always beg him not to tell me, or to have an open and honest conversation with his wife, but he's never relented and I've always felt that is Tom for better or worse.

'I'm certain.'

Annika flops back on the bench and sighs heavily. I'm surprised to see her wiping her eyes and this time I do put my arm around her and she rests her head on my shoulder.

'I'm no fool, David,' she says.

I shake my head rapidly – she is anything but. 'Of course you're not.'

'The only rule Tom and I have is that we must not lie.' I glance sharply at her, not wanting to ask but surprised at what she's hinting at. Does she know what he's done over the years? I realise I have no idea what goes on in their marriage and thankfully, she carries on without us testing that point. 'He's been acting strangely recently, sneaking around, hiding things. He insists that there's no one else, but if I find out he's lied,' she snaps her fingers, 'that will be the end.'

Her voice is harsh and I rub her shoulder, 'Darling, you won't, because he's not lying. He wouldn't do that to you.'

She looks at me again, deep into my eyes, as if she might find the truth buried within, then nods once, 'Thank you, David.'

Getting up, she throws her empty coffee cup into a bin in a perfect arc and gives me a wave over her shoulder, before setting off at jogging pace towards Hampstead without a backward glance.

SEVENTEEN

CATHERINE

Matt and I chatted late into the night but I still wake early, my heart thrumming in my chest as I sit straight up and think, *Nina is dead.* The black hole in my memory still feels like a scorch mark in the earth but I tell myself there is no way I wouldn't remember something as shocking as murder. I'd like to call in sick and make another appointment with Connor to analyse David's visit but I still feel a tight fury whenever I think of our last session and the way he tried to ditch me in my hour of need.

Instead I decide to go into the office early and try to find out as much as I can about the investigation into Nina's death. There have to be some benefits to working in human resources. Deciding to order an Uber as a treat, I get into the back seat and watch the cloudy sky flash by when suddenly something on the radio catches my attention.

'Can you turn this up?' I say, and the driver's eyes slide to me in the mirror, frowning, before he reaches across and turns up the volume.

'... the worker at a London-based television production company who was found stabbed to death in a flat in Bethnal Green has been named. Nina Bello, a 27-year-old who lived alone was killed sometime in the early hours of yesterday morning. We have no further details but police are asking that anyone who may have seen anything suspicious to please ring 1 1 1 and quote the reference number...'

The man's eyes dart to me again and I realise I'm hyperventilating. Winding down the window, I turn my face into the rushing air, closing my eyes as the whole sorry mess comes back to me. What if someone saw me outside her flat? There could be CCTV or footage from cameras in people's cars or homes. My picture could be splashed over the newspapers and it would be only a matter of time before the police came for me. I feel a lump in my throat and a strange throbbing in my head. David would see it and he'd soon know everything – he'd know I'd lied. A warm, prickling feeling of shame runs through me as I close my eyes and try to calm down.

'You all right?' the driver asks and I realise I've been sitting with my eyes shut for longer than is usual.

'Yes, yes, fine.' My voice comes out high and strained and I catch the driver frowning again.

'We're here,' he says flatly.

I realise the car is stationary outside the building and I leap out. 'Thank you,' I call out as I slam the door and hurry across the stretch of pavement to the main doors. Taking the lift up, I try not to think of Nina and her perfect white teeth. I'm hoping that I'll be the first one there so I can spend some time unsupervised on the Portal, but when I scuttle into the office I'm disappointed to see the other three are already in their seats. I feel Matt's eyes on me and my cheeks grow warm as I hurry to my desk.

'Morning Catherine,' Karen says, her clipped voice bringing me back to the here and now.

Kitty, I think, but I mutter a quiet, 'Morning.'

'How are you feeling today?' she asks.

I frown in confusion, remembering too late that yesterday I

left early claiming illness, then say quickly, 'Better, thanks,' but I can see Karen isn't fooled.

'Well, you look a picture of health. No one would know there'd been anything wrong with you.' I hear the jibe in her words but I sit down and busy myself with my computer. It's only then that I notice a small spider plant in a cheery blue pot that has appeared on my desk. I glance at Matt, who meets my gaze and smiles before turning back to his screen, and I feel a rush of warmth that beats the icy glare that Karen is sending my way.

'Stomach bug, was it?' Julie pipes up.

'Yes, one of those 24-hour things.'

'Horrible,' she says. 'My girls are always bringing them home from school. At the start of every new term there's always a new one and we take it in turns to hug the loo. You don't have kids, do you?'

I grit my teeth. 'Nope.'

'Strange, I haven't heard of anything going around,' Karen says.

'I have,' Matt pipes up. 'Nikesh from accounts was off last week and he said the finance team have been dropping like flies.'

I have no idea if that's true but I feel like hugging him.

'I can just about stomach coffee,' I say, wanting to move the conversation on. 'Would anyone else like one?'

'No thanks, I've got to get on with something,' Karen says primly.

'Got one,' Julie says, raising a takeaway cup.

'I'll come.' Matt stands before I can refuse his offer and we traipse to the kitchen where the only thing separating us from Karen's prying ears is a plywood wall. I fill the kettle and hope the sound of it boiling will cover us.

'Thanks for the chat last night,' I whisper. 'And the plant, was that you?'

Matt nods and smiles almost shyly. 'Glad you like it,' he says, and dumps a spoonful of coffee granules into two mugs. As the kettle finishes rattling he asks, 'Are you OK? You look a bit wired.'

The switch clicks off and the sound of the bubbling water fades so the room is silent once more. 'I'm fine,' I whisper, pouring the water and adding milk to mine. Matt takes his black. We return to the office and both Karen and Julie are gone and something makes me wander over to Karen's desk. She's locked her computer but as I walk behind her desk I spot a framed photo that makes me smile. Picking up the silver frame, I turn it around to Matt and he bursts out laughing. Karen has a framed photo of Gary in a romper on her desk.

Putting it back exactly where I found it, I'm about to return to my desk when I spot her pen holder, and a black Sharpie catches my eye. I think of all the snide comments I've put up with, her constant side-eye and the little smirks and snorts that punctuate my day, and something snaps inside me. I pull off the lid and draw glasses and a beard on the glass over Gary's face. Then I return to my desk, ignoring the questioning look that Matt gives me, although we're both smiling and I feel high on the sheer silliness of it. Karen won't be able to prove it was me but I don't care if she suspects me.

Matt and I are working in silence when Karen and Julie return, clasping brown folders to their chests and walking with exaggerated purpose.

'Before you ask us, we can't discuss anything,' Karen says and I just shrug, aware they've probably been speaking about Nina, but I don't want to give her the satisfaction of showing I'm interested. Karen sits at her desk and I hear her typing but I don't dare look at her. There's a strange air of anticipation in the room that I imagine is coming from both Matt and me, waiting for something to happen, and it doesn't take long. After a minute, there's a small gasp before Karen pushes back her chair and leaves the room, the door slamming behind her. I feel a rush of disappointment that she didn't confront me, followed by a niggling sense of guilt that I wasn't expecting as I wonder if I've been unnecessarily cruel. It's not all Karen's fault that my life is falling apart, although she hasn't helped.

She doesn't say anything to me for the rest of the day and I work on the few boring tasks I have, doing them slowly to stretch them out across the whole day, waiting for the clock to tick over to five when I can leave. Matt asks me if I want to join him in the canteen for lunch but I've brought my own sandwich so I sit at my desk as usual and read the news online, poring over the details of Nina's story in the hope of learning something new, but there's nothing I don't already know.

At a quarter to five, I'm close to calling it a day when Karen gets up and comes over to my desk. 'Kitty, would you join me in meeting room six, please?'

I feel heat rising to my face but I tell myself there is no way she can know it was me. I just need to deny all knowledge and she can't prove anything.

Nodding, I say innocently, 'Is there anything I should bring?'

'Just bring a notepad and pen.'

Karen walks ahead and I feel both Julie and Matt watching me as I follow her from the room as if they know something I don't. I tell myself that it's possible that this is not going to be a bad meeting – maybe I'm finally getting the increased responsibility that I crave or even a promotion although something tells me that's not the case.

Meeting room six is the first room along the corridor, and when I follow Karen inside I see we are not meeting alone and my heart drops like a stone. Karen is already sitting on one side of the table and on the other is the petite blonde woman from the agency who looks like she's sucking a lemon. Amber or Amy or something.

'Thanks for coming,' Karen says. 'You're welcome to take notes, and I asked Annabel to join us since she placed you with us.'

I realise I've forgotten to bring a notepad and pen but it doesn't matter. I won't want any record of this meeting since I know exactly what they're going to say. I glance at Annabel and she smiles thinly as if she's on my side, although both of us know that's not true.

'Take a seat,' Karen says.

Sliding into the seat closest to the door, I breathe slowly and steadily, hoping that Karen gets it over with as quickly as possible.

'Firstly, I want to thank you for all your hard work here,' she says in a peppy voice. I don't reply and she goes on, 'However, unfortunately we've decided that you're not quite the right fit so we'll be ending your contract today.'

I glance at Annabel, waiting for her to jump in since I'm sure my contract has a notice period, but she keeps her eyes fixed on the desk and I feel the disappointment radiating off her. How can you get fired for drawing a moustache on a dog?

'Rather than asking you to keep coming in, we've decided that you can leave right after this meeting.' Karen says this like she's doing me a favour, and I force myself to smile as I try not to think about the empty days stretching out ahead of me. 'We will of course pay you in lieu of your one week's notice, and that amount will be included in your final pay cheque.'

It stings that she doesn't even want me to stay long enough to hand over my work to anyone but I can't complain about the pay. Karen is saying something about teamwork, commitment and respecting others, but she's too smart to mention the photo since it does sound petty and as she lists all my failings it doesn't sound good. Perhaps the only surprise is that I've lasted this long. I find myself zoning out until she says, 'Do you have any questions?' and I shake my head.

She gives me a bright smile and stands to leave.

'Well, thank you again.' She holds out her hand and I just stare at it until she lets it fall. 'Please do collect your things and make your way out. You need to leave your pass with security. Annabel, do you have a minute?'

They leave the room together and I sit at the table, staring at the cold, grey plastic worktop and silently saying my mantra over and over. *I am somebody.* No tears come but a deep chasm of emptiness opens inside me. I may have hated the job but it was something, a connection to David, and now I'm back to square one.

After a few minutes I force myself to get up and return to the office, my face feeling like it's on fire. Julie and Matt watch as I pour the dregs of my coffee into the spider plant's soil and shove the mug in my handbag before gathering my few meagre possessions – a couple of pens and a lipstick – and chuck them in too.

'Are you OK?' Matt says, but I just shoulder my bag, put the plant under my arm and walk out, trying not to burst into tears.

EIGHTEEN

DAVID

After leaving Annika, I walk the streets for most of the day, getting close to the office but not having the guts to go inside. I can't face all the gossip about Nina and the truth is I'm worried who might be looking for me. Imagining Detective Hopping waiting in my office is enough to keep me moving whenever I tire. I keep trying Kitty's phone but it goes straight to her voice-mail, and as the light begins to fade, I realise I'm scanning every face I pass for hers – like looking for a needle in a haystack. I keep asking myself, why has she disappeared and why now? Is she safe?

Giving up, I turn for home, stopping on the corner of my street when I get there and peering down before dashing to the front door where the house is in darkness. The moment I open the door, I call out, 'Kitty?' but there's no answer. I know deep down that she's not there, though I walk from room to room to make sure, before returning to the dark hallway and slumping onto the bottom step of the stairs. I will her to walk through the door so we can talk about everything like we used to do and laugh about my ridiculous worries.

My brain is racing through horrible possibilities and lands

on an image of my wife stabbed to death, like Nina. I slap the
wall until my palm stings, wondering what was the point in
trying out all those paint samples to land on this perfect Green
Smoke when we are never here to enjoy it. This house feels like
a mausoleum to our failed relationship, a shrine to imperfection
when we thought we were so fucking perfect.

A message comes through and I snatch up my phone,
desperate for news from my wife, and when I see her name, my
heart soars for a moment until I open the message and read her
words, *It's over, David. Whatever happened with Nina, we can't
come back from this. Stop trying to contact me.*

I let out an anguished yell and try to call her – we need to
talk about this – but it cuts straight to her voicemail and I have
to stop myself from slamming the phone on the floor in frustration. I feel like a trapped animal, unsure what to do or where to
turn, and all I can think to do is open a news app and scroll
through the appalling pieces about Nina, trying to distract
myself from the awful situation with Kitty. The comments are
out of control now, with people speculating what she may have
done to deserve it or throwing out names of random celebrities
as possible suspects as a joke, so I stop reading, terrified of
seeing my own name on the list, certain it's only a matter of
time.

Dropping my head, I push my thumbs into the corners of
my eyes and fight back a scream. Why won't my wife give me a
chance to explain? A juddering in my ribcage takes me by
surprise and sobs ripple through my body. I give in to them for a
while before pushing myself up to pace the short hallway, the
movement helping to distract me. I've called everyone I can
think of and looked everywhere but I have no idea where Kitty
is. Short of continuing to tramp the streets of London, all I can
do is wait for her to come to me.

A loud noise makes me flinch and my heart hammers in my
chest from the shock. It takes me a moment to realise that it's my

phone vibrating against the hard wood floor and I stoop to grab it, stumbling in my haste and landing heavily on my knees, not caring about the sharp shooting pain that runs up both legs. It must be her, surely. I've called at least thirty times and left a dozen voicemails, plus texts and WhatsApps on top of that – she must be returning my calls.

It's an unknown number and I answer quickly, my voice hoarse, 'Kit?'

'Mr Okine?' It's a woman's voice but it's not my wife.

My arm sags with disappointment and it takes me a moment to pull myself together and put the phone back to my ear.

'Don't hang up,' the voice is saying.

'Who is this?' I say, trying to muster some authority.

'David, it's Detective Hopping. Can I ask where you are?'

I don't feel like answering her without asking my own question. 'Did you find out who's been sending me letters?'

'Just answer my question, please.'

Her tone makes me pause and I imagine those sharp dark eyes narrowed. My pulse quickens but I find myself delaying, 'Why is that relevant to your investigation?'

Hopping sighs. 'David, we just need to speak to you. Please, make this easy on yourself.'

I frown as I wonder what she means by that. I haven't purposefully been making things difficult although it was hard to be honest about what happened with Nina when my wife was only one floor down. I will be honest with them but now I need to focus on my wife – I must speak to her before everything gets out. I picture Kitty learning about my infidelity in a newspaper and I find myself backing away from the door, certain that I cannot let that happen. I must talk to her before I speak to the police because if they arrest me, who knows when they'll let me go again? It hits me that in TV shows, the police would be triangulating the phone signal to pinpoint my location, but that's ridiculous because I'm at home – it's not like I'm hiding.

'David?' Hopping asks.

'I'm not making things difficult,' I say tightly. 'I just wish you would get on and find out who's been stalking me.'

'I'm looking into that, David, but these things take time. And right now we have a young woman who has been murdered and we need to talk to you. We've been to your house several times today, and your place of work, and no one has seen you. Just tell me where you are.'

I've always been someone who keeps their head down and gets on with things, and apart from the odd dabble in powders supplied by Tom, I've been fully law abiding. Grinding my teeth, I feel powerless to stop what feels inevitable. I may have lied about some of the details of what happened between Nina and me, but I certainly didn't hurt her and I feel certain that Hopping is going to arrest me the moment she sees me. I can't let that happen.

'David,' she says in a low voice, and I hear the warning in her tone but I just take a deep breath.

'Just find my stalker,' I say, and I let my hand drop and hang up. It takes me another breath to steady my chest and pull myself together; now is not the time to fall apart – I need to move. I'm wearing black jeans and a black T-shirt that will help me blend into the night but it's bound to be cold. Running up the stairs and hurrying into the bedroom, I rifle through my bottom drawer for a dark sweatshirt. My hand lands on a navy hoodie and I tug it from the pile and pull it over my head.

My phone vibrates again and I take it out of my pocket, staring at the screen as the same unknown number appears. I pick up a pair of jeans from the washing basket and tuck the phone into the pocket, dropping them back in and leaving the room, going upstairs instead of down. The police could be coming back here this very moment, or staking out the front door. I may have seen too many TV shows, but I'm not willing to risk it.

My study is at the back of the house and I hurry inside, closing the door behind me and going straight to the sash window. Outside is a small roof terrace so I open the window as wide as it will go and step out carefully into the blustery air. It's higher up and colder than I imagined and I press my back against the window, willing myself not to look down as I draw in several deep breaths. From far below, I hear a repetitive thudding and realise that someone is banging on the front door.

I'm aware that this is a sliding-doors moment – my life is about to go in a very different direction if I don't go downstairs, open the front door and cooperate with the police, but I am unwilling to lose what little control I have left. I'm still a free man and I have done nothing wrong so why shouldn't I decide when and where I speak to them? My wife is the most important thing in the world to me, she always has been, and I owe it to her after that one blip with Nina to tell her directly what I did. Closing my eyes for a moment, I try not to think about my job or my reputation; instead I concentrate on breathing deeply and trying not to be sick. Another loud bang sounds downstairs and I tell myself it's time to go.

Stepping over the railing onto the terrace of the next-door house, I continue along the row until I reach the end house, where I'm stuck with no obvious way down. My whole body is shaking and I'm on the third floor – a slip could kill me but I can't go back. Instead I scan the possible options until my eyes rest on the drainpipe and I feel the horrible inevitably of what I must do. Thankfully, it's an old-fashioned type made from cast iron, and when I test its strength with both hands it feels solid. Saying a silent prayer, I swing myself over the railing and jam my fingers as far around the pipe as they will go, before allowing it to take my whole weight, my knees and feet gripping on like a monkey, and sliding down.

Less than a minute later, I'm on the ground, my body convulsing with adrenaline as I leap the low fence to exit my neighbour's property and leave the street, walking quickly away from the main road and into the residential roads of Barnsbury with my hood pulled up and my head down, my heart thrumming in my chest. The last few hours feel unbelievable – I've become someone I don't recognise – but I tell myself it's all a misunderstanding. Once I've spoken to Kitty, I'll give Hopping a call and clear up this whole mess. It's not like I'm on the run – I'm just buying myself a little more time.

My feet already seem to know which way to go before my brain does and take me west. It's a long walk to Notting Hill but I make it longer by keeping to the side streets where there are fewer cars and people, though I know I'll never avoid all the cameras. London is full of them, and so many homes now have the doorbells that record you, it must be impossible to dodge them. It takes me a couple of hours but I reach their street before it's indecently late. However as I turn the corner towards their house I get a sudden frisson of fear. What if the police are waiting there for me?

Crouching down, I pretend to tie my shoelace while surreptitiously peering at the front door when a noise behind me makes me flinch. My head whips around and I see a man in a suit approaching with a scrawny rat-like dog on a lead. The little bugger comes to sniff my knotted shoelace and I stand quickly, rubbing the corner of my eye to cover my face, but I needn't have bothered – the man tugs at the lead and keeps walking without breaking the conversation he's conducting via a Bluetooth earpiece. The whole exchange leaves me feeling ridiculous, like a budget James Bond, and I shake my head, forcing myself to take the final few steps to their house.

It's a four-storey, powder-blue townhouse with a white trim and a pillared porch that looks grand if a little pompous. Ed has lived here since we graduated, first with a couple of school-friends and later, alone, until Caro finally gave in to his proposal. She moved in a decade ago. He's always been generous with his hosting and I've spent many a late night drinking whisky with Ed and smoking joints with Tom at the kitchen table, or having beers on the roof terrace as the grey light of dawn seeps into the horizon, though the regular visits never truly got rid of the grit of envy I felt at this place. What 22-year-old owns a house like this?

There are lights on both downstairs and up, though the curtains are drawn. Caro's always been a night owl and it's only eleven, so I'd expect at least one of them to be awake. Lifting the curved brass knocker, I rap twice, quietly, not wanting to wake the babies who surely are sleeping, and I listen. It doesn't take long for soft footsteps to approach; the door is yanked open and Ed gives me a confused look.

'Jesus, David, what are you doing here?' He's wearing his work clothes – crumpled grey trousers and an open-necked white shirt with the tails hanging out – and holding a glass of red.

'It's a long story,' I say, and he hustles me inside where we stand in their hallway.

'You gave me a heart attack,' Ed complains. 'It's a bit late for a house call.'

'Ed, darling, leave the theatrics to me.' It's Caro's drawl that comes from close quarters and she appears behind Ed in navy pyjamas with an oriental silk robe wrapped around her. Her dark hair is piled on top of her head and her day's make-up is still on, only slightly smudged. 'Come and have a seat, David.'

I let Caro steer me into their living room and a small pink armchair. The room is bathed in a gentle light from two tasselled lamps and there's a sweet smell of vanilla from a scented candle that's flickering on the walnut coffee table. Their style is the shabby antique look of the English upper classes – the royal-blue rug beneath our feet is almost worn through in places, probably from generations of Ed's family pacing as they practised their court submissions. It's not my style, but then my father was a layabout drunk who left my mother the day he discovered she was pregnant, so we weren't exactly big on heirlooms.

'Drink?' Caro says, sitting opposite me on the sofa. There's an open bottle of red on the table by the candle and another glass with flecks of sediment from the heavy Barolo. My mouth waters at the thought of knocking back a glass, feeling the alcohol course through my body and unclench my muscles one by one. 'Please.'

Ed disappears for a glass and I look at Caro as she regards me, her head tilted to one side, waiting for me to unload the reason I'm here, but I find the words won't come. How can I admit to my dearest friends that I'm wanted by the police – for murder – and I still have no idea where my wife is?

'I'm sorry to hear about your colleague,' Caro says, 'It was on the news.'

'Thanks,' I say. 'It's awful, absolutely awful. She was so young and vibrant and...' I trail off as I notice Caro has raised one eyebrow, but she's still looking at me with kindness in her eyes so I can't believe she could suspect the truth – that I slept with Nina.

Ed returns with the glass and pours out the wine, which I try not to guzzle.

'I haven't seen Kitty in twenty-four hours,' I say eventually, and I see pity shine in Caro's gaze that makes me wonder what she knows.

'She probably needs some time,' she says.

'You know women,' Ed offers, but I can't smile. I'm not sure I do know my own wife any more.

'If you know where she is...' I raise my eyes, pleading, but they both shake their heads and its clear they either don't know or won't tell.

A huge yawn catches me off guard as I realise I have barely slept in the time Kitty has been gone.

'David, you don't look in a fit state to see Kitty now. Why don't you stay here tonight?' Caro says. 'The usual room is made up.'

I'm about to resist out of some misjudged sense of pride but I realise I need my friends right now and I just nod and say, 'Thank you.'

A distant moan sounds from somewhere and Ed and Caro look at each other, concern reflected in their wide eyes. It takes me a moment to work out what is it and where it's coming from but it soon dawns on me that it's one of the babies crying, playing tinnily through the tiny monitor that's plugged into the wall and standing on top of the piano.

'I'll go,' Caro says, sighing and refastening her robe tightly around her as she stands and sweeps from the room. Ed takes her place on the sofa opposite me and bends forward, reaching for the bottle of red and dividing the remainder between the two glasses. We each take a large gulp as the baby continues to wail and neither of us speaks until we hear Caro enter the bedroom and begin soft shushing noises and the baby quietens.

Ed says, 'Any leads on the murder?'

I shake my head, not wanting to admit that likely they have one but they are very much barking up the wrong tree.

'Awful business,' he adds and I nod, realising that as a criminal barrister he probably knows more than most just how awful it is. I want to ask him how bad it is that I lied, what the consequences might be, but I find I'm too much of a coward, not ready to face up to the mess I've got myself in and sure that Ed would try to persuade me to go directly to the police. That may be the most sensible thing to do but I've come this far now, I can't contemplate going back.

Over the monitor, the baby's cries have been muffled to snuffling, mewling sounds, and Caro is singing softly, but there's a piercing shriek that must be the other twin waking. 'Fucking hell,' Ed says. 'I need to help. Feel free to go on up to bed, you look like you're about to crash.'

He strides out of the room and I remain in the chair, feeling awkward as I hear him join Caro in the room and begin a soft hushing song of his own. Closing my eyes, I try to imagine me and Kitty with a child of our own, singing lullabies and rocking them to sleep, but I find I can't. All I can picture is Nina's face, spattered with bright-red blood.

I don't trust my brain any more and I decide to take myself off to bed, determined that tomorrow I will sort out this whole mess.

NINETEEN

CATHERINE

After the meeting with Karen, I set off on foot from the office and wandered aimlessly until I realised that my feet were taking me to a pub, but I didn't resist, deciding I deserved a drink after the last couple of days. Selecting an anonymous pub with a facade unappealing enough to repel the work crowd, since the last thing I wanted was to see anyone from Prestige, I found a table at the back in a dark corner where I set myself up with a bottle of white wine and set about telling my new plant everything I hate about Karen.

I'm barely halfway through the bottle when I find my thoughts wandering to David. It hurts that he believes I'm capable of murder but I find myself trying to come up with alternative theories. David may think I'm the obvious perpetrator, and admittedly, the fact that I was there on the night isn't something I want the police to discover, but I simply can't accept that I was involved. In the newspaper it said she'd been stabbed, and surely I'd have known that already if I'd done it? Or I'd have found blood somewhere on my clothing from that evening? Satisfied I can discount myself as a suspect, I consider David – surely the next name at the top of the list.

I've known David longer than anyone else in my life, and he may have been prone to fits of rage at times, but he's never been violent, and why would he want to hurt Nina? If anything, to me it seemed like they had a rather too friendly relationship. I try to remember if I saw anything suspicious that evening, but my memories seem to end at the corner shop where I bought the bottle of vodka. The only other suspect I can think of is Kitty, and while I may dislike David's wife, it is hard to picture the golden girl, financial powerhouse and all-round well-thought-of woman deciding to murder one of David's researchers. Even if he was sleeping with her, the worst I'd expect from Kitty is divorce.

I'm reaching the end of the bottle and I'm no closer to figuring out anything to do with Nina. My thoughts are muddling together, and I seem to find myself returning to the meeting with Karen and veering between feeling sorry for myself and bitter fury.

'Fucking Karen. Never liked me, always wanted me gone right from day one,' I mutter into my glass, the words running together. 'Stupid dog. Bloody Gary and his bloody skateboard. Never gave me a chance.'

I sense a figure looming over me and a voice says, 'Cheer up, love, it might never happen.'

Looking up, I see a man in his fifties with a shiny grey suit on and a lilac tie with a knot the size of my fist. He's improbably blond, with pink skin like a sunburnt pig and a web of broken capillaries mapped out on his nose. Downing the rest of my wine, I get up and move past him to the bar. 'Excuse me.'

I order another bottle of white and three bags of crisps – I need something to soak up the wine – and juggle them back to the table, where I find the man has plonked himself in my seat with his pint in front of him. He takes a long draught and grins at me, with foam on his upper lip, as I approach. Irritation takes over and I don't bother to hide a shudder; as soon as I'm close enough I say, 'That's my seat.'

'Feisty one, aren't you?' His grin widens and I'm hit by the sudden urge to smash him over the head with the wine bottle, but I manage to resist and sag onto the spare stool next to him.

'Rough day?' he asks.

I ignore him and crack open the screw top on the wine, slopping a large amount into my glass.

'Here,' the man chinks his pint glass against mine, 'cheers. You don't want to be drinking alone.'

A groan escapes my lips and I shake my head, 'That's exactly what I want.'

'Tell me, why is a pretty thing like you so glum?'

Clutching my head , I pray he takes the hint, but I keep my lips pressed together since I can't face an argument, not after the day I've had, and I don't know if I have the strength to keep myself under control. Around me the pub noise becomes like static in my ears, scratching and hissing, but the man's voice still manages to cuts through: 'Come on, love. It can't be that bad.'

A whine cuts through my thoughts like the sound of a lawnmower blade whirring and I wonder whether it's real before I realise it's coming from my mouth. Pressing my lips together, the sound stops but my vision starts to blur and I'm suddenly taken back to being outside Nina's. This was exactly how I felt and it makes me wonder if I saw something inside that filled me with enough rage that I forced my way in and killed her? Sickness rises up inside me as I try to grasp on to the feeling and pull a memory from my mind. What could I possibly have seen that would have made me so angry?

'Cuckoo.' The man waves his hand in front of my eyes and snaps his fingers. 'Anyone at home?'

'Please,' I say through gritted teeth, 'Can you just fuck off?' I see his expression change from amusement to anger in a flash.

'Bitch,' he says, picking up his pint and storming off, as I smile at his retreating back and breathe a sigh of relief. I watch him pass a couple of empty tables before approaching two women sitting together at the front of the pub. They're deep in conversation but that doesn't deter him and he puts his pint down and says something that makes them all glance my way. The women give nervous smiles so I return them with a little wave and take another swig of my drink.

I'm back to doubting myself again and I start to panic that I might have hurt Nina, but I tell myself that just because I was there and might have seen something inside, that doesn't mean I had anything to do with what happened. Perhaps I just saw her and David together, and while I might not have approved of Nina's behaviour, I don't exactly blame her. It takes two to tango, as they say.

What exactly took place in the black void in my memory? Somehow I got from Nina's front doorstep and ended up in a bush in the park and I don't have a single recollection of how. Does that mean anything could have happened? Could I have entered Nina's flat and confronted her? I knock back another swig of wine to try to calm down but that doesn't work. I try my mantra but it's become useless. My panic doesn't subside and I pull my phone from my bag, wanting to call Connor but still feeling angry from our last conversation. I'm about to call him anyway when a message from Matt pops up.

Call me please. I'm worried about... the plant! Remember, it needs water not wine! No, really, I'm worried about you. Just call x

A smile somehow breaks through my dark mood and my finger hovers as I contemplate calling him, but I'm not sure I deserve a friend like Matt. He's nice and uncomplicated and I'm drunk and unemployed, not to mention a possible murderer. I let out a snort at this thought but also somewhere deep inside me I feel a stab of fear that it could be true. Instead of calling anyone, I turn my attention back to my wine and keep drinking, draining the second bottle in record time and munching through the crisps.

By the time I'm on to my third bottle, I can't hold a string of thoughts together and my mind drifts from snippets of David to Nina to Matt and back again to David. Sometimes I let out the odd stream of profanity at Karen or Connor as if they're sitting with me rather than me being alone in the dark corner of a pub. I'm not sure how long I've been there when my phone rings and I see Matt is calling me.

'Hello,' I say, trying to sound sober.

'There you are.' He sounds relieved. 'Where are you?'

'A pub.' I keep it vague as I'm not sure I want to see him yet.

'Understandable. Are you OK? I can't believe Karen did that to you.'

'Doesn't matter.' I realise my words sound slurred and I clear my throat before trying again. 'I don't blame her.'

'You don't sound in a good way,' he says, and clearly my attempt to sound normal hasn't worked. 'Tell me where you are and I'll come and meet you.'

'I'm fine,' I say.

'Come on, Kitty, you need a friend right now.'

'I'm just having a drink.'

'Where? I'll join you.'

It would be nice to have someone to drink with but I find I have no idea where I am. I try to think back to when I arrived, which already seems like days ago. 'It's a bird I think, The Eagle or The Owl or something.'

I'm beginning to feel tired, and as Matt starts asking questions I feel myself drifting off. A little later, I sit up with a jolt and find someone looming over me; I feel a rush of surprise that Matt has arrived so quickly, but as I squint and rub my eyes I see the lilac tie and realise that it's the man from earlier. He leans over me and I'm hit by a warm, sweaty waft of air as he says in my ear, 'Looks like you need some help.'

I try to resist but I feel his arm clamp around my elbow and he heaves me to my feet; I realise I need his help to stand up. Leaning on him, I feel him putting his other arm around my waist and digging his hot fingers into the waistband of my work skirt. We lurch out onto the pavement where I'm surprised to see it's wet, there's a chill in the air and the sky is a charcoal grey. Glancing around, nothing looks familiar, although I know I can't be too far from the office since I came here on foot.

'This way,' he says. 'My place is just around the corner.'

My heart lurches at his words but I find I can't shrug him off, and when I try to speak my words come out slurred and jumbled. We pass a couple who give us concerned looks but the man just says cheerfully, 'One too many, I'm afraid.'

'Please,' I manage to get out, but we're already passed them and the man just gives me a sneering grin and says, 'Oh so she's polite now, is she?'

I try to shove him away and run but all that happens is I stumble and he drags me to my feet. I'm about to start yelling when someone cuts in front of us and grabs the man's arm.

'What do you think you're doing?' a man's voice says, and I'm relieved when I realise it's Matt.

'What's it to you?' the man in the tie says.

But Matt doesn't let go and squares up to him saying, 'I'm her friend. Surely you can see she's in a bad way?'

The man laughs and I see Matt's fists ball by his side and feel a warm glow that he thinks I'm worth putting up a fight for.

'Sorry I took so long,' he mutters to me. 'Dragons may fly but they're not birds.'

I'm not sure why he's talking about dragons or birds but I glance around and spot the pub sign: the Green Dragon.

'Let's get out of here,' Matt says, taking my arm and trying to lead me away, but the man refuses to let go.

'I'm helping her,' he says.

Matt scowls and his face darkens, and I watch him spin around and grab the man by the shoulder with surprising force.

'Leave now or I will knock you down.'

I half expect the man to laugh since Matt is quite short and more tubby than muscled, but he clearly has some authority since the man just slinks away, muttering a stream of insults at us as he goes.

'What a scumbag,' Matt says, stepping out into the street to flag a cab before taking my arm again, 'Come on, let's get you out of here.'

My head swims with gratitude, but also from the booze, and as Matt leads me towards a cab I start to feel woozy. I manage to get into the back seat and rest my head on his shoulder, and the world goes black as I hear him give the driver his address.

TWENTY

DAVID

A piercing shriek wakes me with a jolt and my heart races as I try to work out where the hell I am. It comes back to me in chunks as I glance around and see the familiar floral wallpaper and cream curtains – Ed and Caro's spare room – and realise the noise must have been one of the twins. I stretch my hands across the bed and feel the cold sheets; I remember that I'm here alone and have no idea where my wife is. This thought makes me start to sit up, but then I remember that Nina is dead and the police are looking for me and I crash back onto the pillow. Maybe I should just stay in bed and pull the duvet over my head?

I wish I had a plan to sweep up all these broken fragments of my life and somehow glue them back together again, and more than that, I'd give anything, including all the recognition and money I've earned, to go back in time just a couple of days and go straight home instead of giving in to that deplorable weakness that saw me slip out of the pub with Nina and go home with her. I groan aloud as I think of my own stupidity, and a horrible feeling of shame spreads through me as I feel almost certain that if I'd left alone she would probably still be alive right now and my marriage wouldn't be in tatters.

A feeling of desperation pulls me further into the bed and I don't want to get up, but I force myself to, throwing back the duvet. I get to my feet – I've brought this on myself so I don't deserve to wallow in self-pity; instead I need to get on and fix it. The room has an ensuite where there's a crispy clean towel folded on an antique armchair. Everything Caro and Ed own seems to be a hundred years old and threadbare. Would it kill them to take a trip to John Lewis, I think, as I step out of the shower and dry myself on the rough, hard towel, before dressing quickly in yesterday's clothes.

Taking the stairs down to the kitchen, I hear the soundtrack to a hectic breakfast. One of the twins is screeching and someone is banging plastic against plastic while Caro says, 'No, darling, the yoghurt goes in your mouth not on the floor.'

I take a moment in the hallway, readying myself to enter the scene of their domestic bliss, which is in painful contrast to my own situation. Taking a deep breath, I hear the microwave beep and the door open and close before Ed's voice rings out, 'Porridge is ready, darlings.'

'Put some cold milk in first,' Caro hisses.

There's a pause and then the screeching stops, and I realise the babies must have been hungry. It seems like a good time to join them, but then I hear Ed speak again, 'Do you think he knows?'

'Sh!' Caro says and I stiffen, immediately aware that they are talking about me.

'He must have some idea. How could he not know?'

Frowning, I try to work out what he could be talking about.

'It's been so bloody obvious.'

A ripple of anger runs through me as it hits me that they're holding something back from me. When I asked them last night if they knew where Kitty was, maybe they did and they didn't tell me, but they certainly knew something. I feel like barging through the door and demanding they tell me what they know, but this is their house and I am a guest and whatever else I've lost, I can at least hang on to my manners. I decide I've hovered in the hallway for long enough so I go to move just as the door swings open and Ed strides out.

'David, there are you,' he says, pink circles appearing on the tips of his pale cheeks as his eyes dart from me back to the kitchen, and I can tell he's wondering how much I heard.

'Morning Ed,' I say, not letting my annoyance show. 'How are you?'

'Fine, fine, and how did you sleep?'

'Well, thank you,' I say, lying since I'd spent most of the night awake, my mind whirring as I alternated between worrying about Kitty and feeling frustrated that she's running from our problems. Every couple of hours, I'd hear one of the twins stir and footsteps pad overhead as either Ed or Caro went in to settle them. Looking at the dark shadows beneath Ed's eyes and his unhealthy pallor, I opt not to complain about my own disturbed night.

'I'll be out of your hair soon,' I say.

'Stay as long as you like,' he says. 'I'll be heading to chambers soon and I'm sure Caro would be thrilled to have the company.'

'Thanks,' I say, grateful that they've given me a bed to sleep in and a roof over my head. I have no idea what I'd have done if they hadn't let me in. I couldn't have gone back home and I'd have been nervous about using a bank card at a hotel – Hopping had sounded serious on the phone, perhaps serious enough that they would be checking my transactions. The thought of it chills me and I give an involuntary shiver.

'You look like you might be coming down with something,' Ed says. 'Go through into the kitchen and there's a pot of coffee on the table that will warm you up.'

I give him a nod and comply, opening the door to find Caro at the table spooning porridge alternately into the twins' wide-open mouths.

'Morning darling,' she says, turning her face so I can kiss her cheek as I join them at the table.

'Coffee is here, and there's toast or cereal, or I can make you porridge if this is appealing.'

She raises an eyebrow and gestures at the smeared faces of the twins who give me gummy smiles as I wiggle my fingers and tickle each of their round tummies. They are adorable, even though they seem to have inherited Ed's permanent frown, but luckily they also have their mum's generous lips and big brown eyes. I slide into a chair and pour myself a mug of steaming hot coffee, drinking it black.

'Better?' Caro says, after I've taken several large swallows, and I raise my eyebrows.

'I'm not sure anything is going to make me feel better today but I do feel slightly more human.'

'It's a constant battle,' she says with a grimace and we share a smile, though Caro's face is unlined, and while she may still be in her pyjamas with her silk robe wrapped around her, she's already made up and her hair is artfully messy. Caro's one of those women who can make even the early months of twins look not that bad, and whatever she might say, I know that she's made of strong stuff.

'You would tell me if there's something I need to know?' I ask.

She raises one eyebrow and says, 'Likewise?'

There's a pause while I take another gulp of my coffee, and I realise that as I'm not exactly being truthful about the circum-stances of me being here, it's not fair to expect Caro to blurt out everything she knows. She is Kitty's best friend after all. They were in a play together in their first year, which is how we met Caro. It was some awful student drama that we trouped along to watch Kitty in and there was Caro, stealing the show as the old hag, or something like that. I remember Kitty being quite miffed, actually, that someone had stolen her limelight – she was of course the female lead – but she soon thawed, because who could hold a grudge against Caro?

'Do you think we'll get through it?' I can't help but ask, and Caro doesn't feel the need to ask me what I mean – she just reaches across the table and grips my hand. 'Of course, darling, you and Kitty can get through anything.'

Out in the hallway, I hear the thumps of Ed coming down the stairs and he pokes his head around the door to say, 'Don't get up but I'm off.'

'Have a good day, darling,' Caro calls.

Ed kisses his fingers and blows a kiss towards his family, 'Bye, all.'

'Bye,' I echo, and he steps back into the hallway just as his phone goes off with a ringtone that sounds like an old-school modem dialling up. Caro sighs as the phone spits out white noise until Ed answers it and his voice fades, as he must have stepped into the living room. The twins are done eating and Caro lifts them down onto a playmat in the corner of the room where they flip onto their tummies and start gnawing on a pile of plastic bricks. We laugh as one of them tries to chew on the other's leg until the recipient lets out a whimper and Caro intervenes.

'There is nothing they won't eat,' Caro says.

We're laughing as we hear Ed returning, and when the door opens we both see that his face is drained of all colour and he looks as if he might keel over at any moment.

'Ed?' Caro says with panic in her voice, 'Ed, darling, what is it?'

'Nothing,' he says but his voice is unusually high so he repeats gruffly, 'Nothing, I just need a word.'

'OK,' Caro says, waiting for him to speak, but Ed nods at that door. 'No, out here.'

It's as if everything starts to move in slow motion, and there's a loud hissing in my ears that must be blood pumping around my body as I realise that whatever phone call Ed just received must have been about me. Caro sighs and moves towards the door but Ed blocks her path, his eyes wide, and I follow his gaze towards the chubby babies playing happily on the mat. There is nothing he could have done to hurt me more as I realise that he doesn't want to leave me alone with his kids, but truthfully, I don't blame him.

'Isn't it time for the girls to get dressed?' Ed says.

'I'll take them up in a minute, just—'

'No,' Ed cuts in. 'Let's take them up now.'

He crosses the room in long strides and scoops up both girls, one in each arm, bundling them out of the room as one begins to squeak in complaint at being held so tight. Caro hurries after him and I sit at the table with my head in my hands as I wonder what it is that Ed knows. Squeezing my eyes shut, I try to work out what to do when I suddenly have an idea and leap out of my seat.

I don't feel good about it but I walk as quietly as I can along the tiled hallway and I slip inside the living room we sat in last night. The baby monitor is still on the piano and I hurry over to it, sliding the switch to 'on'. At first I hear nothing, then after a moment a door bangs and I hear a harsh stream of whispers but I can't make out anything they're saying. Turning the monitor over in my hand, I spot the volume wheel on the side and I turn it to maximum.

'There's a fucking warrant out for his arrest,' I hear Ed hiss, and it's like I've been stabbed; a strangled cry bursts from me and I almost lose my balance, but I use the piano to hold myself up as I try to focus on what they're saying rather than let my mind run away with the implication. 'Graham gave me a heads-up since he knows our connection. The police will go public with it soon.'

'Innocent until proven guilty,' Caro replies.

'What innocent man runs from the police?' Ed's voice cracks and I hear a strange breathy sound that I realise after a moment must be Caro crying.

'I know he's our friend but we have the girls to think of,' Ed continues, and again, it hurts but again I don't blame him. Caro says something that's impossible to hear but I tell myself that she's defending me because Ed replies, 'We have to put the girls first. If there's any risk, any at all...' He breaks off and I'm grateful he can't say it.

I wonder what I should do and where I should go. Clearly I can't stay here. Next to where the monitor was is a black and white photograph in a silver frame from their wedding that I pick up. Caro was a glamorous bride in a long red dress and matching lipstick – too contrarian for white – and Ed spent the whole evening following her around as if he'd been pulled into her orbit, which he had, that very first night when he saw her on the stage. The party is in full flow around them with people dancing mid-song, arms and legs stuck out at odd angles, heads tipped back and mouths open as they sing along. Tom is at the back swigging from a bottle of champagne and in the corner of the shot, Kitty and I are dancing close and I have my arm around her waist and she's leaning back, looking right into my eyes.

'I'm going to call it in,' Ed whispers and I tear my eyes from the photo, glancing around the room as if the police might storm in right now.

'Please, no. We can't do that to David.' I silently thank Caro – she and I have always been birds of a feather. I don't catch the next part of what Ed says, only the last few words ring out, '... we don't know what he's done.'

I start edging towards the door. Ed will win the argument –

that's the problem with marrying a barrister – and I can't be
here when the police arrive. I'm not running because I'm guilty,
I tell myself, I'm running because I love Kitty. I'm doing this for
her. Back in the hallway, I shove my feet into my trainers that I
left at the bottom of the stairs, and I'm about to leave when I
stop in my tracks at the sight of a shiny, slim black iPhone,
sitting on the hall table.

Picking it up, I press the 'home' button and the phone
springs to life revealing a photo of the twins curled up together
in a single Moses basket, their hands intertwined, and almost
without thinking, I tuck the phone into the pocket of my hoodie
before slipping out of the front door, promising silently that I
am only borrowing, not stealing.

Hurrying along the street, aware of how conspicuous I must
look wearing all black, including the sweater, on such a warm
day, I turn off the road at the first chance I get and go through
the gate into one of those lovely shared gardens – a green oasis
in the centre of all the brick and masonry, surrounded by leafy
trees with benches placed in shady spots. I fling myself down on
the first one I come to, ensuring I'm facing away from the street,
and turn my attention to the phone.

Of course it's passcode-protected, but Caro and I go way
back. I've been there for every milestone in her life since she
was eighteen – surely I have a good shot of guessing it. First, I
try her birthday, the day and month, followed by Ed's and the
kids', then I try Caro's year of birth, the year we started university, the year we graduated and '1234' because it's Caro, but
nothing works and I feel tears of frustration pressing against my
eyes. What am I doing? It's humiliating enough that I'm being
falsely accused of murder but now I'm trying to break into one
of my closest friend's phones. In disgust, I toss the phone onto
the grass and bend forward, pushing the heels of my palms
against my eyes and trying to block everything out.

I'm not sure how long I sit there, but a while later I hear a jaunty tune that makes me lift my head and I realise Caro's phone is ringing. I guess she's calling it to locate it and I go to pick it up, deciding that I will answer and sheepishly admit what I've done, but when I lift up the phone I see a name on the screen that makes my heart soar: 'Kitty'. I fumble the phone and almost drop it but I manage to hang on and slide the button to answer.

'Caro, hi,' my wife says, 'are we still meeting later?'

I clench my teeth but I can't be angry with Caro since she's done her best to help me. I try to work out what to say so Kitty doesn't hang up, but I'm quiet for too long.

'Caro?' she says sharply, sounding suspicious.

'Kit, it's me,' I say, and she draws in a breath. We're quiet for a moment before I add, 'Please, don't hang up.'

'I don't want to talk to you,' she says, sounding sad, if anything, rather than angry.

'Please, just—'

'No, David,' she cuts in. 'I won't "just" do anything. I need to look after myself now.'

Closing my eyes, I wince at her words. I should be the one looking after her but I've failed. The sun must have gone behind a cloud because the world feels gloomier, and as I look up, there's only heavy grey overhead.

'Isn't there anything I can do?' I ask, and there's a silence so long that I pull the phone from my ear to check the screen and make sure the call is still open. When I return it, I hear her voice say softly, 'Just talk to Tom.'

'Tom?' I ask, confused, but when I check the phone I see she's hung up, and I sit on the bench until the sun reappears, wondering what Tom has to do with any of this.

TWENTY-ONE
CATHERINE

Sitting up with a jolt, I glance around at the unfamiliar living room, wondering where the hell I am and feeling a sharp pain in my head and a churn in my stomach that tells me I had far too much to drink last night. A couple of memories hit me in quick succession: first, that I was fired, and second, that this is Matt's flat.

I'm stretched out on a stylish charcoal-grey sofa and wrapped in a soft blanket. There's a glass of water on the table and a bucket on the floor that makes me flush with shame. I try to remember whether I said or did anything that I need to apologise for, but nothing particular comes to mind and I'm quickly distracted by a musty, earthy smell that seems to be coming from elsewhere in the flat. It's not entirely unpleasant but it makes me push myself up and take a proper look around, and that's when I see that almost every surface is covered with plants.

The coffee table is crowded with succulents. Vines tumble from a bookcase, spilling over each shelf, obscuring the books and brushing the floor. Suspended over a wooden dining table is a chandelier-type thing, only instead of lightbulbs, the metal frame holds rows of potted plants. As I stare open-mouthed, I hear footsteps and Matt appears wearing his *Stranger Things* T-shirt that's a little too tight around his doughy middle, and his mousy hair is mussed up from sleep.

'Morning,' he says, giving me a sleepy smile and yawning widely.

'Morning,' I manage to stutter.

'Water?' he asks, acting as if it's entirely normal to be living in a greenhouse.

'Yes, please,' I say gratefully, since the alcohol has left me parched.

Collapsing back into the sofa, I stroke the leaves of a tall palm in a pot next to me while Matt goes into the small kitchen area at the opposite end of the room. In a moment, the silence is broken by the sound of the tap and I use the cover to breathe in hard through my nose, getting another earthy hit, trying not to worry about the excess of vegetation and telling myself that there's nothing dangerous about plants. Maybe it's the opposite of a phobia – I rack my brain for the word but I'm hit with a sudden terror: I hope whatever obsession this is, it's not something sexual.

Matt reappears with a tall glass of water and sits beside me on the far end of the large sofa as I down it in several noisy gulps.

'Thirsty,' he says with a laugh, before adding, 'Now you know my secret.'

I frown a little, not sure what to say.

'And now I'll have to kill you.'

I must look alarmed because he laughs again. 'I'm joking, come on. You didn't think my whole life was about computers, did you?'

Shrugging, I don't say that's exactly what I thought.

'So are you a keen gardener?' my voice wavers with uncertainty.

'It's a bit more than that.' Matt runs his hand through his stringy hair, and it's the first indication that he's uncomfortable. 'It's a bit embarrassing, really, but it's fun and it keeps me busy.'

I glance around, wondering how embarrassing tending plants can be, but Matt's not finished.

'I'm a greenfluencer,' he says.

My eyebrows shoot up and I try to keep the note of incredulity out of my voice. 'A what?'

'I do videos online about plants.'

'Plants?'

Matt laughs, 'Yes, plants.' He reaches across to stroke the leaves of a spider plant that's exactly like the one that appeared on my desk at work, and sits and pets it like a dog.

'And people watch these videos?'

He laughs again – a looser, more relaxed laugh, 'Yes, actually, a fair few. I've got around fifty thousand followers.'

My breath sucks in sharply and he ducks his chin and gives a boyish grin.

'It is a bit mad but people like plants and they seem to enjoy me talking about plants. I've always been into gardening because I used to do it with my granddad.'

'What sort of things do you do in the videos?' There's an edge of uncertainty in my voice that I can't hide. I've always taken Matt's quietness for shyness but here he is, sitting in his flat, broadcasting to fifty thousand people, and it's left me wondering whether I've totally misjudged him. Perhaps he's a secret exhibitionist and craves the attention of strangers on the internet.

'Pruning, watering, deadheading – you know, gardening,' Matt says. 'I give people tips on keeping their plants alive and sometimes companies pay me to talk about their products, though not enough for me to say goodbye to Karen just yet, sadly.'

The mention of her name makes me gasp and I cover my mouth with my hand. 'Imagine if she knew. There she is, posting daily about Gary's exploits to seventy-three people, and here you are...'

I let my words hang and Matt smiles, his face pink as if he's a little embarrassed by his success.

'I did try to tell you last night but—'

My hands fly to my cheeks, 'I'm so sorry, I was drowning my sorrows but that's really no excuse. I hope I wasn't too awful...'

'You were fine, no need to apologise. It's entirely understandable after yesterday,' Matt says.

I feel like I owe him an explanation but I wish we could keep talking about Matt's love of plants rather than embark on any serious topics like my lack of a job or my failed relationship with David.

'Thank you for letting me stay over,' I say sheepishly.

'Hey, no problem at all. We lesser members of the people team need to band together for strength.' He gives me a grin.

'Former member,' I say.

'Still counts,' he says. 'Look, it seems like you've got a lot going on, and you don't have to tell me anything, but if you ever want to talk, I'm totally happy to listen. And now you know my secret alter ego, you've got something over me so you know I'll keep anything you tell me to myself.'

'Well, I haven't actually seen one of your videos...'

Matt groans. 'OK, one video while I make a pot of coffee, and then you tell me your deepest, darkest secret,' he laughs, 'or reveal your top fantasy humiliation for Karen. Either works for me.'

Matt hands me his phone with the Instagram account open and returns to the kitchen, heating coffee in a fancy pot on the stove while I scroll through his photos and videos. In the most recent video he's wearing his yellow Snoopy T-shirt and looking down beneath his stringy fringe at the spider plant, caressing the leaves and talking about how they are one of the easiest plants to look after. This plant he rescued from a skip, its leaves yellow and drooping, and he brought it back to life with soft light, sips of water and some TLC. There are some before-and-after photos that are pretty astonishing, and at the very end of the video, he looks up and gives the camera a flash of his shy smile, thanking the viewers for watching. Glancing down to the comments, I see rows of fire emojis, and someone has written, *You can give me some TLC anytime.*

'You promised not to laugh,' Matt says, returning with a full mug and a plate of shortbreads.

'I'm not.' I try to smother my smile but it breaks through. 'You've got fans.'

He puts the biscuits on a stool, taking one for himself before he sits back down. 'You know, the comments do get a bit much actually.' He lets out a little self-deprecating laugh. 'You should see some of the stuff that comes through. It's absolute filth.'

I'm trying hard not to laugh; Matt spots the smirk on my face and protests. 'Really. I need my day job to stay sane. There are some real lunatics on the internet.'

Reaching across the gap between us, I pat his arm. 'I understand what it can be like, I really do.'

It's on the tip of my tongue to tell him everything. How I've lived with the same fears, that I've seen the boom of social media and its impact first hand, the way it gives every little person a megaphone and lets them bellow in the ear of anyone they choose. It's hard to ignore the comments, the emojis, the DMs; there are some that probably float in front of David's eyes at night as they drift shut, screaming at him just as he's going off to sleep. I'd love nothing more than to round up every one of the trolls, haul them to court, and have them say those words in front of a judge.

'Hey,' Matt's voice is gentle. 'You OK?'

I give myself a little shake. 'Sorry.'

He shrugs and I can tell he has no idea what I'm thinking.

'You know I'm married?' I blurt out.

'You've never spoken about your husband but I did notice your ring.'

I try to twist the slim silver band but it's so tight around my finger it won't budge. 'It's complicated. He's in the public eye so we don't talk about our relationship.'

Matt's eyes narrow in confusion and he opens his mouth to ask a question, but I'm not finished. Now that I've started, I find I want to talk about David. After our confrontation, I wonder if it will help to talk about it. Perhaps a different perspective is what I need.

'He works for Prestige, actually.'

Now Matt's blue eyes flicker wide and surprise etches onto his soft features. 'And he's someone famous?'

I nod and he draws in a breath.

'Does Karen know?'

'Of course not and it needs to stay that way.'

'Deal.' Matt smiles but he's still shaking his head in disbelief. 'Who is it?'

My heart pounds and my mouth is dry. It's so rare that I talk about David to anyone other than Connor, and I can't remember the last time I spoke about him to someone new. In fact, I can't remember the last new friend I made, full stop.

'David Okine,' I say.

There's a beat before Matt lifts his hands to his head and mimes his brain exploding.

'Now I see why you've had so much on your mind with all that's going on. My God, is that how you know Nina Bello? She was in his team, right?'

I nod and grimace, not wanting to go into detail about how well he knew Nina. 'It's been pretty complicated between me and David for a long time and we're not exactly together right now, but that doesn't mean that I don't care about him.'

'Of course not,' Matt says. 'It must be a really tricky situation. Man, I can't believe I was complaining to you about being noticed. Me with my fifty-one thousand, two hundred and twenty-three followers, and there you are, married to Mr *Confessions*. Is it two BAFTAs he's won or three?'

'Four,' I say, and Matt groans.

'They're not just his. They're for the whole show and the documentary series he did, but maybe you didn't see that—'

'*David Meets David*,' he says excitedly. 'The Attenborough thing. Of course I saw it, I bloody loved it.'

Matt goes off on a tangent, talking excitedly about the programme, and I find my hangover rearing its head as Matt fanboys about David, but suddenly he looks at his watch and breaks off mid-sentence.

'Shit, I have to get to work or Karen is going to spend all day sighing whenever I say anything.'

I start looking around for my things but Matt says, 'You don't have to rush off. Honestly, make yourself at home, watch a movie or two. You really are welcome to stay as long as you like if you need to lay low for a while.'

I feel a rush of warmth at his generosity but I'm not sure how to respond – I can't remember the last time someone made me such a kind offer and I do feel drained. Staying in this comfortable flat far away from my real life suddenly feels very tempting, especially as somewhere in the back of my mind a little voice whispers that the police would have no idea where I am, and it's possible that their attentions may shift to me at any moment. All it would take is for one CCTV image to be released and my whole life would change.

Pushing down the panic that suddenly threatens to

consume me, I give Matt a smile. 'Are you sure I wouldn't be intruding?'

'Please,' he replies. 'Intrude away.'

He rearranges the blanket across my legs and I sit back on the sofa, resting my aching head, and think how lucky I am to have found Matt.

TWENTY-TWO

DAVID

Setting off for Hampstead on foot, I quickly realise that being out in the daylight is too risky for me since almost everyone knows my face, so I make a quick decision and dart down the side alley of a house where the front windows are shuttered. Leaping a gate, I find myself in an overgrown back garden. When I peer through the back window of the house I see that the furniture has been cleared and everything is covered in a thick layer of dust, so I feel safe to wander around and look for somewhere to lay low. Halfway along the long stretch of grass is a small summerhouse with a grubby little porch that I decide looks as good as it's going to get so I slump down, sitting with my back against the door and wondering if I've hit rock bottom or if it's possible to fall any further.

The day passes slowly and I spend it thinking of all the things I've already lost. *Confessions* – that will surely be cancelled now. TV shows don't survive a scandal like this. Ditto all my upcoming TV appearances. My marriage? I'm not certain, but it's not looking good. At least I still have my friends and I'm hopeful that Tom will find it in him to speak to me again, since Kitty must have told him I'm coming. We can't let a disagreement over Dick Bell ruin a twenty-year friendship. Kitty must think that Tom is the best person to help me in my predicament, but I fear even Tom may not have a way out of this one.

When the sky finally starts to darken, I pull up my hood and leave the garden quickly, veering back onto the main street and putting one foot in front of the other, walking north. Whenever I pass someone, or a car's headlights slide across my face, I turn away, praying for more time, but knowing that at any point, a police car might pull up and arrest me. It's a long way across London from Notting Hill to Hampstead, but eventually the busy streets give way to tree-lined roads with huge houses looming behind tall security gates. It's picturesque but uninviting, and at this time of night, most people around here are locked up inside. It's eerie as I walk towards the Heath and the streetlights become less frequent and the shadows seem to darken.

Tom and Annika's house has a purposely rusted gate that's seven feet high and twelve across, blocking the whole house from view. As I approach, I briefly consider trying to climb over, but I realise how ridiculous that would be so I sidle up and press the buzzer.

In a moment, there's a crackle of the intercom and I hear Annika saying, 'David, what the hell are you doing here?'

I look up at the camera and give a sheepish grin, hoping she will let me in, and a few seconds later there's a click and a whir as the gate opens. I find Annika waiting by the open front door, her fair hair gleaming like a halo in the porch light, wearing a crisp white shirt with a long gold chain that has a rather gruesome anatomical heart pendant that I remember Tom bringing back for her from Paris after one of his wild weekends. I thought he said she hated it, but she squeezes the heart in her fist as she shows me through into the kitchen at the back of the house.

'Thanks for letting me in,' I say.

Annika sighs impatiently and walks around the kitchen so the large marble island is between us. I pull back one of the chairs at their blond-wood table and slump down.

'What are you doing here?' she asks.

'I need to see Tom. Is he in?'

She lets out a short bark of laughter that makes me glance at her sharply and I notice there's something off about her. If I didn't know her better I'd think she was drunk – there's a slight pinkish tinge to the whites of her eyes, and her usually perfect mascara is smudged.

'No, he's not.'

'Are you OK?' I ask, and she laughs again, muttering something in Norwegian before saying, 'No, I'm not. You were wrong, you know. Tom has been having an affair.'

I feel stunned and can't help but ask, 'Recently?'

Her eyes narrow. 'Yes, recently. Probably this very minute.'

'God, I'm sorry,' I say. 'I really had no idea. Where is he?'

'I kicked him out. I told him to choose between her and me, and if he chose her he was not to come back into this house.' Her eyes flash with anger and her jaw is set but I notice a tremble in her shoulders and a sob judders through her. Leaping up, I hurry towards her to give her a hug but she darts away, moving around the island so the wide expanse of hard stone remains between us.

'Annika?' I say, my voice high with surprise.

Her eyes are wide and it takes me a moment to understand that what I'm seeing is fear. 'Stay away from me, David,' she says. This is my best friend's wife who I've known for ten years. I'm godfather to one of her children. 'Annika, it's me,' I say.

'You think that means fucking anything?' She raises her voice and I shush her, imagining one of the children, or worse, their nanny coming downstairs.

'Don't tell me to be quiet – this is my house!'

'I'm sorry. Just tell me what I can do.'

She rakes her fingers through her hair. 'Just go.' She bends over the marble worktop and rests on her elbows, her body shaking with emotion. I walk around the island and place my hand on her back and she lifts her head, grief and sadness shimmering in the depths of the blue pools of her eyes, before she stands up and allows me to hug her. She sobs into my shoulder and I say nothing. What is there to say? I've always known there would be a moment like this – a time when Annika's perception of Tom would crash into the reality – but there's nothing that could have been done to avoid it. Tom was never going to change.

After a minute or two, Annika falls quiet and her body stops quivering. She extricates herself from my hug and pulls away, smoothing the front of her shirt and wiping the mascara smears from beneath her eyes with her fingertips.

'I'm sorry,' she says.

I shake my head. 'You have nothing to apologise for.'

'Not for me,' she says. 'For you.'

I frown, trying to work out what she means. 'What—'

'You really don't know?' She tilts her head on one side and peers at me in her way that seems to look right through you. Already her composure is back and I feel like I'm the one disintegrating.

'Know what?' My mind is whirring but it slowly grinds to a halt as if a spanner has been jammed in the spokes of a bike. I know what she's going to say the second before the words leave her mouth, and I feel as if I've stepped off the edge of a building and the floor is rushing up to meet me. I brace myself but there's no way to stop myself shattering into a million pieces.

'It's Kitty,' she says, and my whole world tilts. 'Tom's been having an affair with Kitty.'

And it feels at that moment like my life snaps in two.

TWENTY-THREE

CATHERINE

Matt returns from the office later in the day and finds me where he left me, though I have had a good snoop around his flat in the meantime. Beyond the plants, I found nothing unusual, and it's a relief to discover that Matt doesn't appear to have any other kinks or quirks. He cracks open a couple of beers and joins me on the sofa, seeming happy to find me still there.

'What are they saying about me at work?' I ask, picturing Karen and Julie talking about me all day.

'Not much,' Matt replies, and I feel sinking disappointment that I'm not even deemed worthy of gossip. 'All anyone can talk about is Nina Bello.'

I duck my chin; of course, that's the headline news.

'And David, of course,' he adds, dropping his gaze.

I swig my beer but it takes me several tries to swallow it.

'We can talk about something else?' Matt asks. 'If it's too difficult for you.'

I shrug and he takes this as a green light to continue. 'I didn't want to upset you but you should know that everyone thinks he did it. He's got a nasty temper – all these stories have come out about him raging when he didn't win the first BAFTA, and I hope you don't mind me saying that a few people mentioned that he and Nina have been spending a lot of time together recently. People are convinced she must have knocked him back and he's flipped out.'

I raise my eyebrows but I don't respond; David may have his flaws but failing to hide his disappointment about losing out on an award hardly indicates he's capable of murder, and I don't need Matt to tell me about him and Nina – I've witnessed that relationship first hand.

'An Uber driver has come out and said he drove David to some fancy house one Friday night and apparently David was eyeballing him in the mirror the whole time, giving him evils.'

I nod, but it does sound a bit tenuous; watching someone is hardly a crime.

'And there's a photo of him and a blonde woman hugging on Hampstead Heath in the papers today, looking very cosy.'

He's lost me there, but I just shrug since David is always surrounded by women.

'You seem very interested,' I say.

Matt's face flares red and he turns his attention to his beer. 'I'm just looking out for you,' he says defensively. 'Anyway, there is one thing...'

'Yes?' I say.

'I couldn't resist doing some googling and, well...' He runs his hand through his hair and I want to tell him to spit it out but I keep my expression in a bland smile. 'You have to do a bit of digging, but it says online that he's been married to Kathryn Kennington, the former Prestige finance director, for years.'

I open and shut my mouth, feeling my face grow hot as he stares at me. 'I did say it's complicated between us,' I say, sounding defensive now.

'Try me,' he says gently, and I shut my eyes for a moment,

trying to arrange my jumbled thoughts before I speak, stumbling over my words.

'We first got together back in college and it got serious pretty quickly. We *were* all but married – he even gave me a ring,' I thrust my hand under his nose and he glances at it but it's plain that he's more interested in my story than the band of metal around my finger.

'But then he went on to marry someone else?' he says, his voice filled with uncertainty.

I feel a surge of anger that I bite back, knowing that if I don't tread carefully this could push Matt away – I've lost friends before over David, since people don't like to hear the truth about us, and I realise at that moment that I don't want to lose Matt; he means a lot to me, actually.

'He did, but I'm ashamed to say it's been on and off over the years, even as recently as this year.'

Matt looks shocked, 'What a bastard.'

'I know I should have moved on but I truly believed he was going to choose me over her, and you know the saying, "young love never dies" – I can't remember who said it but it's true.'

Matt shakes his head and busies himself with opening a large bag of crisps and pouring it into a bowl.

'Does his wife know about you?' Matt asks.

I meet his gaze and freeze for a moment, unsure what makes me look better or worse, but finally I decide on the truth and nod. 'She's known for years.'

Matt shudders. 'What a creep. He's strung you both along all this time and now he's wanted for murder.'

I shrug but it's not pleasant hearing Matt's potted summary of our relationship.

'Do you think he did it?' Matt asks, shovelling a handful of crisps into his mouth.

I choose my words carefully. 'I wish I could say no, but who knows what he's capable of.'

'Well, the police certainly think so. There was a couple of officers patrolling the office all day today just in case he turned up, but he's probably halfway to Rio right now.'

'He wouldn't run,' I say with certainty.

'Where is he, then?' Matt asks, and then bursts out, spraying shards of crisp all over the sofa, 'You don't know, do you?'

'Know what?' I'm frowning now, confused by the turn the conversation has taken.

'Have you not turned on the news today?' he asks.

I shake my head, not wanting to admit that I've spent most of the day sleeping off my hangover, as Matt picks up his backpack and roots around inside, pulling out a folded copy of the *Evening Standard*. I immediately spot the headline: 'Wanted: David Okine'. My heart lurches and I reach over and take the paper, my fingers already shaking as I try to smooth it out.

I read that the police have named David as a suspect in Nina's murder and warned the public not to approach him. There's a lovely large photo of him next to the story – a black and white shot that really shows off his bone structure – and as I stare at it a horrible feeling rises inside me. It's impossible to think that a man as smart and as handsome as David could be involved in anything as sordid and grotesque as murder. David may be many things, but I can't believe him to be a murderer.

'It can't have been him,' I say.

Matt doesn't respond right away, but when he does I hear the doubt in his voice. 'People do sometimes surprise you. It would be strange for the police to release a public statement if they didn't have something on him.'

'Well, they're wrong,' I say, and my voice sounds angrier than I intended.

There's a tense silence before Matt changes the topic. 'You hungry?'

'Yes, please,' I say, hoping to return to the calm I felt before as Matt grins and sets about cooking us dinner.

I move to a high stool at the kitchen island, watching him expertly slice vegetables with a Japanese knife as he chats away, and though we're both relaxed, I begin to wonder how long I can stay here. It's hard to imagine returning to my empty flat where I'll be forced to confront my role in what happened to Nina – I can't deny that there's a black hole in my memory but I'm starting to feel less afraid that I did something. Would someone sitting here, eating teriyaki salmon, drinking a crisp Chardonnay, really be involved in murder? It feels utterly impossible as I swirl my wine in the glass and take a small sip.

Surely if I'd done anything wrong, the police would be on to me by now. It would be my picture splashed all over the papers, not David's, and though it's hard to imagine him being violent, I have come to realise that maybe I don't know him as well as I thought I did. Some of the things he said when he came to my flat didn't make sense. I certainly haven't been sending him letters. I learned my lesson about putting my feelings on paper the last time when he threw them back in my face. Perhaps someone else is involved, since it's unlikely David would send letters to himself, but that's not really my problem.

'Where were you?' Matt waves his knife in front of my face and I snap back to the present.

'Sorry, just thinking about David.'

Matt falls still for a moment, his hand pausing in mid-air before he returns to slicing an onion.

'Old habits,' I say, trying to joke about the situation. I'm not sure exactly how much Matt understands about my relationship with David – whether he truly gets the importance of it – but I decide it doesn't matter. He seems to accept me for me, and that's exactly what I need. A friend who isn't going to judge me or try to change me.

'I hope you're hungry,' Matt says as he makes a dressing from ingredients I've never heard of.

'A man of many talents,' I say, and he bobs into a curtsy, making me laugh before plating up and lighting a squat candle in the centre of the scrubbed wood table.

We sit opposite each other and he fills our wine glasses.

'Do you mind if I ask you something personal?' he says, and I worry at how much of myself he's going to ask me to reveal, aware that there are parts that I've kept hidden from almost everyone that I don't know if I can share.

'OK,' I say, lowering my fork as I brace myself.

'You seem a bit overqualified for the admin role at Prestige. Why did you take it?'

Taking a big bite of salmon, I give myself time to try to find the right words but then I swallow and decide that honesty is the best policy. I want Matt to know the true me, since he already knows about my relationship with David.

'After I left university, I got a job in a bank and worked my way up. I was actually the head of recruitment for the whole of Europe for a couple of years so I have had some pretty big jobs, but my mental health hasn't always been up to it. I've had to dip in and out of work, and in the last couple of years I really struggled so I decided to take voluntary redundancy. When the Prestige job came up, I already had my flat and my savings, so it was more about confidence. I wanted to ease myself back in.'

'Do you think you'll look for more responsibility next time?' Matt asks.

I open my mouth to answer when we're interrupted by the sound of my phone ringing.

'Saved by the bell,' Matt says, and I hop down from the stool and hurry to the living room where I left my phone on the coffee table. I refuse to acknowledge the ripple of hope that passes through me but my heart sinks when I see it's not David's name on the screen. Connor is calling me and I frown, since we didn't exactly leave on the best of terms. Glancing back at Matt,

I make an apologetic face and hold up one finger – *one minute* – before pressing the button to accept the call.

'Kitty, so glad you picked up,' Connor says, 'I've been worried about you.'

I make a non-committal sound but secretly I'm pleased he's been thinking about me.

'I felt awful after our last session and I want to apologise,' Connor launches in. 'I never should have questioned your relationship with David. That was unprofessional of me. I've had a few things going on personally but that's no excuse.'

I answer with another grunt but he's right – what David and I have is special, and who is he to judge?

'When I saw the news today about David, I immediately thought of you and how much you must be suffering, and I wondered whether you'd like to come in for one more session? I will make myself available any time. I owe you that much.'

I'm smiling as he's speaking, and nodding, since he does owe me that much, but I realise I haven't said anything and Connor is waiting for an answer.

'Tomorrow would be good,' I say slowly.

'Brilliant,' Connor says, and I hear genuine happiness in his voice. 'Morning, afternoon, evening – take your pick.'

Something about an evening session piques my interest since I usually see Connor first thing in the morning. It would be interesting to see him ruffled from a full day of work; I wonder whether he'll be the same cool, calm person or whether he'll be more fractious after he's listened to other people's problems from morning until night. I must admit that the thought of him seeing other patients makes me feel a little jealous.

'Evening,' I say, decisively.

'Seven?'

'Seven it is.'

I hang up and glance over at Matt and see he's concentrating on his plate, but he must sense I'm watching him because he looks up and smiles and I feel an odd little ripple like something fluttering inside me. It takes me a moment to realise just how happy having dinner with Matt is making me feel; it's something I vow to discuss with Connor, since he'll surely be interested to hear that I've met a man who makes me feel a tiny fraction of what I felt with David all those years ago.

TWENTY-FOUR

DAVID

I don't know how long I stand in Annika's kitchen, trying to make sense of her words and clinging to the kitchen island to hold myself up until Annika breaks the silence. 'I'm so sorry, David. I thought when you came here that you must know already.'

Shaking my head, I try to picture Kitty and Tom together but I just can't see it. Surely they wouldn't do that to me? But even as I'm rejecting the very idea, fragments of memories force their way in and pierce my armour. I see them together at the barbecue in this very house, sitting close together, Kitty confiding in Tom the way she used to in me. There's always been something between them, a shared experience of never wanting for anything, that drew them together – a private bond that I was never in on.

I remember Tom on our wedding night, the drunkest man there, barely able to stand, and yet he sought me out on the dance floor to grab my arm and splutter in my ear, 'You don't deserve her.' I laughed as if it was the funniest thing in the world, and dismissed it as drunken ramblings, but I always knew Tom had a thing for Kitty back when we were all nineteen-year-old cauldrons of hormones, and it amused me more than anything. I enjoyed having something that he didn't, but my relationship with Kitty developed into so much more than that. I thought we'd left our schoolboy jostling long behind us.

I lift my head and look over at Annika. 'Are you sure?'

'He told me yesterday. It's been going on for months, apparently.'

I think back to all the times Kitty has been missing. Her unexplained absences and chaotic returns, at times clearly nursing the mother of all hangovers. It's hardly a surprise that Tom was the cause. The last man I know to leave a party; still clinging to our youth with his weed vapes and weekends in Amsterdam. I picture them together and my whole body jerks violently as if I've been punched in the stomach. The betrayal feels like a thousand sharp knives digging into my skin while my insides are engulfed in flames.

'I can't believe they would do this to us,' I say, but Annika gives me a hard stare.

'You can't?' she says with a harsh laugh. 'It's their nature.'

I don't like to think of Kitty and Tom as similar but it's hard to deny that they're both enigmatic and charming and utterly selfish. Part of my attraction to her has always been my certainty that she could weather any storm and I see that she's found her way through this one; only Tom's been her life raft, not me.

'I always thought he'd fight for me,' she says, and I see tears sparkling in her eyes once more. 'If I threatened to kick him out, I was sure he'd beg to stay with me and the kids, but this time it was like talking to a stranger. There was no Tom behind the eyes. He didn't even want to say goodbye to the kids.'

She sobs once but sniffs and pulls herself upright. 'Enough of this. Now you know. Tom isn't here and you need to leave.'

Glancing at the large, stainless steel clock on the wall, I see it's only 9 p.m. but it feels much later because the sky is black outside with no stars or moon visible. The idea of walking aimlessly until dawn makes me shudder and I think of the spare room upstairs where Kitty and I have stayed when we've drunk too much to make it home, with its vast bed and marbled ensuite. 'I hate to ask...' I say softly.

She silences me with a sharp look. 'The kids...' She doesn't finish the sentence but I know what she's saying. It's another blow, but I understand.

'You know what they're saying?' she asks.

I nod once. 'I know the police want to question me.'

'You're on the news.' My stomach lurches and she continues, 'They've said the public shouldn't approach you. That you're dangerous.'

I dig the heels of my hands into my eyes and hold in a yell. All my hard work to build up my reputation ruined in a few days. After the Dick Bell show I was dreaming of my next award – I could almost feel the weight of the gong in my hands – and now it's gone, my whole career reduced to ash, but the main thing I care about now is finding my wife and righting my wrongs as best I can. Kitty is all I have and she's still my wife, whatever has gone on between her and Tom.

'Why don't you go to the police, David?' she asks.

Things are simple for Annika. She looks at the world in black and white. She gave Tom an ultimatum and now that's done, and I wouldn't be surprised if the divorce lawyer is instructed in the morning and the house put up for sale by the afternoon. For me, life isn't so binary. I can already feel myself making excuses for Tom and Kitty, finding a way to justify their behaviour in order to avoid my life cracking in two.

'Are you hungry?' Annika says.

At the mention of the word my stomach gives an almighty groan and I remember I haven't eaten all day.

'There's a lasagne in the fridge that you can put in the microwave while I get you some clothes. You have ten minutes.'

I nod, understanding that she's taking a risk having me here, and I feel a rush of gratitude. 'Thank you, Annika.'

She makes a dismissive sound and leaves the room as I open the fridge and locate the lasagne wrapped in cling film. Once I've microwaved it, I sit at the island on a high stool, shovelling mouthfuls of scalding pasta into my mouth and burning my tongue in the process, barely tasting it but not caring. Delving into the fridge once more, I crack open a beer, figuring Annika won't begrudge me one, given the news she's just broken; I drain the can in five or six gulps. Annika reappears with a backpack, and adds a box of cereal bars from a cupboard and a bottle of water from the fridge before pressing the bag into my arms.

She's done more than enough but I need to ask one more favour. 'Annika, can you send Kitty a message for me, please?'

Already, she's shaking her head but I can't let her refuse. 'I need to talk to her before I go to the police.'

She won't look at me.

'Please.'

She shuts her eyes and sighs. 'What do you want me to say?'

'Tell her to meet me where we got engaged, tomorrow at noon.'

'David, I don't know—'

'Just let her decide,' I say. 'Please.'

Eventually she nods and I realise I should leave – I've pushed my luck far enough. She follows me to the door and takes a black windcheater and cap that both look expensive from the cloakroom cupboard, holding them out to me. 'Tom's,' she says. 'Bin them when you're done.'

Resting the backpack on the polished concrete floor, I pull on the jacket and cap, before hoisting it onto my back. Annika and I face one another and her eyes seem to search my face, boring right into mine. 'You didn't hurt anyone, did you, David?'

'No,' I say truthfully. 'I didn't.'

She doesn't look away and after a moment, she nods. 'No, of course not. You don't have it in you.'

It crosses my mind that this may be the last time I see her; I wouldn't be surprised if the kids were enrolled in school in Norway before the summer is out. I give her one last hug and after a moment she relents, her body loosening as she squeezes me back. The thought of leaving the comfort and warmth and stepping back into the unknown almost makes me fall to my knees and beg her to let me stay, but I know she's done more than enough, and I can tell she wants me to go.

'Thank you,' I say as I open the door and step out into the crisp night, slipping through the gap in the gate as it opens, and turning towards the Heath.

* * *

It's broad daylight when I stride along the pavement towards King's Cross station, my body aching after a night spent sleeping in a hollowed-out bush and my paranoia levels high with so many people around. It's not just that I fear being recognised – though of course that is constantly on my mind – but I'm twitchy because I feel uncomfortable in my own skin. There's a thick layer of grime on me and my stubble is now three days old, making my face itch where the hairs are poking through, and I'm aware that I'm starting to stink.

Tugging self-consciously at the peak of my cap, I pull it lower in the hope of avoiding eye contact, silently thanking Annika for her foresight. King's Cross must be one of the busiest stations in London, and it was probably a stupid place to suggest meeting near, with a face as recognisable as mine, but I needed somewhere that only Kitty would know and I wanted somewhere that meant something to us. Perhaps coming here will remind my wife of what we have. I haven't let myself think that she might not come, as it would be too crushing.

I planned our engagement weekend meticulously, booking the Eurostar tickets months in advance and speaking to a friend who'd moved to Paris to find a romantic hotel and the perfect restaurant. The morning we were due to depart, I stuck a chilled bottle of champagne in my bag and two plastic flutes along with the ring – on Tom's advice, a bigger diamond than I could afford, which I paid for with a loan that would take me the next two years to pay off.

I'm sure Kitty knew what I had planned and we were giddy with excitement when we arrived at St Pancras station, but when we joined the queue, I heard an announcement that made my heart plummet: 'Would all passengers have their tickets and passports ready for inspection at the front of the queue.' In my anxiety to remember every little detail, I'd forgotten my bloody passport. I half-heartedly searched my pockets though I knew it wasn't there, and as we neared the front I insisted that Kitty go ahead and I would catch the next train.

'Absolutely not,' she said, taking my hand, and we both left the queue together. As we walked outside towards the taxi rank, Kitty tugged me outside onto the main road in front of King's Cross station and across the junction, leading me into the McDonald's on the corner with a grin, proclaiming, 'I'm starving.' She's always been an enigma, comfortable in the swankiest restaurants but equally happy to nip into a fast food joint when the mood takes her, confident in her own skin. It's one of the things that drew me to her. We ordered Big Mac meals and sat at a table upstairs, across from one another, and I retrieved the champagne from my bag.

'It will only get warm otherwise,' I said.

Kitty laughed as I popped the cork and we each managed half a glass before the security guard threw us out. We were both in hysterics as we spilled out onto the street and I wrapped my arms around her and said in her ear, 'Will you marry me?'

She said 'Yes' and kissed me, long and hard, and we never did make it to Paris.

The station has changed a lot in fifteen years – the front has been modernised with a wide expanse of pavement and new café pods outside – but the McDonald's is still there. The station clock, high on a pillar above the concourse with its golden face sparkling in the sun, ticks past noon and there's no sign of Kitty. My body is tense and I keep flinching as people in high-visibility jackets catch my eye, and it takes me a moment to establish they are a construction worker or security guard and not the police. I've avoided the news, but my name and photo must be all over the media by now. I don't want to know what they're saying about me but I'm sure my reputation is shattered beyond repair. I wonder if I've achieved international fame and let out a snort – Stanley always wanted me to crack America.

My back is aching after a night spent sleeping outdoors on the hard ground, so I slump onto a stone bench and survey the crowd. I start to wonder if Kitty will come, my confidence eroding as the minutes tick by. After everything we've been through – so many years, the good and the bad – I wonder if Tom will be the final nail in the coffin. My closest friend and my wife – it still doesn't feel real – more like the plot of *East-Enders* than my life.

Spotting a blonde woman walking along the street, I sit up straighter, ready to rush across to her, but she passes the McDonald's without slowing. I squint into the sunlight and it takes me a moment to work out that she's too short for Kitty, too squat, and I feel a hit of disappointment until a woman's voice comes from close behind me saying, 'Don't I know you?' and I'm filled with terror.

Turning slowly, I come face to face with an unfamiliar older woman in a floral dress that looks like a sofa cover and she narrows her eyes at me, scowling.

'I thought it was you,' she spits.

I wonder whether I should run, but there are too many people around – if she shouts I wouldn't get far.

'Do I know you?' I try to sound casual.

'No, but I know you.'

I open my mouth to answer but she continues before I can speak, jabbing a finger into my chest. 'You are the man that humiliated poor Dick Bell. That man's been nothing but an upstanding citizen and just because some little upstart—'

'Excuse me,' I say quickly, feeling a rush of relief since she clearly hasn't seen the news and I move away, desperate to avoid a scene.

I'm scanning the street again as I walk when a voice comes from behind: 'David?'

My heart leaps because I instantly recognise my wife's voice and I glance behind sharply and there she is, looking pale and wan and dressed in a black shirt dress, making her look like she's on her way to a funeral. She doesn't smile when she sees me and her face contorts with something that looks horribly close to disgust.

'Why are you still doing this, David? Look at yourself. You need to hand yourself in.'

I get up to go over to her but she frowns and hisses, 'I'd rather we weren't seen together. You sit down.' I obey her command and she sits next to me but with her legs on the other side so she's facing the road while I'm facing the station. It hurts that I'm someone to be avoided now but I understand of course, and part of me is relieved that I don't have to look at her face.

'How could you?' I say softly.

There's a long pause and I hear Kitty let out a sigh. I wasn't expecting tears or for her to beg for forgiveness, but when she speaks, her anger disarms me. 'How could I? How could *I*? You can't sit there and pretend you're squeaky clean when you're wanted for fucking murder!' She lets out a harsh laugh. 'You know how difficult this year has been for me. I've been doing whatever it takes to try to have a baby while you've been cosying up to your hot young colleague. And now this.'

I start to protest but she cuts me off. 'How am I supposed to know what to think, David? It's like trouble is permanently stuck to your back like a shadow. First, there was Catherine McCollum – we had to move house, for God's sake, after everything she did, and at the new place, who do you think was dealing with the decorators and the interior designer, making sure everything was perfect for you.'

'I thought you enjoyed doing the house.'

She snorts as if that's the most ridiculous thing in the world, and continues, 'And then, when I needed you, when the IVF really started to take its toll, all you could think about was your fucking TV show...'

'It's been an important year.' I realise how lame that sounds and change tack. 'Kitty, you slept with my best friend.'

She flinches but she doesn't back down. 'You weren't around and I needed someone.'

I don't know how to respond to this wholly inadequate excuse and we sit in silence as the world moves around us. People rush for trains, buses trundle by, cars and taxis and bikes whiz around the corner, and the McDonald's has a constant flow of customers. I tip my head back and see that overhead the sky is a perfect blue.

'Do you love him?' I ask.

A cloud passes over the sun at this moment and it feels like someone has hit pause. The silence stretches and I can hear my heart beating in my ears as the blood rushes around my body until the cloud moves away.

'Do you?' I prompt.

'Do you remember what I did on my gap year?' she asks.

I frown, confused about how that could possibly be relevant, but nod. 'Yes, skiing in Verbier and then sailing in Bali.'

She laughs sardonically. 'The perfect year.'

I open my mouth to ask what she's talking about but she goes on. 'That's what I told everyone, but what I really did was spend eight months in hospital recovering from bulimia. It was a hard slog but I got through it, and when I arrived in Oxford, finally, I was fragile but determined to start a new chapter. And there was you...'

I smile at the memory of spotting her across the quad. Her red scarf flapping in the wind behind her, hair flying as she tried to contain it.

'... and there was Tom. I met you both on that first day and you were both attractive in your own way.'

A horrible pain starts in my stomach and I clasp my arms around my waist. I don't want to hear her 'what ifs' about Tom.

'Can we just—'

'Let me finish,' she says. 'I don't suppose you have any idea how hard he pursued me? Drinks, dinners, expensive presents – it was a constant whirlwind, while you just made me laugh so easily. He was disappointed when I chose you, but I never once regretted my decision. I needed someone who would lift me up, not pull me down, and whatever he said, Tom would have done that eventually.'

Though we are facing away from each other, I feel her hand touch mine and I let her wrap her fingers around mine, but my whole body feels cold. How did I not know Tom felt that way?

'He never gave up, and in these last few months I've been...' She searches for a word and lands on, 'desperate,' and sighs heavily. 'I needed someone and Tom was there.'

'What about me?' I ask.

'I'm sure you'll admit that you've been distracted.'

I should be furious with her but all I feel is sadness that we've ended up here. I can't deny it, the show has demanded a lot of attention, 'and Nina' a little voice whispers inside my head but I won't say that aloud, and the letters have been a big drain, but the worst thing has been trying to get my head around the fact that Kitty and I won't be parents. I've never told her how much it hurts because I know she's struggling too, but maybe it's time to be honest? There's nothing else to lose.

'I need to tell you something,' she says, as I open my mouth to speak.

I tense, my mind freewheeling as I wonder what else she could have to tell me. I'm not sure I can take much more. Before I can wonder too much, she blurts out, 'I'm pregnant.'

My mouth falls open. I didn't expect her to say that and a huge smile breaks onto my face as I think back to the last time we slept together and realise that the maths works, but quickly the smile dies on my lips. We've been trying for years and now here she is, pregnant, after a fling with Tom, a man who already has three kids of his own. Blood rushes up my neck to my face, and suddenly I feel too hot in the glaring sun.

'Is it Tom's?' I manage to get out.

The pause is like a knife in my heart and when she says, 'I don't know,' I sit silently gasping for air as I try to compute how I feel. Surely it's more likely that it's Tom's than mine, but something inside me makes me want to fight and I feel like if there's even a shred of hope I will cling to it for all I'm worth.

'How far along?'

'They think almost twelve weeks. It's been such a shock. A wonderful shock.'

There are tears in my eyes but I blink them back. 'Do you want a divorce?'

'No,' she says quickly. 'I want this whole mess to be sorted out. David, will you go to the police? Please, for me.'

I hear the sound of her softly crying and my heart aches. 'I need to speak to Tom. Give me one more night and then I'll call Detective Hopping and explain everything.'

The sound of her crying doesn't stop.

'What's wrong?'

'I'm scared. I don't want you to go to prison.'

'I won't,' I say with much more certainty than I feel. I have no idea what happened to Nina, and the police clearly haven't discovered the truth or they wouldn't still be looking for me. 'They'll find who did this to her and I'll do what I can to help. Just let me talk to Tom first.'

'Why?' her voice is almost a wail.

'I've come this far, a few hours more aren't going to make much difference, and Tom is my best friend. I need to ask him face to face how he could do this to me.' I don't tell her that Tom knows things about me that even she doesn't, things that I think would be better for both of us if they remain between us, but she seems to accept my explanation.

'Do you know where he is?' I ask.

'We've been meeting at his flat,' she says sheepishly.

'His flat? I thought it was rented out?'

'The tenant left and I think he saw the potential in keeping it empty.' She lets out a hollow laugh but the thought makes me angry for my sake and Annika's. Pushing myself up, it's time to leave.

'I'll go there this evening,' I say. 'And Kitty, even if I'm not the father, I'm happy for you – you were always meant to be a mother.'

TWENTY-FIVE
CATHERINE

It's dark when I arrive at Connor's office and Camden has an edge at night that isn't present in the daytime. Every pub I pass is full and the pavements outside are crowded with people smoking and yelling at one another in the way they do when they're drunk. I hurry along the main road with my eyes downcast, trying to be inconspicuous. Matt almost persuaded me to cancel my appointment and stay for dinner again this evening but I decided that it's a good idea for me to see Connor, and it's better not to outstay my welcome.

Matt worked from home today and I spent most of the day on his sofa, pretending to look at job adverts on the internet but mostly watching the entire history of his Instagram account and laughing at all the in-jokes. I'll admit he is very watchable, but I wonder what Connor will say when I tell him about Matt. I'm smiling to myself when I reach Connor's front door and I buzz and it clicks open without him saying anything over the intercom. A flurry of nerves surprises me as I step inside. I'm not sure whether it's the evening revelry that's put me on edge but as I take the stairs, using the handrail to steady myself, my nerves continue to jangle.

Pushing open the door to Connor's office, I'm hit by a blast of cool air, and the first thing I notice is that the windows that face onto the street are wide open. The noise from outside drifts up and I hear the traffic and voices of the people out and about as clearly as if I'm down among them. Connor is standing by the window with his back to me and I'm surprised to spot the glass of red wine in his hand. It's not like Connor to be so unprofessional, and when I clear my throat, he doesn't turn around. I begin to wonder if he thinks I'm someone else.

'Help yourself to a glass of wine, if you like,' he says.

'No, thanks,' I say.

I edge closer to his desk and spot his large leather notebook beside an open bottle of red wine and I find myself drawn to it, my hand moving towards it and hovering above it. I'd love to read what he's written about me but I know it's a breach of our professional relationship. Glancing up, I see he's still looking out of the window, his eyes fixed on the pavement below. I stroke the soft leather cover of the book but something makes me freeze. As I look at Connor I notice something that makes my whole body tense – Connor's hair is blond today.

I edge backwards, taking small steps towards the door. I don't know what's going on but something tells me I need to get out of here, fast.

'Where are you going?' Connor says.

For a fraction of a second I'm paralysed with fear before I turn on my heel and sprint to the door, but before I can open it, the whole weight of Connor's body slams against me. We land hard on the floor with him on top of me and the air is squeezed from my lungs. I find myself making a strange noise like the suck of water from a blocked drain as I try to catch my breath while tears stream from my eyes.

'Sorry, that was rude,' he says in a plummy voice, all trace of his Irish accent gone completely. 'But I couldn't let you leave; we're only just getting started.'

He moves off me and I slide to my knees, bending over until I manage to suck in some air, and I turn slowly to face him, opening my eyes wide with confusion as I take in his ruddy face and sweeping blond fringe. He smiles and I see a flash of teeth that seem whiter than before. The only thing that's familiar is his blue eyes, and I search them for any hint of compassion, but all I see is a smirking, overgrown man-child.

'What's going on?' I ask, and his grin widens. 'Who are you?'

'Don't you know?' He chuckles softly and the hairs on the back of my neck lift. This is a man I've cried in front of and told all my secrets to, and here he is, laughing in my face. A surge of rage lifts me to my feet and I find I'm breathing hard, looking around the room for anything heavy or sharp to arm myself with. The wine bottle is next to his computer but he's between me and it, and when he follows my gaze he raises one finger and wags it at me. 'Not a good idea, and I think I should hold on to this.' He snatches my bag from my hands and, after a brief tussle, removes my phone and tucks it into his pocket, tossing my handbag across the room.

'Now, why don't we get comfortable?' He gestures to the sofa. 'One last session, for old times' sake.'

His fingers clamp around my arm and he gives me little choice, marching me over to the sofa and shoving me roughly so I land hard on the sagging cushions and sink in deeper than I'd like, as if I'm being swallowed whole. He kicks the table out of the way and it hits the wall with a sharp crack as he drags the armchair forward and sits opposite me, so close that our knees are touching. I wonder if anyone would hear if I scream, but the clamour from the street below makes me think it's unlikely.

'It's such a relief we can finally sit here and be our genuine selves,' he says with a smirk. 'You don't know how hard it is living a lie.'

I look away from his face and keep searching the room for a

way out. The stranger opposite lets out a giggle and I can't help glancing at him, wondering what is going on inside his head.

'Actually,' he says, 'what am I talking about? You know more than most, since you've been play-acting the part of David's wife for the best part of two decades.'

I want to tell him to shut up but I press my lips firmly together as I keep looking for something that might help me. People never understand what I have with David.

'It is rather disconcerting to hear you talk about him, so let's be frank with each other – you don't honestly believe that the two of you are in a relationship, do you?'

I frown and my gaze lands on the standing fan that's only a couple of feet from me and is probably heavy enough to do some damage. I wonder if I could grab it and swing it before he stopped me.

He lets out a strangled laugh. 'Oh, you do. It really is tragic how deluded you are.'

While he talks, I edge closer to the fan, moving millimetre by millimetre and nodding along as if I'm listening.

'You know, it was the make-up that I really detested. The foundation and pressed powder that made me look like the undead and stained all my collars. Ended up costing me a fortune because I had to replace all my shirts.'

The fan is only just out of reach so I shift in my seat, pretending to scratch my foot so I can get closer.

'The whole get up didn't look too bad, actually, you have to admit. A make-up artist I was seeing a couple of years ago showed me how to comb the dark gel through my hair, which really was very effective. She thought she was helping me for some amateur dramatics, and I suppose she was, in a way.'

He lets out the strange laugh once more. 'It was the Irish accent I really regretted. I have no idea why it popped out of my mouth but it did, and I had to keep it up for a whole year. I can't believe you didn't notice it slipping.'

I make a sound as if I find this funny, all the while preparing to leap forward and grab the fan before he realises what I'm doing.

'I know what you're thinking, and I'm telling you, don't bother or you will be hurt in ways you can't imagine.' His words chill me and he bends forward, puts both hands on my shoulders and shoves me hard into the cushions. The sofa is soft against my back, but I'm off balance once again and Connor takes the opportunity to jump up and roll the fan over to the wall. 'Let's remove all temptation, shall we?'

He grabs the wine bottle on his return to the armchair and takes a long swig as I stare at him through narrowed eyes, desperately trying to place him.

'Who are you?' I ask again.

Raising his eyes to the sky, he laughs gleefully and knocks back another swig of wine. 'I love it that you don't know. It must feel strange, the shoe being on the other foot. Shall I give you a clue?'

I don't want to play this man's games but I nod, making up my mind to launch myself for the door when he's next distracted.

'That ring,' he gestures with the end of the bottle towards my hand and I glance down. 'You know I found it, not David.'

This man must be a friend of David's, someone from Oxford. I think back to that night when David extracted the ring from his pocket and offered it to me, his pupils unnaturally large and his words tumbling over one another in a nonsensical patter.

'Harrow?' I mutter the word that David said over and over, and the man opposite lets out an angry snarl.

'Don't call me that.'

It hits me that this must be David's best friend, the louche posh boy that David befriended from the start who I quickly learned to avoid. He must have been twenty-one the last time I saw him and he's aged like a man who's sampled too many of the finer things – he's swollen and pompous and his head looks like a stuffed pigskin.

'David has insisted on dragging out that little nickname for almost twenty years. One schoolboy slip of the tongue...' He drains the rest of the bottle in his pique, but some goes down the wrong way and he splutters. Taking my chance while he's bent double, I hurl myself out of the seat and sprint towards the door; there's a brief moment where my heart lurches and I think I'm going to make it, before I feel his arms around my waist and we crash to the floor. Using both hands, he flips me over, his whole face purple with fury, and he swings back his hand.

'I'm sorry,' I say, just as the blow lands across my cheek and my head explodes. My vision turns black then red, before exploding into fuzzy white granules that slowly come together and form his face, inches from mine.

'This isn't a game,' he says, hauling me up and throwing me back onto the couch where I put my arms over my head and whimper.

'Why are you doing this?' I manage to get out, and he lets out another hard laugh that turns my insides to stone and I know for certain that this man is not going to help me. 'I've never done anything to you.'

'It always has to be about you, doesn't it? You don't know how deathly dull it's been sitting here, listening to you whine on and on about how you feel.'

I trusted him, and now his words are like sharp knives sticking into my ribs. I suck in deep breaths, not wanting to give him the satisfaction of seeing me cry. 'I only come to these sessions because the police said I had to do a year of therapy with you to avoid being charged.'

He lets out another harsh laugh. 'And how did the police communicate with you?'

I frown at the question. 'Email,' I say slowly.

He's smiling a horrible grin that makes me wish I could do something to wipe it from his face. 'Detective Brian Army, was it?'

'I don't remember,' I say, although the name does ring a bell.

'Oh I do,' he says. 'Detective B. Army. Barmy. It may be silly but David and I fell about when we came up with that.'

A strange squeak comes from my throat as I try to unravel what he means.

'So the police didn't arrange these sessions?' I'm confused as I think of the stern emails I received, informing me that I would be prosecuted unless I attended therapy.

'You really don't get it, do you? The police know nothing about these sessions. David and I concocted them in the pub one day because he wanted to keep tabs on you and, I must admit, I was tempted to find out what was going on inside that addled mind of yours.'

My stomach roils as I take in that this whole thing has been a set-up, one big joke for David to laugh about down the pub. I've been spilling my darkest secrets to someone who actively detests me and I begin to feel hot and cold all over, but then another thought turns me to ice.

'Was Kitty in on it?' I ask, thinking of the real Kitty with her gleaming golden skin and matching hair, like she's been dipped in molten honey. Kathryn Kennington. She stole everything from me. David and I were happy until she arrived at Oxford and it all fell apart. I bet she'd find it hilarious to imagine me wading through the detritus of my life, dragging up every sordid detail for them to turn into a comedy routine at my expense.

'What a bitch,' I mutter, and he responds by pulling his hand from his knee and whipping it across my face, this time making tears spring to my eyes.

'Don't talk about her like that,' he says. 'She's far too good for the likes of you.'

Sitting up, I look into the man's eyes and a name suddenly bursts from my memory. 'Tom?'

He lifts his hands and the sound of him slow-clapping rings through the room like gun shots.

'Now she gets it.'

I try to work out why this man has sat here hour after hour, wearing make-up and speaking in a false accent, but it's like an impossible equation that doesn't make sense no matter how hard I try.

'Why would you...' And then I stop and think about Kitty and my stinging cheek. She's one of those women that men go to the ends of the earth for, not like me. It isn't the most ridiculous notion that this could be about her. 'Is this about David's wife?'

I shrink back, bracing myself for him to hit me again, but he seems to shrink, his eyes dropping to the floor, and he says gruffly, 'It's always been about David's wife.'

I keep my mouth shut as he goes on, 'Part of the reason I agreed to act out this charade was to hear exactly what it is about David that's got you so hooked.' He puts on a falsetto voice: *'He's so handsome. He's so special.* Let's just say, you didn't exactly reveal great depths.'

Running back over the times I've sat here, I remember the things I've told him and my face grows hot. How did I not realise this man was a fraud? He seems utterly repellent now but perhaps he was able to deceive me simply by giving me his undivided attention, something I receive so rarely. I feel a rush of shame at how pathetic I've become, but I decide that enough is enough and I grit my teeth, determined to make my move if he gives me even the smallest opportunity.

So just as he lifts the wine bottle and takes another glug, I try to escape one last time, diving from my seat and rushing for the door. I make it across the room, almost within touching distance, when he slams into my back and we land against his desk. Crying out in pain, I slide to the floor, holding my side, and his leather-bound book lands next to me, falling open at a random page. My eyes widen as I see his scrawls – the word 'bitch' written in capitals – but it's not the words that shock me the most, it's that everything is written in purple ink.

Looking up slowly, I see him leaning against the desk, watching me, and I huddle into a ball against the wall like a wounded animal. The purple ink forces me to remember something else that fills me with shame, as if I'm sinking into a cold bath, as I think back to the time I used to spend hours crafting my own declarations of love, believing they were eloquent and the purple ink romantic, but over time I realised they were crude and childish and David did not react in the way I'd hoped. But that was years ago.

When David came to see me, he asked me if I'd been back at my old tricks, and now something else falls into place. It can't be a coincidence that Tom is filling his book with scribbles in purple pen.

'Have you been sending David letters?' I ask, my voice barely above a whisper as the shock almost squeezes my throat shut.

'You're good at this. Perhaps it takes one to know one,' he muses, and I try to ignore the insinuation, given how damaged this man clearly is. 'It started as a prank. He'd just won his third BAFTA and he was growing tiresome so I planned to take him down a peg or two, and since you're the only thing that's knocked his confidence over the years, I decided to emulate your behaviour. Just the odd loopy letter through his front door when I was passing – it started as a bit of fun, but when his paranoia started causing problems between him and Kitty, let's just say I saw my opportunity.'

'With Kitty?' I ask, not able to hide my surprise, since David has more charm in his big toenail than this man does in his entire body. As hard as it is to imagine anyone preferring Tom to David, I feel a brief hope that perhaps he and Kitty will get together and David will be left alone, heartbroken, needing a shoulder to cry on. Even trapped in this room, I feel buoyed up at the thought.

'Yes, with Kitty,' Tom says, sounding bitter again. 'But that's all over. She's chosen him over me, again, despite him being wanted for murder.'

He laughs but there's nothing funny about this as I suddenly remember Nina and it feels as if the temperature has dropped a few degrees. This man is clearly deranged, and I've sat here and talked about Nina, speculating about her relationship with David, putting ideas in his head. God knows what he's done. I can barely bring myself to ask but I force myself to speak, telling myself that it's time to be brave, for David.

'Did you do something to Nina?' I ask, a shiver running through me.

His eyes shine and I can almost see his excitement; I can tell he wants to tell me something.

I manage to croak, 'What did you do?'

'When the letters didn't work, I started to wonder what else might get to David. You mentioned Nina so many times that I started to think that maybe it wasn't just a figment of your imagination, so I followed them the night Dick Bell appeared on *Confessions*.'

My mind is whirring and a rush of desperation makes me blurt out, 'Did you see me?' I can't help but ask, having spent the last few days wondering what the hell happened that night.

A strange smile spreads across his face. 'I saw you, and you being there gave me a delicious idea. I saw a way to get rid of David once and for all. Yes, there was some unpleasantness – the woman had to be dealt with – but it really was the perfect crime.'

My mind goes blank and I'm terrified as it dawns on me that he killed Nina, and after telling me, he probably isn't going to let me leave this flat in one piece. I try to hold myself together

but a deep sob judders through my body as I huddle by his feet.
He ignores me and I bite down hard, trying to stop the tears,
since I can tell he's not a man who reacts well to weakness.
Keeping quiet, I decide then and there to do whatever it takes to
stay alive. I may have had moments where I wondered if I'd be
better off out of this world, but facing this man I realise that I
want to live more than anything – not as Kitty and not for
David, but for me.

'I was very careful when I went inside the flat, but David –
not so much; he left his DNA all over that place and all over
her. I knew it wouldn't take long for the police to arrest him but
I wasn't sure if the DNA would be enough.'

I feel a cold dread rising up inside me, sensing what is
coming next.

'I needed a witness and then you stumbled up.'

I frown, wanting to keep him talking while I desperately try
to think of a way to escape. 'Why would I say I saw something I
didn't?'

Tom laughs, 'Because if you don't, who do you think they're
going to blame? The police will place you at the scene. There
will be CCTV from the corner shop where you bought the
vodka and probably driver cam or doorbell footage when they
really start looking.'

'I never went inside.'

'Here's the best bit. I took a bloodied tissue from Nina's
place and then I stopped by your house when you weren't home
and let myself in. You really ought to get a better lock on your
patio doors. I found a nice place to leave it, in among your
clothes, and I don't suppose you'll ever find it, but the police
will, if they really look. They're trained for that type of thing.'

It's like ice water is trickling into my veins as the horror of
what he's saying sets in.

'It's not going to look good, now is it? Given your history.'
He's grinning again and I wish I could wipe the smile from his

face, but he's a lot stronger than me and I've tried all the possible exits. 'But there is a way out for you. All you have to do is tell the police that you saw David kill Nina.'

I nod. 'OK,' I say, thinking that as soon as he lets me go I will tell the police the truth.

'I know what you're thinking,' he says.

'I'm not thinking anything. I'll do what you want, I promise.'

He reaches down and grabs a handful of my hair, dragging me to my feet. I whimper but I have no other option than to stand.

'Imagine if you tell the police that I was involved. There'll be no DNA, no CCTV – I was very careful. It will just be your word against mine. Me, a well-connected banker and father, and you, well, we don't need to go into that, now do we?'

Before I can respond, the buzzer goes and Tom's head whips up. He gives my hair a sharp tug and puts his finger to his lips. I want to defy him but the stinging pain in my scalp and the torrent of noise rolling in through the open windows stops me. We stand frozen to the spot while the buzzer goes again and again, and Tom's phone starts ringing. He seems flummoxed for a moment, then he drags me across the room to the back window and says, 'Out!'

My body tingles with fear as I think he's telling me to jump, but when I peer through I see there's a metal fire escape outside. His powerful body forces mine to move and he pushes me out into the blustery night air. It's balmy and, down below, the streets of Camden are jam-packed with people embarking on a night of revelry.

'Up there,' he points to the metal stairs that lead to the roof.

TWENTY-SIX
DAVID

There's no answer to the buzzer but I lean on it anyway and try Tom's phone again. After I left Kitty, I found a quiet park where I walked in loops and tried to work out how I feel about Kitty's news, but I'm too much on edge to think straight.

Jabbing the button, I consider what to do if Tom fails to answer. I don't want to sleep another night outdoors but I'll have no choice but to find somewhere to hide out and to return later since there is no way I can enter a prison cell without confronting him. After everything we've been through, the highs and lows, two decades worth of adventures, and he's betrayed me with my own wife. Feeling a deep chasm of self-pity open up, I turn to walk away but there's a crackle on the line and Tom's voice rings out, 'Who is it?'

'Harrow, it's me,' I say.

There's only the briefest of pauses before I hear the lock click open and I slam my hand on the door. Inside, I stop in my tracks at the sight of his former living room, which has been redecorated to look like a doctor's waiting room, complete with white walls and a women's magazine. I knew Tom was gaining Catherine's confidence, but I never expected him to take it this far. To be honest, I tried not to think about what he was doing too much, only checking in infrequently to get his reports on her behaviour. Now I realise I shouldn't have trusted a word that came from his lips and I feel a deep-seated guilt that I've dragged Catherine into this.

Taking the stairs, I reach the hallway at the top and draw in several deep breaths. I haven't worked out exactly what I'm going to say to Tom, but I know I need to look him in the eye when I ask him what excuse he has for the ultimate betrayal. The door to the master bedroom is open a crack and I call out, 'Tom?'

'In here,' he replies from inside, and I enter, seeing immediately that this room has been transformed into a consultation room for his one and only patient. Something about the lengths he's gone to sends a chill down my spine. As I step inside I see him straightening furniture. He bends to pick up a large notebook that's fallen onto the floor and returns it to the desktop, carefully brushing the leather clean, before turning to me. His lips, stained from red wine, stretch into a smile. I clench my fists and rush towards him, overwhelmed by the urge to punch him in the nose, swinging my arm wildly. I've never been much of a fighter and he ducks, shoving me into the middle of the room where I swing back around, hands balled by my sides, breathing hard.

'You look like shit, mate,' he says.

'Fuck off.' It's not the most eloquent of replies but it's all I can manage as emotions swirl like a hurricane in my chest.

As he stares at me, I can't help but study his face and wonder what Kitty could have seen in him. His skin is taut and shiny, I suspect with a little help from Botox, though he's never admitted it, and his floppy hair falls with a little more care these days as he attempts to cover the receding hairline. There's a puffiness to him that comes from overindulgence, and a nasty

set to his mouth that transforms into a horrible smirk that I want
to wipe from his face.

'How could you?' I ask, but the smile doesn't drop from his
face and I wonder how much he's had to drink.

'About as easily as you ruined Dick Bell's career.'

I shake my head, refusing to accept that. 'Dick ruined his
own career by trying to shag everything in sight, but leaving me
aside, how could you do it to Annika and the kids?'

He turns on me and fury seems to shoot from his eyes.
'Don't you lecture me about my marriage. What about yours?
Somehow the mud always sticks on me, but from you it seems to
slide like shit off a shovel.'

I frown but Tom comes closer and jabs a finger into my
chest. 'You're just as bad as I am, only I don't pretend to be
anything else.'

Anger simmers inside me but I manage not to swing for him
again. 'You don't know what you're talking about. I have respect
for my wife.'

'She had very little for you when she was in my bed.'

A strangled scream comes from deep inside me and I throw
myself at him, swinging my arms and diving on top of him. We
both hit the floor with a thump and begin wrestling as we each
try to land a blow. There's always been a competitive edge
between us, something akin to that between brothers, I always
thought, but now it feels hateful, as if we are true enemies. We
have always ribbed each other for our perceived weaknesses –
I've teased him for his sense of entitlement and he's needled me
for my working-class upbringing; remembering some of his
taunts gives me a spurt of energy to pin him down with my
knees, drawing back my arm to land a fist in his face.

'Stop!' a woman's voice rings out. 'Stop this at once!'

I falter and Tom bucks me off. Kitty is standing by the door,
holding a key and staring at us with horror etched on her face.
She's changed into white jeans and a white shirt, and her

blonde hair is pinned up from her face where light make-up highlights her perfect bone structure. Even though her face is almost as familiar to me as my own, her beauty still shocks me. She's one of those people in life whose faces have been carved from generations of perfection – it's not just wealth that's inherited.

'Get up, you fools,' she says, and Tom scrambles to his feet. I get up more slowly and look from her to him, revolted at the thought of them together. 'Can't we talk about this like adults?'

Tom smiles his strange smile again and reaches for a bottle of red in a crate under his desk. 'Good idea. Why don't we go up on the roof and have a drink?'

I haven't been on the roof of Tom's building in years, not since he lived here before Annika, when we'd return from nights out in Camden and stagger up there, swigging from bottles of whisky and smoking hash. It's not even a roof terrace, just a fire escape that he co-opted into some extra living space, and I remember that it's four floors up and the building is surrounded by a low wall that comes to knee height – a trip hazard rather than protection.

'I'm fine here,' I say, but Tom is already stepping out of the window, ushering Kitty ahead of him, and I close my eyes for a moment before following.

It's bloody windy on the roof, and by the time I get up there, I see Tom is standing too close to the edge, peering down, while Kitty tries to pull him back to the middle. It's a flat roof with a chimney stack in the middle that provides the only shelter, and when Tom finally takes up a safer position, leaning with his back against the brick chimney, he calls, 'You can come out now.'

Kitty and I look at each other, frowning, and I try to work out what Tom means. It's only us up here, but he's been acting strangely since I arrived and now I wonder if he's taken something.

'What...?' The question dies on my lips as a flicker of move-ment behind the chimney stack catches my eye. At first, it looks like a cat, unfurling from the shadows and stretching out, but quickly I realise it's much too big, and almost at once I see it's a person, then a woman, and as her face turns to mine I realise it's Catherine. Her eyes are wide with what looks like fear, and she looks like she's been crying.

'What is *she* doing here?' Kitty demands.

Tom turns to Kitty, ducking his head like a sheepish little boy, all trace of the cocky smile from earlier gone. 'I'm ashamed to admit it, but David's had me pretending to be Catherine's therapist for almost a year. I know I never should have gone along with it but I thought I was helping to protect you.'

Kitty swings round to me. 'David, is this true?'

'Yes, but...' I try to think of a justification but realise there isn't one. 'Yes, it's true.'

'She's been sending him letters again,' Tom says.

Catherine just stands there, her mouth open, her hands on her face as if she's watching a car crash.

'I thought you said—' I begin, but Tom cuts me off.

'And she's been following you. Catherine, tell Kitty what you told me.' He gives her a gentle push towards Kitty. 'Tell her what you saw.'

Standing next to her, Catherine looks like a pale imitation of my wife, a cheap lookalike. By anyone standards, Kitty is infinitely more attractive, but the most striking difference is the way they hold themselves, the poise and confidence in Kitty's straight back compared to the self-loathing evident in Cather-ine's slumped shoulders and weak chin.

'I... I...' Catherine stammers, and Tom pushes her gently again. 'Tell her.'

Catherine glances at me and I see tears sparkling in her eyes as our gaze locks; she gives her head a hard shake before throwing herself on Tom, beating her fists against his broad chest. He's off balance for a moment and the wine bottle slips from his grip and smashes on the ground beneath our feet, splashing red wine in a large puddle and sending wine fumes into the wind, but Tom manages to stay on his feet and spins away from her, leaving Catherine to fall to her knees where she gasps in pain.

'If she won't tell you, I will,' Tom says. 'Here.' He pulls out his phone and taps on the screen before holding it out to Kitty. My heart lurches as she accepts it and I dart forward trying to snatch it back, but she turns, using her body as a shield.

Her face is lit up by a circle of light as she looks at the screen and her expression changes from confusion to disgust.

'What is it?' I ask, not wanting to know the answer.

Kitty shoves the phone into my hand and I see it's a photo of me and Nina, taken through a window: we're on her sofa, both of us naked, our bodies tangled together. I stare as blood pounds in my ears and I can't bring myself to look at Kitty.

The world seems to slow down as I realise that the photo was taken the night Nina died. Someone else was there, and this could be the proof I need to take to the police – not an alibi exactly, but evidence that someone *was* following me that night and that person could have killed Nina. Glancing at Catherine, I see she's buried her face in her hands and is moaning softly. Was she the one who took the photo? Could she have forced her way inside in a fit of rage and murdered Nina? As I'm watching her, she lifts her eyes and looks at Tom, not me, and her face transforms into a mask of terror.

'Stay away from him!' she screams, but Kitty just stares at her as Tom puts his arm around my wife's neck and pulls her in close. He's muttering something in her ear and she listens for a moment before shrugging him off.

'I told you it's over,' she says.

All trace of triumph deserts Tom and he rounds on her. 'Is there nothing he can do wrong? He treats you like shit and still you go back. You're more pathetic than she is.' He swings an arm to gesture to Catherine and manages to catch Kitty's wrist in the process, making her grasp her arm to her chest. I move to protect my wife, stepping forward to get my body between them.

'David! No!' Catherine screams from behind me.

Tom bends down and scoops up something from the ground and flings himself at me. At first I think he's punched me in the chest as the air is knocked from my lungs and a dull pain hits my sternum, but then the pain turns sharp and my body turns to jelly. Finding myself flat on my back, my hands go to my chest and I feel something warm and sticky leaking out of me that I know immediately is blood.

Catherine gasps and throws herself down beside me, her hand snatching up mine as I search for my wife behind her. Kitty is standing like a statue, looking down at me, fear etched on her face, and her hands holding her stomach protectively. Tom is beside her and I hear him saying in a fast, urgent stream, 'He slept with her then killed her to keep her quiet. You have to believe me. He's dangerous. I was protecting you. Ask Catherine, she'll tell you.'

I look at Catherine and she shakes her head. Even after everything we've been through, I know she won't betray me.

'Ambulance,' I croak.

Tears fall from Catherine's eyes and she shakes her head. 'He took my phone.'

We both look up at Kitty, who's watching us, wide-eyed, while Tom is beside her, still muttering but now to himself. I feel cold all over and oddly calm, though I'm certain life is draining from me like water from a bath. Staring up at the sky, I try to make out a star or the moon in the murky blackness overhead as I wait for my wife to make the call that might save my life.

'Kitty!' Catherine yells. 'Do something!'

Kitty glances at me and I see the anguish on her face as she mouths a single word, *sorry*. Then she lifts her chin, her hands still spread on her stomach, and looks directly at Tom.

'Come away,' she says gently. 'We don't need to see this.'

He doesn't need asking twice and the two of them step over me and Catherine to a spot on the edge of the roof. They embrace and a slight smile lifts the corners of his mouth. Kitty bends over and rests her hands on her knees, taking steadying breaths, and I find it's too hard to keep my eyes open.

'David, stay with me!' Catherine slaps my cheek and I force my eyes open.

Behind her, Kitty lets out a yell that seems to come from deep within her, and then throws herself at Tom from the half-crouch position she is in. It happens in a moment and there's no time for him to react. Panic fills Tom's eyes as she connects with his chest and he goes backwards, tottering several steps, before his ankle catches on the low wall and he falls over the edge. We don't hear the crash from here, but I know he'll have hit the pavement that must be thirty feet below. Kitty peers over the edge before hurrying over to us, and I wait for her to come to me, certain I don't have long left, but she seems to be stuck and her movements are so slow it's like she's wading through treacle.

'It's time for you to listen to me,' she says, and it takes me a moment to work out that she's not talking to me.

Catherine sniffles beside her and Kitty grabs her arm. 'Listen to me, Tom and David fought. Tom stuck the bottle in David's chest but in the process he went over the edge. Got it?'

Snot drips from Catherine's nose as she looks up at Kitty.

'Do you understand me?' Kitty demands.

Catherine nods but she croaks, 'Why?'

Though I don't feel any sadness for the man surely lying dead, cracked and broken far below, that's the question I want to ask. Kitty's hand moves to her stomach again and she says, 'If Tom is the father, I can't have a man like that in my baby's life.'

Catherine judders violently and they lock eyes, nodding once, before Kitty takes out her phone. When she speaks her voice is filled with anguish and desperation. 'Please, we need an ambulance, my husband's been stabbed, he's not moving...' A deep, animal wail escapes from her lungs and fills the air as finally I feel her cool fingers take mine.

EPILOGUE
CATHERINE

I stand at the sink, looking out of the large window across the park where white and pink blossom is bursting from the trees, filling my view with a riot of colour. On the stove behind me, a copper coffee pot burbles and the rich aroma wafts through the flat. It's become my morning ritual – no more instant for me – and it's hard to imagine starting the day anywhere but here.

Footsteps pad on the wooden floor behind me but I don't turn, waiting as they approach and I feel arms around my waist and a soft kiss on my neck.

'Morning,' Matt says, his voice thick with sleep. 'Good to see the daffs are holding on.'

Matt planted the window box with a jumble of spring flowers and the daffodils came up proud and early. We've been watching their progress, waiting for them to wither as the later-flowering crocuses burst through, but they haven't disappointed us yet. I never noticed plants before I met Matt but it's been a joy to get to know something as alive as we are, that breathe and grow but are constant in the way that humans can never be.

'Shall we record the herb planter video today?' Matt asks as he takes the coffee pot from the stove and decants it into two earthenware mugs.

'I've got my group this morning,' I say, reaching for an avocado from the fruit bowl on the table and testing the give of each one, before selecting the ripest and slicing it carefully down the middle, twisting it open to reveal the vivid green flesh. 'This afternoon?'

'Great. Shall we take a picnic to the park for lunch? Looks like it's going to be a nice day.'

'Lovely.' I bring the sea-salted butter and the plate of sliced avocado over to the table. When the toast is ready, Matt slots it into the rack and joins me. Our morning routine has become one of my favourite parts of the day. There's no need to rush since we both work from home these days. Matt handed in his notice two weeks after Karen fired me and asked me to move in with him that same day. It was a leap for both of us, but he was my lifeboat in the storm during the whole period when I was dealing with the police and the press. It took a couple of months for things to die down and Matt gave me the space I needed to sort out my head, but then I noticed he could do with some help responding to his followers on Instagram, and things snowballed.

These days, we're a team. Matt is in front of the camera of course, and he plans all of the content, but I run the admin for the account and handle his PR. A few months ago, a video he did on growing vegetables went viral and his following grew by a hundred thousand in a day. That week he appeared on *This Morning*, and Karen got in touch to ask if he'd do a post with Gary her dog and we laughed like drains as he composed the message to gently tell her that Gary isn't quite on brand.

I've just taken a big mouthful of avocado toast when I sense Matt looking at me, his head on one side, and I can tell he's thinking. Chewing and swallowing, I say, 'What?'

Matt looks away, 'Nothing.'

'What is it?' I ask.

His blue eyes slide back to me, 'I just wanted to say that I think you're doing so well, after everything.'

I hold his gaze and we both smile. It's been a tough few months – in fact it's hard to believe that the summer is approaching and soon it will be a year since it all happened – but we've got through it. 'Thanks,' I say.

'We don't have to talk about it if you don't want to, but I did wonder how your group is going?' Matt's always so considerate, never pushing or asking me difficult questions, which makes things easier. I hate thinking about those dark years, all of those things I did; now that I think back, I can hardly recognise myself in that person – perpetually the other woman.

'It's good, thanks. The format works for me. I'm not sure I could trust an individual, not after Con—' I start saying his name, then check myself. 'Not after what Tom did.'

Matt reaches across and covers my hand with his. We sit by the window for a moment with the warm sun on our backs before he leans over and kisses my cheek and we both carry on eating our toast. 'I'm just glad you've found a support network.'

'And I'm glad I found you.' I kiss him on the lips, and then over his shoulder I spot the time on the stainless steel clock. 'Shit, I need to go.' I push back my chair and start clearing the table but Matt takes the butter dish from my hands. 'Leave this. You get ready.'

After one last kiss, I hurry through into the bathroom and take a quick shower in the large walk-in, even in my rush taking a moment to enjoy the home-made jasmine body wash Matt made – another semi-viral hit – and the rainfall effect of the huge showerhead. Dressing quickly in a soft, floral dress that I got a few weeks ago, something the old me would never have worn, I pop on a slick of lipstick and a coat of mascara before returning to the kitchen to collect the tin of flapjack I made yesterday. There I find Matt sitting on the scrubbed wood counter, munching one of the golden oat and apricot bars.

'Hey, those are for my group.'

He grins mischievously. 'They won't miss one. These are delicious.'

I give his arm a playful tap and put the lid back on the tin as he reaches for the windowsill and picks up the card I stood there yesterday.

'Cute kid,' he says, looking at the front before flipping it open.

I murmur in agreement because it would be impossible not to agree. If there was ever any doubt about whose child it was, the moment he popped out it must have been apparent to anyone who knew David – the boy is his miniature. I wonder if it's hard for Kitty to look at him with David dead and the resemblance so strong, or perhaps it makes her love him even more, but that's not a question I feel like I can ask.

'What did we get him?' he asks.

'A Babygro. Grey cashmere with a yellow duck on the front.'

'Fancy,' he says. 'It's nice that you stay in touch.'

I make another sound of agreement but really I'm not sure 'nice' is the right word. What happened on that rooftop bound us together for the rest of our lives, and though I know she didn't want me there, Kitty inviting me to David's funeral was the first step in our new relationship. She stays in touch because she needs to make sure I'll stay silent, but she needn't worry, I'll never tell.

It didn't take long for the police to put together that Tom killed Nina, not once Kitty made her statement and showed them the photo Tom took of David and Nina that he brandished on the roof. Kitty admitted their affair and his motive was attributed to jealous rage, but the police never worked out that Tom wasn't the only one following David that night and I plan to keep it that way. Being seen as a victim is much nicer than the scrutiny one faces when words like 'stalker' are bandied around. To me, what happened to Tom may have been rough justice, but it felt like justice nonetheless and I feel like I deserve a fresh start after everything he put me through.

Tucking the tin under my arm, I give Matt a wave.

'What time will you be done?' he asks.

'I'll be back around noon,' I say, factoring in a leisurely stroll and time for chatting after the session.

'Shall we meet in the park? I'll bring the picnic.'

'Sounds great,' I say, giving him one last kiss before forcing myself out of the door and down in the lift. There's a gentle warmth in the air when I get outside, and after a few minutes of walking, I take off my cardigan and my long skirt flaps in the breeze. I've grown out my shoulder-length style and my hair hangs long and free down my back. The ashy highlights have been covered up by a packet red that makes me feel younger but my lipstick is still the same shade of red and it hasn't let me down yet. As I stroll along, I slide off the intricate silver ring that Matt gave me and admire the curls of metal and tiny sapphires that look like flowers. It's not an engagement ring but a promise, given to me a few days after that awful night so I had something to look forward to. That's when I knew that Matt was a keeper.

Unzipping my handbag, I slide the ring into the tiny inside pocket and dig around until my fingertip touches the cheap silver band I keep inside and I hook it out. This ring doesn't sparkle in the sunlight; the metal is a dull pewter and always leaves a dark-green line on my finger that I have to scrub off with soap. Jamming it over my knuckle, I force the band back onto the fourth finger of my left hand with difficulty and hold it up for examination. It's not beautiful or impressive, but it takes me back to my youth, and of course, it reminds me of David.

I glance at my watch and see I need to hurry to make it on

time. The church is further along the street and I hear the bell begin to toll. Picking up my pace, I hurry the last few steps and push open the heavy wooden door just as the bell falls silent. As ever, it's a few degrees cooler inside and I go straight over to the trestle table, popping down my tin of flapjacks before shrugging my cardigan back on. Several women greet me with smiles and hellos, and a tall ginger lady named Sally wraps me in a hug.

'How are you, my lovely?' she says.

'Today's a good day,' I say, and we both smile, her eyes crinkling kindly.

Ellie is leading the session today and she claps her hands to ask us to take our seats in the circle. I sit between an older man with a salt-and-pepper beard and a woman who, by rights, should be far too young to be here. We exchange nods and smiles and little shrugs as if to say 'well, here we are' as Ellie stands and says, 'Welcome everyone. I would say it's great to see so many of you, but we all know that Wonder Widows is the best group that you never wanted to be part of.'

A few of us chuckle, though it's the same opening remark Ellie makes whenever it's her turn.

'No, really, I'm so glad you're all here and we can be part of each other's support networks. Today our good friend, Catherine, is going to speak to us since it's been almost a year since she lost her darling husband, David.'

Everyone looks at me, smiling kindly, and I feel a warm flush rising from my chest to my neck and face. Of course I haven't told them any of the details or even David's last name, but it's such a treat for me to be able to talk about him openly, without judgement. I smooth my skirt, readying myself for their full attention as the room breaks out in applause and I smile, though my eyes flood with tears, and I clear my throat, ready to begin.

A LETTER FROM HOLLY

Dear reader,

I want to say a huge thank you for choosing to read *The Other Woman*. If you did enjoy it, and want to keep up to date with all my latest releases, just sign up at the following link. Your email address will never be shared and you can unsubscribe at any time.

www.bookouture.com/holly-down

I hope you loved *The Other Woman* and if you did I would be very grateful if you could write a review. I'd love to hear what you think, and it makes such a difference helping new readers to discover one of my books for the first time.

Thanks,

Holly

ACKNOWLEDGEMENTS

I'm thrilled to have had the chance to publish my second novel and I'd like to thank the whole Bookouture team for bringing it out into the world, especially my editor, Claire Simmonds, whose feedback has really helped whip the book into shape.

I'm very grateful to my early readers for their advice and encouragement – Jodie and Isabelle, thank you. Without your support I'm sure this book would never have been finished.

Thank you to my agent, Daisy Parente – your support, expertise and enthusiasm are really appreciated.

And thank you to my wonderful family and friends, for listening to all my plot ideas and not telling me how boring that is, for supporting me and for not complaining when I abandon all household chores in favour of writing!

A final thank you to anyone who has read the book – I really hope you enjoyed it.

PUBLISHING TEAM

Turning a manuscript into a book requires the efforts of many people. The publishing team at Bookouture would like to acknowledge everyone who contributed to this publication.

Commercial
Lauren Morrissette
Hannah Richmond
Imogen Allport

Contracts
Peta Nightingale

Cover design
Toby Clarke

Data and analysis
Mark Alder
Mohamed Bussuri

Editorial
Claire Simmonds
Jen Shannon

Copyeditor
Seán Costello

Printed in Great Britain
by Amazon

43946650R00142